WATER
WITH
BERRIES

Other books by George Lamming

WATER

WITH

BERRIES

GEORGE LAMMING, 1927-

Holt, Rinehart and Winston

NEW YORK   CHICAGO   SAN FRANCISCO

for
John and Dorothy Figueroa
and in memory of
Willy Richardson and Claudia Jones

Part One
The Fall

I

One

The fog was breaking up. A moment ago he had marvelled at the huge edifice of blue air which occupied the street, obliterating houses and the telegraph poles. His gaze had grown weary with looking for the first row of houses which would announce the heath. It was such an unlikely start to the day: this black dawn erupting from the heart of September.

But Teeton was in a mood to welcome it. He was in a mood to forgive any extravagance. And after seven years he had learnt to live with the lunacy of the seasons. Teeton had set himself a little apart from them, trusting to some private temperature of the blood. He had let the seasons rub him on the outside. They pushed him about a little, like an amiable crowd drawing attention to their waiting. They might tread on him now and again. But he had never felt any panic amidst their mob; no gales had yet come to tear his skin away. He had been growing without much notice from anyone; a plant which had defied some foreign soil, coming to fruition without a name. He liked it here. London had been a city of welcome, the safest harbour for his kind of waiting. But he was about to bring this pilgrimage to an end. After seven years it was now over.

The sun started a web of light in the corner of his window. There was a tremor of water on the pane. The morning was turning on. He saw a pair of hands divide the curtains in the house across the street. A nose was probing the glass. The fog had begun to crumble; its subtle carpentry of air and smoke was coming apart. Two neat little chimneys of brick emerged as the wind swept the last parcels of dirt up from the roof. He saw the hands withdraw from the window. The nose had disappeared. Now he turned away from the weather and looked to his room like a farmer alerting himself to the needs of his livestock. He might have been putting it up for auction.

Two windows and one door.

A pair of chairs at opposite ends of the table.

Twin divans that stretched the whole length of the wall.

There was a white plaster head of Columbus on the mantelpiece.

A black tree trunk rose from the far corner.

The folding maps were his only curtains.

He loved this room. Spare, solitary, without any trace of fuss. It was beyond improvement.

Teeton knew what he was going to do with the maps; but it seemed more difficult to decide on the fate of the black tree trunk. It was resting beside the large wash basin, no taller than a man of average height with its twin branches struck out on either side like arms cut off at the elbows. He had salvaged it from the back of the garden more than a year ago.

That's where he had always hung his wet underwear. It was the neatest place for his overcoat. It was the masterpiece of his furniture, this complex of laundry and cupboard: a versatile log of wood which had grown on him like regular company. Now it was quite naked, and he could see how the bark split open round the trunk like a skeleton of ribs. He had fought many a battle to bring it up to the room. When he had got it there, the fight went on to keep it. At first the Old Dowager thought he had gone out of his mind. Next he would be asking to grow vegetables in the carpet; or turn the loft into a chicken farm. But the tree trunk remained.

The Old Dowager had relented; and the tree trunk had won. But she kept an eye on it just in case 'things' began to accumulate. This was, in the end, her only condition. She sprayed it every day; explored the grains of bark for 'things' that might have got away. And Teeton did come to think of it as a nuisance when 'things' began to crawl over him in his sleep. Teeton didn't let her know his reason, but there was a time he wanted to return the tree trunk to the garden. But the Old Dowager wouldn't hear of it. She thought it a perfectly harmless addition to the room. She heard every argument, but she wouldn't yield an inch to anyone who wanted to dispose of it. This ordinary black portion of a fallen tree had become a necessary piece of the furniture, a natural element of the household. And Teeton had to agree. The room could never be the same without it. But he was going. Now it would be the Old Dowager who would have to decide. He glanced at the map and saw the island smile and sink under the shadows of the early morning.

There was a muted knocking at the door. Teeton answered yes and waited. He was smiling at her delay. He knew there would be no need to speak again; no need to enquire who was there. The Old Dowager was simply rehearsing her apologies. It was their game, an example of the formula they had made for being together. She had heard him say come, but she would not enter until she was ready. Teeton saw the maps stare at him from the window frames like a warrant authorising his return. 'I've almost left it too late,' he thought as he waited for the Old Dowager to appear. 'I must tell her I'm going home.'

"As luck would have it," the Old Dowager said, making her way straight to the table. She had passed him the habitual gift of morning tea.

Teeton greeted her with a gentle complaint against the weather. An instant frown appeared on the Old Dowager's face. She agreed. Neither really thought there was much cause for complaint; but this had become their routine of welcome. For as many mornings as they could count in six years, that's how they had observed their ritual of greeting. The Old Dowager saw the sizzling blaze of an ocean spread out on the maps, and prolonged her scolding of the English air. There was a mild bite in the draught which had blown in. Teeton was making an effort to hold the hot cup up to his mouth. His bottom lip was on fire, but his eyes were laughing.

"I didn't think you were in," the Old Dowager said.

Unnoticed, she had started dusting the mantelpiece. Soon she would extend her campaign to the divans and the carpet, leaving the black tree trunk until everything else was over. But the room had a slightly different shape this morning. It looked a little smaller where the blanket was draped over the high stack of paintings in the corner. She reflected that her stay would be much longer.

"Didn't think you were in," she said again.

"Didn't think I'd be in!" He knew she must have thought up some charge against him. "And where would I be at this hour?" He was in a mood to defend himself; even to offer himself up for mockery.

"I've never known you to work by the clock," the Old Dowager said.

Soon she would be taking him on a tour of his habits; but it would be done without any reference to himself; almost without any trace of curiosity about what he did; or where he went when he wasn't in the room.

"So what would a man be doing out at seven o'clock on a Sunday morning?" Teeton said and held the map up to give the Old Dowager a better look at the weather.

"Seven o'clock of a Sunday morning," she said, playing echo to his surprise. "Why, I've known some people who get home much later. Very dear friends of mine."

"I don't suppose I know these friends?"

"You might and it's just as likely you might not."

"They work nightshift, I suppose."

"I can't be sure what work they shift," the Old Dowager replied, "but Saturday can be a long night from home. For some people."

Teeton suddenly felt a little clot of air harden like cramp in the pit of his throat. He might have laughed it away, but his glance had found the Old Dowager smoothing the sheets over the divan; now she was cuffing the pillows into shape, plucking at the corners so that they stood erect like a dog's ears.

He watched her and wondered what miracle of affection had turned this room into a home. Cosy as a cave when he wanted to be in hiding; it had also acquired certain characteristics which had nothing to do with its size. It could be like a fortress in the morning: harsh and cold with neglect until the Old Dowager came in and took it over. Soon it would be converted by her hands back to its more normal state: a mixture of workshop, playground and garden. She never came back after this stage of her duty was over; but some signature of her presence was left behind. He had almost come to think of the room as a separate and independent province of the house. The house was the Old Dowager's; but the room was his; and house and room were in some way their joint creation; some unspoken partnership in interests they had never spoken about. He had changed lodgings nine times during his first year in London. Six years ago he had discovered a home in the Old Dowager's house. But it was time to go. The lump was thawing in his throat. He would have to tell her soon of his plans to leave.

The Old Dowager was moving in reverse, passing slow verdict on the angle of the covers; giving herself a second opinion on the way they fell, and a third on whether they shouldn't have come right down to the floor. Teeton wanted to distract her; he wanted really to distract himself from this emotion which the Old Dowager's chores had aroused. He felt he could now speak without risk. The lump had thawed; and his throat was free. She looked over her shoulder when she heard him call; but she hadn't quite settled her verdict on the bed. Perhaps she could adjourn the issue of the covers until tomorrow.

"Yes, I was saying," said Teeton, restoring the balance of the maps, "I'm going to be away for a couple of days."

She came towards the table.

"Just a couple?" She asked. "You need a lot more than a couple days' rest."

She was getting ready to collect the cup; but she waited for Teeton to go on. She wanted him to offer more details; but she could never let him know that she was trying to calculate how long his couple of days would last. She thought he might have been a little more precise; but it would have been inconceivable for her to ask.

"I'm not here if anyone calls," said Teeton, preparing the Old Dowager for her assignments. "And you don't know where I've gone —or when."

"Which wouldn't be a lie," she reminded him, and quickly added, as though it were urgent and a matter of principle, "I'd only be telling the truth, wouldn't I?"

"I wouldn't ask you otherwise," said Teeton, and caught the Old Dowager's glance reminding him that he should think again.

He turned away; gave himself a moment to extinguish all evidence of his smile before facing the Old Dowager again.

"I know you can handle it," said Teeton.

"The trouble is your friends don't always believe me," she said.

"Which friends?" Teeton had become cautious. He had to be sure the Old Dowager was returning with a name from the right compartment. She had noticed the change in his voice.

"Well there's the actor to begin with," she said, sorting the names before taking any risk that she might be wrong.

"Oh Derek," said Teeton. He looked relieved.

"And Roger is much the same," she added, now she was sure where the names belonged.

"They wouldn't hold it against you," said Teeton; and his caution was no longer there.

Roger and Derek belonged to the compartment which the Old Dowager was free to enter. For a moment he had wondered whether there might have been some breakdown in the agreement which he shared exclusively with the other friends who kept the strictest censorship on what they knew about each other. It would have been against every code of safety for any member of the Secret Gathering to call for him at the Old Dowager's house.

The Old Dowager was making a loop with the duster. Her silence had focused Teeton's attention on her wrists. They were wide with a high tide of veins which converged round the sharp white stump of wristbone. Something had delayed her; for it was unusual to see her stand still. She was waiting as she often did when there was some occasion for apology.

"I don't know what's come over me," she said, "but I don't seem to remember a thing these days."

She turned to let Teeton judge the truth of her regret.

"What have you forgotten now?" he asked; and smiled so that she knew he had already given her the benefit of the doubt in any charge she was about to make against herself.

"His wife called yesterday," the Old Dowager said.

"You mean Nicole?"

"Twice," she answered. "It must have been important."

"She's Roger's wife," Teeton said, helping her to fix the names where they belonged.

She had caught his meaning; but she showed no reluctance in admitting her failure to remember the names.

"He's the tall one, isn't he?"

"Looks Indian," said Teeton, "as indeed he is."

"She called twice," the Old Dowager said promptly.

The loop had come undone; and the duster trailed like the tail of a kite down her side. Teeton watched her turn away to inspect the wrinkles in the black tree trunk.

"She didn't leave any message?"

"Now I wouldn't have forgotten that, would I."

She was looking at him again, confident that she was now free from any lapse of memory. He had often had complaints about her reluctance to let messages through, but he had never brought this to her attention. She was an obstacle he was often glad to have between him and the telephone.

"She is American, isn't she?"

"All of her," said Teeton.

The Old Dowager might have been trying to gauge his interest in the message she had given him.

"Twice," she said again, as though she were drawing attention to danger. "I hope there's nothing wrong."

"I'll see Nicole before I go," he said.

"Well don't forget now," she warned again, trying to curb her curiosity about the telephone calls. "You might be gone longer than you say."

"Exactly two days," Teeton said quickly, as though he had to dispel any doubts the Old Dowager might have about his absence.

He had changed her mood by letting her know; it made life so much easier to manage when you knew. She was almost gay; ready to let her irony go sparring at him again. But Teeton had become a little more sombre once more. He was looking at the stack of paintings in the corner, wishing some miracle would pack and transport them where they belonged. The gallery had started to complain about his delay.

'I'd better tell her now,' he thought, 'you'd better tell her you are going home.'

"In that case," she was saying—and Teeton was startled; felt almost catapulted out of his skin—"we'd better start getting the paintings ready today. It's not a long time, two days. And there's a lot to do. No point waiting, I say. Now, is there?"

And Teeton had remained still as though her question had forced a guilty silence on him. 'You'd better tell her now.'

"I agree," he said, "why not start on them today."

"Then I'll take this if you're through," she said, collecting the cup, at last. "We'll just let Vulcan know. He won't be too pleased I daresay."

"Bring him back with you," Teeton said.

"Most certainly not," the Old Dowager insisted. "There's work to be done." Then she relented; as though there might have been an injustice in such exclusion. "Moreover, he isn't that kind of dog.

Not Vulcan. Likes to go his own way. Follows his own nose, I'd say."

"As you like," Teeton was offering.

"Definitely not."

And Teeton realised the matter had been concluded. The dog would not be invited this morning.

Two

The Old Dowager had hardly got past the door when the feeling seized him. It came on like an attack of nerves. He had once deserted his comrades in San Cristobal. It was desertion. There was no other name for his escape from the island. After seven years the word had lost none of its terror. It seemed to drag its echoes up from the deepest roots of his being. Seven years ago he had been arrested after a minor revolt in the San Souci plains. The island was never to be the same. But he had got away, leaving some of his own cell-mates behind. Two were now dead. And the charge had pursued him ever since. How was it possible for him to get away? And when did he decide to go? After seven years he could still hear that martyrdom screaming in his ears. It was desertion. In the notorious plains of San Souci they couldn't have found any other name for his escape. He heard the Old Dowager on her way; and he looked up at the window. The maps were coming to his aid.

Now the island rose in a blaze of morning, riding at ease through treacherous currents of wind and water. Hurricanes had often disfigured its face. Floods were regular when he was a boy. They would carry huge portions of soil into the sea. But it would grow again, as though its hopes were never wholly out of favour. Its history had been a swindle of treaties and concessions. Its sovereignty was no more than an exchange of ownership. There had been no end to the long and bitter humiliations of foreign rule. The battles for ascendancy were too numerous to be remembered. But its habits of submission had suffered a terrible blow. The meek flame started at San Souci had spread beyond his wildest expectations. Now this name San Cristobal had become a warning everywhere.

But the ocean was too narrow a stretch between San Cristobal and her northern neighbour. There to the north, a nightmare away, the stupendous power of America sent a shiver through every nerve; shut every eye with fear. The ocean was innocent, an amiable killer beside those urgent executioners who kept vigil over the fortunes of that hemisphere. It was no longer safe for a man to remember his name. But the island was there, erratic with rage; pugnacious as its legendary fighting cocks, and vulnerable as air. The hills were shadows unfolding tediously before his eyes. He could hear the murmur of landslide coming down the mountains.

He glanced at the black tree trunk and then across at the canvases stacked high in the corner. The Old Dowager had already taken the blanket away. A week today these objects would be on display somewhere. They were no longer his. He smiled when he recalled the letter which stated the contract for this sordid, little barter. He had astonished the merchants at the gallery by his offer. Five hundred pounds for the lot. Now they could fix whatever price they liked and he wished them luck. He was grateful the matter was no longer in his hands. This premature fruit of a rotten crop was about to pass out of his ownership for all time. They were an innocent betrayal of the island which was dancing about, filling the space of the window. He turned to look at the maps again, inviting the island to pass some verdict on his escape. And the blue ink of ocean looked so troubled, so utterly indecisive where it should go, what it should let him hear. The island was smiling under the monstrous shadow of its northern neighbour.

He heard the Old Dowager's voice tapping on his ear. She had shaken him out of his dreaming. The catalogue, she was saying, you get on with the catalogue and I will get on with the cleaning. Everything had to be clean. She was an enemy of dirt. Teeton watched her body bend; now it was straight again. She was young again; and it made him cheerful. Now she's in her element, he thought, the Old Dowager is in her natural element. Her mind was busy as an engine.

There was work to be done this morning; but it gave pleasure to the Old Dowager's hands. It put a joy on every memory which was working its way back from the past; and her memory was always bright at this hour, sharp and sure as a magnet attracting every particle of gossip that had gone astray in the Mona bar. Hardly an angry word might pass in that pub, but what a cremation of character took place over the passing drink. Yes, she had heard many a marriage go up in flames; watched many a dead heart flutter back to life at the sound of a famous name. It was a minefield of risk for courting couples. An abominable place whose clientele were always persuading themselves to go elsewhere; might have been on their way out forever, almost through the door, when the power of a new scandal suddenly caught them by the ears and swung their attention back into play. 'He's never told me,' the Old Dowager was thinking, 'never told that he had a wife. Never a word after all these years.'

Teeton's voice must have detected her secret thinking.

"The Wednesday evening visitor," Teeton was laughing. "You know that's what they call you at Mona. You're the Wednesday evening drinker. Only on Wednesday in the evening."

Teeton had started to invent a tune that might carry his refrain, only on Wednesday. And the Old Dowager looked up briefly and smiled. It might have been the start of a compliment to his voice; but she had decided to withdraw it. She had a slight shudder at the thought of being caught between the tongues of the Mona firing squad.

"What's wrong with Wednesday?" She had come to her defence. "You know very well why I go on Wednesday."

Teeton said nothing because he knew. The Old Dowager was really a lunch-time regular, visiting every day from about twelve until she had finished her large gin fizz. That was her limit, served in a glass with a round, wide barrel of a belly. It looked like a chimney at the waist. The Old Dowager would nurse her gin and tonic for the better part of an hour; and if the talk was not too dull, she would make it stretch past the hour. But the evenings were out; except on Wednesday which was, she had warned Teeton, the most tolerable night of the week. It was the night wage earners were likely to be away. The Old Dowager didn't know what happened elsewhere because she never drank in any other bar. But Mona had its own curriculum of traffic; and its own categories of professional spongers. You were not likely to be attacked for a loan on Wednesday because it was the day which fell, according to the Old Dowager, bang in the middle of two extremities: of receiving and disposing. That is—she would explain to Teeton, schooling him in every contingency which Mona might spring on an innocent passer-by—having what you earn and having it not.

"Halfway," Teeton was teasing her. "Halfway between the two extremities."

But you see, and the Old Dowager was in delight, rehearsing the days she put her pupil through this exercise, they have to take time off that night. It was a bad day for anyone to negotiate a loan. Much too near the previous Sunday for the sake of dignity; and not near enough to coming Saturday. It put too great a strain on the memory, having to think from Saturday back to midweek. Only the prudent would appear on Wednesday; and then it would be for five minutes or so before closing. Just the right margin of time to escape the expense of company. Thursday was much safer. And Friday offered almost total protection against such emergencies. Except in the event of disaster, like the sudden arrival of O'Donnell; and then you might be caught shamefully, without your guard.

"He's a man who's suffered," Teeton had said. "You can't be too hard on O'Donnell."

There was a case in point, the Old Dowager was about to concede; but she felt it necessary to defend the value of her instruction. O'Donnell would have been an exception anywhere. His solicitations were never of a simple nature. He would descend like a vampire, literally from nowhere. You didn't see him enter. But there he was, all tears and whisky in his whisper: 'can I have a word with you, such a terrible thing to have to share'. And how could you resist? He had already got you in his fat embrace; and for the sanctity of your ear alone, that dreadful newsflash of his misfortune fell. A fiancée was on O'Donnell's heels. Breach of promise, never given according to his oath; but perjury can have a terrible success, even in an English court. And what was a poor man to do? Flight was the only answer. Immediate and without further meditation. Flight if a good man of catholic charity were to be saved. Destination two pounds and a coin or so less than ten shillings away. He would make it if the publican's clock wasn't telling a lie. From Vancouver to the underground of North West London the bailiffs had continued to live in his shadow.

"Mona's not all that bad, you know."

Teeton seemed inclined to hoist a flag in praise of something. He was feeling a little merry with the sight of the Old Dowager. She didn't make any challenge, although she heard the cremation fires burn her loyalty into silence: 'you don't know what they say about you ... and where is his wife, who knows? who knows?' That's the song the urn was singing when Teeton's ash came floating down. The Old Dowager wanted to put a curse on Mona, if only for Teeton's sake; but some better judgement advised her to hold her peace. She was careful not to trespass on his past.

"That's what is so nice about you," she was observing. "It doesn't take very much to cheer you up. One good day is grace enough, as they say, for a whole, grievous year."

"It's not a bad place, the Mona," Teeton insisted. "No worse than any other pub. And a good deal better than most. There is such a nice cross-section."

The Old Dowager didn't want to take a break from her work; but Teeton had forced her into argument again.

"I don't like sections," she said sharply, "neither cross-sections, intersections nor any kind of section. That's the trouble, isn't it? Mona is nothing but a section. When it isn't a section of this, it's a section of the other, and a section of the next. It's a rare sight to come across anything whole at the Mona."

"But you love it." Teeton was irrepressible with his teasing. "You love the place. Admit it, Gran. You love it whatever they say about you."

It was difficult for her to make any prompt denial.

"The prices are fairly high," she said. "And you hear the strangest things in that place."

Teeton looked bored with the chore of making a catalogue of the paintings.

"What a strange couple, the cartoonist and his wife." The Old Dowager was doubtful whether she ought to go on.

"She wants him to be a millionaire," said Teeton.

"Does she?" The Old Dowager's contempt began to simmer. "Well, well. I couldn't find my breath when I heard her introducing him to her ex-husband."

"Didn't know she was married before," said Teeton.

"Nor did he," said the Old Dowager.

"Nor did who?"

"Her husband."

"Which husband, Gran?"

"Her present husband," the Old Dowager said. "The cartoonist, I mean. It was he started the introductions. He was introducing her to this couple I'd never seen before. But the woman was his ex-wife."

"The cartoonist?"

"That's right."

"I didn't know he was married before."

"Never mind," the Old Dowager said. "Both women knew."

"They were all ex-'s," said Teeton.

"But the men never knew," said the Old Dowager. "Not until then."

Teeton jerked his head up and stared at the Old Dowager. The duster was waging war over the picture frames as she tried to sort out these marital complexities, divided between her loyalty to order and a restrained passion for the bizarre.

"It was a right musical chairs," she said.

"Hell of a thing when you don't know whose chair you're sitting on." Teeton was laughing; but it was hardly in keeping with his mood.

"It wasn't so funny," the Old Dowager said. "I think the men felt a bit awful." She paused to judge the truth of this.

"I'd think so," Teeton agreed. "But I don't suppose you can throw away your chair because somebody's been sitting there first."

"Come off it, Teeton. What would you have done? Finding yourself in that position." She had begun to regret the direction her gossip had taken.

Suddenly Teeton seemed to retreat from answers. What would I have done? The Old Dowager was in time to see the change of expression when he spoke.

"I don't know," he said as though he couldn't be sure of anything.

"Well it must have taken some doing," she said. "The publican caught what was up when some terrible looks started to pass, and called for a celebration. A bottle of champagne was off the shelf. On the house."

"On the house?" Teeton exclaimed.

"Couldn't believe my eyes," the Old Dowager said.

"But Millet is not a publican who gives anything away," said Teeton.

"But he did last Wednesday night," she said. "You should have been there."

"I'd have liked to see that." Teeton's voice had almost lost its sound.

"It was like a repeat performance of the honeymoons," the Old Dowager said.

Teeton didn't respond. It seemed he had lost his enthusiasm for this drama which had enlivened the Mona bar. He was looking at the maps, so lavish and vivid in their detail. His eyes had caught the peaks which were calling from the window frame. He had forgotten the Old Dowager for a while. His glance was loitering over that blue solitude where the forest grew, freezing at night; a circus of wandering birds by day. The mountains drifted away like clouds, hopelessly out of reach. The Old Dowager's voice was coming back.

"The new couple had just returned from India," she said.

"That's a long way," Teeton said, recovering the lost half of his attention.

"The whole thing seemed so remote," the Old Dowager said. "But it's a privilege to travel. Such a great privilege. It never came my way."

Now Teeton gave her all his attention. She seemed so forsaken the moment she spoke of things that hadn't come her way.

"It's never too late," said Teeton.

She leaned the frame away to get a better look at him. She was laughing. A magic of former times had illuminated her face. Her eyes had been washed clean of the mist which often showed the room to be miles away. Now it seemed the maps had come forward to receive her gaze. She would have liked to believe that every word of Teeton's was a prophecy that would come true. Teeton knew what an appetite she had for promises; and he wasn't going to let his offer fall on incredulous ears. Expectations were so scarce at her age. Teeton had always inspired her with the feeling that it was the extraordinary circumstance which would reward her for any loss of opportunity she had suffered.

"You may laugh," he said, "but you'll see. It's going to happen. One day, just like that (and he snapped his fingers like a player at dice, sniffing his luck) one day, out of the blue, your chance has come. Just like that. And you're away. The Old Dowager up in the sky, taking herself off to foreign parts."

"No plane for me," she said, "they are an abomination. All that noise. And you never can tell. Suppose anything goes wrong. Like engine trouble and not so much as a garden plot anywhere in sight. Where would I be? At my age? You can keep your planes. And all that noise."

"Then we'll fix you up by ship," said Teeton. "It's even better that way. Don't have to lose your sleep."

"Oh you get away," she smiled, "where would I be going?"

"You'll see," said Teeton, moving closer to the map.

The Old Dowager had gone back to her work. She was polishing the frame, begging her arms to give all their strength. There was still a lot of living in her hands. Yes, she would show a preference for the boat. But she would want to manage on her own. No, thank you, it's all right. You look after yourself. I can look after mine. She was already getting herself ready for these eventualities; learning the various courtesies that should go with saying no. There would be many instances in which she would have to face these offers of help. In rough weather, she had seen boats slide down on one side as though the waves would turn them over. Now there was a case in point! She'd have to learn how to stand like sailors do, shifting the balance the other way. And if, perchance, she stumbled. Then there was a case in point! She would have to practise the right words for saying she refused.

She had paused to change her grip; she wanted to rest the frame on its other side; but her eyes had caught a view of the yellow bars of sunlight plunging out the corner of the painting. She stood the canvas up to look at it again; and the colours seemed to change the more she looked. Now there was a shade of tangerine peeling away from a ledge of cloud that crumbled slowly out of view. A fleet of small boats lay idle on the shore. The sea was blue serge in colour; it was crowded with huge towers of rock leaning high above the surface of the water. She thought of danger; the frightful wreck that could befall a ship which failed to navigate the neck of water which stretched between the bigger rocks. It seemed so absolutely real with peril: those open jaws of rock, waiting to swallow anything that had come into collision there. The sky felt safer now. At least the clouds gave way to the flight of airplanes. There was wickedness in these rocks. She didn't believe that boats would trespass there. But the small boats looked firm enough. Perhaps they were no longer in use. They must have been abandoned after years of service; and brought here until it was time for burning.

Teeton was watching her. He was fascinated by her total absorption with the painting; the gradual stages of her viewing, a little puzzled at first; then hopeful that whatever she had lost couldn't be far away. Then his voice gave her a double shock.

"I can show you exactly where it is," Teeton said.

He made her tremble. She felt as though she had been caught in the act of stealing; the slight alarm of someone who had just failed to escape in time.

"Did you say something?" she asked, putting on her housekeeper's face: the eyes generously open to his request.

Teeton never failed to indulge her in these moments of prevarication. Could this be an element of hypocrisy? But it gave him great delight. He would never surprise her with the truth; because he felt it was her privilege to be free of all embarrassment; so he would let himself enter into their little game of harmless deceptions, supporting the Old Dowager whenever she felt it a matter of dignity to misplace her memory. Now she was accusing her ears of being idle; of going to sleep when her hearing should have been alert. Teeton didn't hesitate to show that he was on her side.

"Do you want anything?" he asked.

"No, no. I thought I heard someone call."

For a moment they both pretended to speculate on the chance of unexpected visitors. The Old Dowager had raised a hand to consult with the ear which should have been on duty. Teeton let his attention stray leisurely back to the map. He had given her time to recover from the shock of his voice; to adjust to the realisation that she must have let herself get carried away by the painting. It was a cardinal rule of living that she shouldn't ever let enthusiasm take charge of all her attention. Some portion should always be placed on guard, keeping her aware of what was happening elsewhere. Now it was over. They had come to the end of their game; and it was clear that she had suffered no loss of face. The rules came to her rescue.

"I would swear I heard someone call," she said, returning her attention to the frame. She had resumed her polishing.

"It must have been me," said Teeton. "I talk to myself now and again."

"Not to worry," she assured him; and she was in control again. "Everybody does it some time or another." She considered the arch of the frame. "Of course it's a habit that can go too far."

"Don't scare me, Gran."

"God forbid," she said. "What could be farther from my thoughts. And you of all people!"

This phrase was a bond of her affection for Teeton: 'you of all people'. She would put it on, as it were, at the end of the sentence; as you might fix a label to make sure that no one could be in doubt. It was a phrase which had come to mean more to Teeton than she could have imagined. It was not only protective in its tendency to select him from others. Her age had given it a more lasting assurance. It made him hear again the echo of voices which had mothered his childhood; the exceptional pride of place which infancy occupied in the attention of any who came near.

"I wish you'd start painting again," the Old Dowager said.

It might have been a message she had forgotten to deliver. There was a hint of embarrassment in her voice. She wasn't sure she would wait for an answer. She hadn't raised her head from the painting. Teeton was looking at her. But he wasn't going to be drawn into a reply. He couldn't tell the Old Dowager what he was thinking as he watched the crop of canvases gathered in the corner.

He was judging the dead harvest of his youth. They might have had some value as a record of his own lack of foresight. The effortless braveries which had passed for courage. The farce of heroism had been dignified by the subtle briberies of an art which had led him astray. There were subtle and cruel dangers in every natural talent. His brush had been an aimless eye wandering always beyond himself, a glance intended for others. He had been plodding through experience without any pause, collecting pleasures like a royal tramp. But he had brought these frivolities to an end. A look at the Old Dowager was sufficient proof that his youth was over. In seven years time, he would be on the other slope of living, descending tamely towards his natural end.

The Old Dowager was still under the spell of the painting. Teeton looked away. He saw the map shivering against the window pane. A draught had found its way up the backside of the island. The ocean shook. He thought he had to show the Old Dowager where the boats would have been at anchor. He was shading the map with one hand while the other became a telescope under his eye.

"Can you spare a moment ... ?" he asked, closing one eye in order to sharpen his vision.

"Would you be wanting anything?" The Old Dowager was already on her feet.

"Over here," said Teeton. He didn't look up from the map. "It's just about there. The red lines with the squares. That's where it is."

"The sea," the Old Dowager exclaimed, letting his finger guide her eyes.

"The boats," said Teeton, making room for her to be near. "That's where I was born. Cattlewash we call it."

"The scene for the boats," the Old Dowager said. "I daresay you could draw them with your eyes shut."

She had shoved Teeton gently aside; and her eyes devoured the red squares which ran in a crooked line along the coast. "What with the sea so near."

"On the door step," said Teeton, continuing his view over her shoulder.

"On the door step," the Old Dowager intoned, as though she had got a vision of her own journey at hand. "Must be beautiful there." And taking her head away, she glanced towards the divan where she had left the canvas. "It's a pity to spoil such places."

She frowned; and then returned to her scrutiny of the map.

"I hear they are spoiling such places. Those who can afford to get on them."

She continued to read the map, dipping her glance where the dark line traced the course of the river. She lingered over the names, Chacachacare, Potaro, Saragasso and San Souci, feeling the slight tremor of her lips which were eager to give them sound. Her imagination had grown vivid as the sun: her vision was crowded with superb specimens of a race she could not name; she heard the flow of music, loud and steady as rain, cascading down the mountain range. Nature had gone on holiday before her eyes: a splendour of plants overwhelmed the earth; the flowers were chiming like new bells. She had covered every mile of road; climbed the tallest peaks; explored the dark, unpeopled interior of the forest; and like the travellers in her reading she had survived. She had come back. She was safe.

She looked up from the map, no longer worried that enthusiasm had swept her away. Teeton saw a list of questions in her eyes; but he wasn't at all prepared for the adventures which had troubled her most. She looked tormented by some keen delight.

"I think we ought to sit," said Teeton.

"I think so too," she said. Her agreement was prompt; but it showed no trace of worry about her strength. It was rather a curious feeling of tranquillity which made her welcome his advice.

"Do you believe in another world?" She checked herself in order to make some correction in this turn of phrase. "What I mean is this. When we talk, like we are talking now, it never gets lost. The voice, that is. Wherever it goes, however far, the words never disappear. You follow what I mean, Teeton? The same sound will always keep the words together."

Teeton had walked over to the divan. He sat directly opposite the Old Dowager. He was halfway to a smile, but it was halted by the expression on the Old Dowager's face. He had seldom seen such a mood of serenity come over her.

"You think," said Teeton, weighing his words with excessive care, "that somewhere, in San Cristobal, perhaps, they can hear what we are saying now."

"Not quite, not, not quite that way," she said, lifting her chin to ponder the spaces of the ceiling. "Perhaps it could be, I don't know. But I was thinking more of a lapse of time, if you follow me. Some time in the future, heaven knows where you and I might be, this conversation, word for word, will travel back to you. And every sound, every note of the voice, yours and mine, intact."

"Just as we're hearing each other now?"

"Word for word," she said. "Every note intact."

Teeton watched her with an increasing sense of wonder. She looked suddenly younger, and free from all restraint; as though she hadn't a care what this new enthusiasm would entice her to say. A girl's blush had startled her cheeks.

"I've known it happen," she said and paused as though her natural caution was about to get in the way. "It's happened to me," she went on, now careless of all consequence. She might have been talking to herself. "Some years after his death," she said, "my husband, that is. He's been dead twelve years to be exact. I was alone when I heard his voice plain and clear as you hear me now. And every word exact as I remember it. And there was his voice, just the voice. No presence as might happen with people who see things, nothing of the kind. Just the sound of his voice, word for word, as it was that morning."

She brought her hands to rest on the table, pondering this mystery of sound; the extraordinary power that could preserve everything that had been said. Teeton had got over his early amazement. Now he looked credulous, almost converted to the certainty of the Old Dowager's experience.

"And you could hear yourself as well?" he asked. "Were you saying anything?"

"Yes I did," the Old Dowager said, as though she had been expecting his question. "Both voices were there, each talking in turn exactly as we did that morning. It gave me quite a shock hearing myself as I did. At first that is. But the longer it went on the more I started to feel at home. And of course I knew exactly how we had come to get into that painful scene. A good twelve years after. Would you believe it?"

Recollection was beginning to lose its hold over her; and Teeton noticed her face was resuming its normal pallor; the droop of the eyelids had returned; and the little pleats of flesh ran like stitches down to her chin.

"Then the other voice began."

"A third voice?" Teeton intervened.

"Yes, there was. You see, Teeton." But she wouldn't go on. Some fear had warned her to be quiet.

Suddenly she got up from the table and signalled Teeton to get out of the way. She wanted to get back to her task of dusting the paintings. She appeared fretful and full of rebuke at this lapse of duty. Teeton gave way to her sudden change of mood. He skipped aside, and watched her stoop over the divan to prepare her attack on the picture frames.

"Fancy wasting such precious time," she said, working her hands over the frames. "And it isn't as though it belonged to us. It's just on loan as I always say. That's why you've got to make the most of it."

"Shall I get you some tea?" he asked.

"No you won't," she returned without the least hesitation. "What have I done to deserve it?" She was always decisive in her refusal.

And Teeton had learnt not to persist with his offer. This was another rule of their living game which she wouldn't allow him to violate. He wasn't supposed to offer her tea. It was not on the list of favours which she was prepared to accept. This code was complex. Once he had brought her a large bar of chocolate which she refused. No argument could make her change her mind. She thought it was a gross extravagance; and she couldn't accept because that would have been a form of encouragement. But she had surprised him by taking a single peppermint from a pack which he had bought for himself. When he offered the rest, she took a second as though it was enough to confirm him in his right to give; but that was the limit. After long debate he had achieved the freedom to help her with the garden. But even this triumph had to go through several stages of resistance before he could put his hand to the fork.

He sat at the table and tried to recollect those moments which had assured him of her welcome in this house. During the first three months they had hardly exchanged a word beyond the normal habit of greeting when they met on the stairs. Always warm and brief. It gave no opening either way for prolonging the comments that might have followed. Then she had missed him for two mornings—and it seemed this habit of greeting was a natural ingredient of a day. The omission had come over her like a violation of custom. For her it would have been an extreme aberration to enquire why she hadn't seen him on the stairs; but she had dared all the rules to find out why this omission had taken place; and discovered that he was down with a cold. Teeton was in no mood to resist her attention. That's how the offer of tea began. And she continued as though his recovery was a matter which she alone was able to decide upon. He hadn't noticed how this simple morning service had passed into ritual.

There was regret in every glance which he now turned on the Old Dowager. He didn't know how he would begin to prepare her for his departure. He couldn't settle with any certainty for a time of day which might make the news more bearable. And he feared—improbable as it seemed—that the actual day would arrive before he had found a way of telling her that he had to go. And then it would be too late. No confession of weakness would spare her the shock.

The Old Dowager was shifting the pictures from the floor to the divan, nursing them with gentle strokes of the duster; but she didn't realise that this was the last time that she would set eyes on them. In a way she was speeding Teeton's departure; for the removal of the paintings would almost be the last stage of his preparation for going; the final links of possession to this room. He would leave her the maps.

He was going to distract her; to forget his habits of discretion and impose whatever favours he chose on her attention. He had to make himself heard like someone in command. It would be necessary to violate the code.

"Now listen," he said, displaying authority in the wide, elaborate spread of his hands. His grip came firm at each end of the table. She had looked up, a little wary of the tone in his voice. Then she wheeled her body round to face him; and wondered what was holding him back.

"I'm waiting," she said.

"I'll do the talking," Teeton said—straight face, eyes in a militant stare. "And I won't have no for an answer. Or else, and you can take it from me, I shall have no alternative but to leave this house. Bad as it will make me feel, I'd have to go."

"But what's come over you?" the Old Dowager intervened. She was perplexed by this show of petulance.

"I do the talking," Teeton retorted. "The Exhibition is a week away. And on that day, in the afternoon, I want you here. As my guest. And I'm going to make tea. And you will not refuse a crumb, not one single crumb of what I offer when we celebrate the sale of those paintings. Here. Just you and me. Right here. In this room." Now his arms were folded across the table. In a moment of grave consultation, Teeton finished: "I will not ask you for an answer now. And if you say no, that leaves me with no alternative. I will go."

The Old Dowager was trying to recover from these threats; but Teeton rose and came towards her. His mood was slipping into compromise. He was standing before her, his hands offering a stroke of comfort to her shoulder.

"You don't have to give your answer now," said Teeton. "I think that's fair enough. Seeing the circumstances. So you can hold your answer. Just for a day."

There was such a long interval that Teeton had given himself time to turn away; so he couldn't tell what the Old Dowager was doing. Then he heard her voice pleading for his attention. There was no sign of distress; but it was full of enquiry.

"Did you hear something fall?" she asked, "like a noise in the garden."

Teeton knew how this moment had to be answered. He walked to the window and looked out towards the end of the long brick wall.

"I'd swear I heard a crash," the Old Dowager said.

"I'd better go down and see."

"No, you won't."

"It's all right, I'll go."

"Well, as you wish."

"Back in a minute," said Teeton, slipping behind the door.

"I'll be along," the Old Dowager replied. "Just in case."

Three

Vulcan had followed close on their heels. He had been waiting for the Old Dowager at the foot of the stairs. They came along the passage which brought them on to the brief ladder of wooden steps that led into the garden. Teeton had gone ahead. The dog raced up and down, flexing its tail like a whip, supervising every movement Teeton made before chasing back to be the Old Dowager's guide.

The Old Dowager seemed to measure each step as she made her way over the narrow asphalt path that stretched like a lane through the grass. They stood in the centre of the garden, trying to discover some reason for their visit. The Old Dowager made no further reference to the noise. She was inspecting the pots of geraniums to the west, now heavy with shadow from the hedge. It grew high and even all the way from the house to the fence of barrel staves at the back. Beyond there was open space which you entered through the small gate in the fence. But the Old Dowager never bothered to go that far. It was over-run with bush; and the huge trunk of the tree, fallen many a year ago, had become a fortress of ants. A tool shed rose where the fence met the red brick wall that made a frontier against the encroaching heath.

The crate was safe above the roof of the shed. But Teeton had been trying to ignore it; for this was also the Old Dowager's gift. She had remembered it when she heard him making arrangements for the transport of the paintings. It must have been around for years, a souvenir of some forgotten removal. But the Old Dowager had called it back to service. In a few days he would lower it from the shed and make it ready for packing. He couldn't avoid thinking of the crate as another contribution to his departure.

"What are we going to do with that tree trunk?" the Old Dowager asked.

She was gazing over the fence at the wilderness of bush that obscured the rotting body of the tree. But Teeton didn't answer. He might not have heard; or he might have been resorting to the rules of their private game. Silence was allowed as a form of protection against any further question. The Old Dowager seemed content to go without an answer ... She could feel his mood, and she didn't speak again. She was going to give her attention work elsewhere. She began to stray towards the wide cultivated expanses of the garden.

Teeton looked a little alarmed by his own silence. He was thinking of the journey he had made across the garden when he carried the portion of the tree trunk to his room. He was yielding to the sudden intrusions of the past. He could hear the Old Dowager in some dialogue with the plants. But he was careful to exclude her from this sudden recall of their first meeting. In that year of vagrancy when he walked the streets in search of shelter. It felt like an eternity away: that slow, interminable routine of days when living alternated between nervous enquiry and the apologetic reply that he had arrived too late. He was out of luck. He had been exhausted by those journeys. He had often had that curious experience that his feet had gone ahead; his feet would be waiting outside some door until he arrived.

Was it really six years ago that he had made his first visit to the Old Dowager's house? This garden would always remain a part of that event. The shed must have been their witness; and the fallen tree trunk. It was here his vagrancy had come to an end. The event was to confirm his own sense of expectation. You could never really know the future of an error. For this was not a call to enquire about rooms. He was giving himself a rest from those journeys. He was simply looking for normal company.

He was calling from Roger's room where he had been in hiding from the landlord for more than a fortnight. He could feel again the tremor of the telephone receiver in his hands. The conversation had hardly started before it was over. It was too brief an exchange for him to anticipate the welcome he might receive. But he would depend on the Bensons and the party. They were his credentials. He was sure he had spoken with her then. Yet the voice had surprised him.

"Is that Mrs Gore-Brittain?"

"Yes, speaking."

"I'd forgotten the voice." He had found the tone which might suggest their previous acquaintance.

"Who is it?"

"I met you at the Bensons two nights ago."

"Oh yes." The voice had grown suddenly warm. "What a crowd Theodora got together."

"Too many," he was protesting. He had established his claims to be known. "Theodora thought I ought to drop in on you one day."

"By all means."

He didn't know how he should treat this reply. It had come too soon. Her tone was precise, yet free of any specific intent. It didn't say come; and you couldn't accuse it of saying no. But the habit of vagrancy had made him bold.

"Whenever it suits you." He was making himself free for the asking. "Today or tomorrow?"

There was no reply. The wires might have gone dead. But it was more likely she might have been trying to escape from his intrusion. He was going to put the Bensons' suggestion out of mind. He was too indifferent to plead for entry anywhere. But the voice had suddenly restored his interest. The receiver was about to make him an offer.

"Tomorrow," she was saying. "After six."

"Six thirty would be fine." His mind had been enlivened by the prospect of a meal. But some instinct warned that he should make his position clear. The honour of his credentials might be at stake.

"After supper might be better for me," he was saying, and heard Roger's laugh intercept her reply. "Seven thirty, perhaps."

"As you like."

He had established his claim to be remembered.

Teeton felt a certain relief that the Old Dowager was occupied. He was grateful to the plants for keeping her there. She couldn't see his face, or she might have guessed what he was thinking. The slightest sound of her voice might have brought the cramp back to his throat. The air seemed to weigh over his eyes. He couldn't resist the demands which his first visit now made on his feeling. 'But she must have known,' he was telling himself, 'and not a word. The old witch never said a word about what was happening.'

No trace of astonishment had showed in her eyes. He might have been a face come back from her own past. Superb in her control, she was guiding him down the passage. Then she stood back and let him go ahead into the huge living room. He was like a puppet that moved at the sound of her voice. He didn't take the seat which she indicated. He had lost his daring. His boldness was not enough to help him settle in the chair. He wanted to explain that there had been a mistake. She was not the person he had spoken to at the Bensons' party. It was necessary to insist that his arrival was not a hoax. There was no mischief in this visit. She must have been at the Bensons' party; but he had never seen her face before. Theodora must have got the names mixed up. Now he understood why the voice had surprised him on the telephone. He couldn't understand why she showed no interest in exposing his error. She must have noticed his reluctance to sit. He was bursting to speak. He was straining to make some apology; but his mind was distracted by her calm. His honour demanded that he should explain. But her response had startled him. It came between him and his duty. He was trying to detect some hint of apprehension in her control. But there was no interval in her welcome; no evidence of the slightest misgiving as she offered him again a free choice of chairs.

"A little sherry?"

It was then he sat; and she must have treated this as his acceptance of the drink; for he didn't think he had answered yes. He watched her fingers thread round the glass as she walked back from the cabinet to his chair.

"I've known Theodora since she was a girl."

He was saying thanks for the drink.

"But I hadn't seen her for years. Yet she has always been like that. Her friendships never spoil."

He was rebuking his socks where a rent showed the knuckle of his ankle peeping through.

"Have you known them long?"

He was slow to recognise that the question was directed at him. Then he jerked himself out of his stupor; he had made his presence seem normal. He began to speak with an excess of candour. He hadn't known the Bensons long, a matter of two months at the most. That was enough to settle the agenda. They spoke of nothing else all evening until he rose from the chair to say that it was time he went. After three hours she had confirmed his faith against all previous counsels of despair. For the first time since he left San Cristobal he had discovered how it felt to be gay. Like Theodora Benson he might have known her all his life. She saw him through the door and paused to let him lead the way down the passage. She was wishing him a safe journey when she noticed his uncertainty about the street.

"You know the way to your place, I hope."

He started to laugh.

"I have no place, but I know the address."

And she could hear his laughter long after he had gone.

A week later the Bensons informed him that he had found a room; and their astonishment seemed even greater than his. They had never known it happen before: that the Old Dowager would condescend to have a tenant. But they didn't let him know their fears. They were sure the arrangement couldn't last. They had given it a month; then the novelty extended its lease for another month. They were amazed he had survived three months. And finally they forgot that it had ever happened.

Teeton looked a little alarmed by his own silence. His eyes had found the fallen trunk of the tree, but he hadn't recovered from the perplexities of that first visit. It seemed to contain all the elements of initiation: the disciplined gifts of secrecy which had transformed his error into a friendship that would remain a permanent part of his future. For their friendship had achieved the force and delicacy of a secret. It was never stated; and no strangers shared it. 'Not a word,' he was muttering to himself, 'she never said a word about my mistake. Even to this day.'

He had often tried to explore the nature of her silence that night. Now he reflected on the value of negative statement; for it wasn't a silence which he had witnessed, nor was it a form of refusal, but rather the positive and disciplined act of not-speaking. What, then, was the name for such an exercise in concealment? That concealment which continues to work when everything is known; remains transparent to all. It seemed thoughtless to regard it as hypocritical. This struck him as too weak a word to support all the possibilities of the Old Dowager's intention. For experience had shown that it was an act of protection; a generous intervention between him and his embarrassment. She had refused to ruin his visit. She had halted his error from slipping deeper into a feeling of disgrace; and she had done so in the only way she knew: by refusing to call attention to what she was doing. Her behaviour, like its meaning, had become invisible. He couldn't see what she was doing although it was happening under his eyes. Now he could see it as an example of discretion which made any charge of hypocrisy unjust. 'Never a word,' he reflected again, 'even to this day.'

The Old Dowager was walking in and out among the rose beds, pausing to sniff the scarlet petals which had arrested her glance. Teeton watched her straighten her body again as she made progress towards the neighbouring row of tulips. They might have been aware of the homage her visit had paid them. They seemed to resist the push of the wind as they waited for the Old Dowager to pass, a guard on parade, now meek and grateful for the honour of her gaze. She was bending low, her hands in a tender hug round the head of the stalk. And he saw her lips move. She was in conversation with the little school of tulips which rose like yellow fists at the near end of the bed.

And Teeton thought this must have been the world her childhood had known: this effortless intercourse with nature. It had never been learnt. No fashion of taste had influenced her affection for the soil. She would end as her infancy must have begun. There was a pride of ownership in her eyes as she watched over the obedience of her plants. That's how he saw her now; how he would probably remember her always. Her instinct for authority would survive long after her power had become extinct. The habits of command had always ruled her blood. Now her last battles had begun. Old and alone, she would soon be entirely on her own.

Teeton felt the little cramp of air come to his throat again. His departure would strike like an act of desertion. Gradual as an illness you couldn't detect, her loneliness had become a part of his fears. He thought it strange that he had never done a portrait of the Old Dowager after all these years. It was an omission which seemed to defy explanation. Now it was too late. Yet he wondered how he would have gone about that face. He caught a glimpse of her eyes, pale and still as an autumn evening, and soon he could hear a call like trumpets shake the wide, high dome of her brow. He saw her hands when the wind billowed the sleeves, and he heard a clap of sails over her shoulders.

Vulcan started to bark. It must have been a warning to Teeton that they should return to the house. The Old Dowager was emerging from the shade of the trees. Teeton turned away from the fence and came forward to meet her.

"It's too much," the Old Dowager said, sweeping her view across the turf of garden and over the roof of the shed.

"We could have started a little farm here," said Teeton, agreeing about the size of garden.

He had always come to her defence when others complained that it was a waste of land. There was space for two cottages at least, and there would still have been garden enough for the Old Dowager's use. Speculators had grown tired of arguing with her that it was a waste; that she was being wicked at a time when land was scarce. But Teeton had always admired her resistance to their numerous offers for purchase. It made him proud of the Old Dowager; the way she defended her own style of comfort. She had settled for what money she had already; and enough was, in her view, the extent of what anyone should require.

"They'll make you sell one day," Teeton said.

"That breed of pest," she said, making her way up the asphalt path. "They would buy the sky if they could reach it. But nobody is having this. I don't care what currency they come with."

She scratched Vulcan's head. They stood at the centre of the garden, like a family getting ready for home.

"So you won't sell?" Teeton continued to tease her.

"I'd rather they buried me first," she defied him. "Rather be buried right on it."

"But it's too much land for a single grave," he said.

"Makes no difference," she answered.

Teeton was enjoying her triumph against the speculators. And suddenly he began to wonder what would happen if the Old Dowager died. But he couldn't pursue this speculation; for the thought now made him guilty. He heard himself wishing, please don't die, at least don't die before I leave.

"You're not going North again this year?" Teeton enquired.

She didn't conceal her surprise. He had taken a step beyond the rules of the game; but it was a violation which now seemed to please the Old Dowager.

"I couldn't afford it," she said. "One holiday a year is quite enough."

Teeton didn't know why he had raised this question; except that there might have been some sinister hope at the back of his mind. He might be gone while the Old Dowager was away. But it couldn't have been the reason; for he had no intention of deceiving her; couldn't think of any circumstance in which he would yield to such a deceit. Now the question was beginning to reveal itself. It had come as an escape from his feeling of guilt that he would be leaving her alone. Perhaps there might have been the earliest groping of a wish that death might come gently and relieve the Old Dowager of any grief which might afflict her after he had gone.

The sun had set a patch of diamonds on her hair; and Teeton felt he had suddenly had a glimpse of the girl who was now buried with age in the Old Dowager's body. Teeton was going to ask about her youth; to bait the Old Dowager with some flattery that would make her bring the girl back to life. But the Old Dowager had stolen his cue.

"Why are you trying to send me North?" she asked. "Am I in your way?"

"I'm doing no such thing," Teeton protested.

"But you know I go once a year."

"Of course you're in my way," said Teeton, trying to escape her scrutiny, "and that's where I want you to be."

Now she saw the geraniums laugh. The grass had gone incredibly green; and the garden was like a wayward island floating further and further out to sea; in search of its own ledge of ocean.

"The maps," she said, and felt an unruly joy in the wind. "You've always promised to get me some of those maps."

"I will, I most certainly will," Teeton accepted.

He was under the spell of her delight. He couldn't quite understand what he had done to make the Old Dowager look so young.

Four

The basement is like a cell the Secret Gathering have tunnelled deep underground, shut away from the chuffing of trains, a proof against sound. It's a freedom which the size of the city allows: this secret cover which emerges like a cave under the solitary bulb which lights them from above. Potaro, Santa Clara, Chaca-Chacare, San Souci. They are waiting for the delegate from the Midland cadres to arrive. Their agenda will last for two days. But time is like luxury in their hands.

"Four hundred and seventy-six pounds seven and sixpence," Teeton says as he burgles the briefcase up from between his legs and lays it on the table. It swells like a stomach where the zip slits it open and spills its fat.

"The harvest is here," says Potaro and smiles to hide his amazement. Their voices collide in a chorus of assent.

CHACA-CHACARE: A day is coming when the rich in San Cristobal will eat grass.

POTARO: It is near. Almost here.

CHACA-CHACARE: Will it be good grass?

SANTA CLARA: Grass is grass an' the degree can't make no difference.

POTARO: They build the world on all kind of scheme. Teach the poor their duty is to endure like a man who feel his only ambition is to lose.

SANTA CLARA: Poverty is a bad habit, a kind of epidemic with some people.

Each answers to the name of the province where his assignment will take him; as though the place and the man must be inseparable: a discipline which trains them to identify with the river and the plains they will soon inhabit. It's the same discipline which makes them go blind if they meet by chance in any street. They will never acknowledge each other by daylight. No disaster can be sufficient reason for them to break this rule.

"San Souci," Potaro exclaims, summoning Teeton by the name of his province.

Teeton smiles at the older man's bewilderment. Potaro weighs a packet of notes in both hands, and struggles with his emotion. He compares the inscription on each note; but his reading is slow, tedious, like an adult deprived of schooling, a man who is making his first, laborious discovery that he is literate.

But Potaro is a man of sound though simple education, a voracious reader of biographies and any manual which deals with the business of war. It is not ignorance which delays his reading. It is rather the sight of money in such a quantity which amazes his literacy. It seems that each note reminds him of some obstacle rising like a roadblock across his youth; some previous hazard which has defied his passion to overcome the iniquities of his past. Now he sees knife and gun, fruit and lint, dispensary and supermarket sparkle and shine where sceptre and crown adorn the face of each English pound. And suddenly his familiar laugh overwhelms the basement room. The men respond to Potaro as they have always done; for he is the veteran of the Gathering. He has been hunted in every corner of San Cristobal, sought in almost every major North American city. Until, three years ago, he deposited his weariness like unregistered cargo in this hidden berth of the basement room.

"What planet you born under?" Potaro asks, talking vaguely to a shadow on the wall.

CHACA-CHACARE: The crab.

POTARO: That's why you so familiar with grass. An' what you, Santa Clara, what you born under?

SANTA CLARA: I don't know.

CHACA-CHACARE: How you mean you don't know?

SANTA CLARA: I say I don't know.

CHACA-CHACARE: Then when you celebrate your birthday.

SANTA CLARA: When I feel like.

POTARO: But your birth must be in a register somewhere.

SANTA CLARA: It ain't.

CHACA-CHACARE: But it got to be. It must be.

SANTA CLARA: My mother didn't bother to make me known till I was nine. An' then the place they register birth look so far away. The only transport was by foot. So we leave it at that.

CHACA-CHACARE: Santa Clara, what it is you trying to say.

POTARO: You mean the law don't know that you alive.

SANTA CLARA: The law know I alive but it can't verify I was born.

CHACA-CHACARE: What a camouflage that can be.

SANTA CLARA: I just lose my birthday if you want to put it that way.

POTARO: But you start life with a very fine privilege. To know that your name from birth was never between police covers. A fine privilege, that. No trace or recollection o' this human who choose his own birthday. Can change his name without fear o' contradiction.

CHACA-CHACARE: I call that a self-made man.

Potaro releases his cannon of laughter again and looks at Teeton as though he wants to hold on to the star that has brought them luck. But Teeton is occupied. He is removing the rubber band from a bundle of notes. He lets them slither over his hands; and the men observe his smile give way to a look of incomprehension. He shares Potaro's feeling about the money: the element of chance which may provide it, the impudent privilege which it allows. He has always been at a loss to grasp the intricate arrangements which say: *pay to the order of.* The words startle him, force him to contemplate the machinery of partnerships which support the order to pay one pound, five pounds; the unholy conspiracy which confers such power on this fragile piece of paper.

It can set off the most violent plague of longing; create some special chemistry of need in a man's desire; betray the most disciplined appetite; or nurture a moment of supreme confidence in the most cynical heart. And to think there may be no connection whatsoever between its source and the end which it pursues.

He sees Potaro smiling up at him, and for a moment the crop of paintings falls like a shadow over the table. But it's really theirs, he tells himself; it's really those bitter memories of San Souci which made the paintings which brought the little harvest here. It's less than Potaro deserves, but it is the decisive contribution to their funds. Everyone agrees about that. They hear Chaca-Chacare grumble an oath, as though the money has unearthed some burden he finds it hard to bear.

"Which devil after you now?" Potaro taunts him. And they tease Chaca-Chacare to observe the code.

POTARO: Come straight, Chac. What's worrying you?

SANTA CLARA: You know the rule.

CHACA-CHACARE: Small matter from the past.

SANTA CLARA: Small or large any personal problem is also problem for the Gathering. What is private secret today may be public scandal tomorrow.

POTARO: You ain't kill nobody in this town.

CHACA-CHACARE: Not yet.

POTARO: Some men braver than some. But you just plain fearless. That I know. You fight like a man who had no life to lose.

CHACA-CHACARE: Not without reason. For years I been living a next man's life. Hang by law for what he didn't do. You remember the Belvedere case in Half Moon Bay. The jury sit up eleven nights before agreein' to what never take place at all.

SANTA CLARA: But all the evidence was there, Chacare. The only question was whether Scar Face beat her first an' rob her after. Or the other way round.

CHACA-CHACARE: The old girl was dead before Scar Face get there.

44

SANTA CLARA: Where you learn that from? It was common knowledge Lady Belvedere always carry cash, an' as the jury say Scar Face would be let free if they didn't find the same notes in his place.

CHACA-CHACARE: That money was for me.

SANTA CLARA: What it is you talkin' 'bout?

CHACA-CHACARE: The Belvedere case in Half Moon Bay. I was the only man with evidence that could set Scar Face free.

SANTA CLARA: But I don't see how you come in the picture at all.

CHACA-CHACARE: I was there when she drop down dead.

SANTA CLARA: You mean it was you who kill Lady Belvedere?

CHACA-CHACARE: In a court o' law you could put it that way, but how it happen was different. I believe her heart gave way.

Teeton makes an effort to smile but his lips hang open in alarm. He recalls the Belvedere case with some misgiving. Found at daybreak on the beach and naked to the waist with the stripes of a cane which had bled her back. It was regarded by the jury as a political murder. The Belvedere case and his own internment made the news of the day.

"Did you know Lady Belvedere," Teeton asks, and studies the black shrub of beard which shakes over Chaca-Chacare's chin.

CHACA-CHACARE: For over a year I used to meet the Belvedere lady in secret. Once a week at the private end of Half Moon Bay. She was living alone in the Lightbourne manor then. But I couldn't show my face in such a house as you know. She used to drive herself out every week to that end of the Half Moon beach. It was her money help me escape when the army move in on San Souci.

SANTA CLARA: You say her heart give way?

CHACA-CHACARE: I know for sure it happen so. She was getting old; but her taste was still wicked, rough wicked, I tell you. It was a tamarind whip that make those marks. The only marks the post-mortem find. That was her favourite fun, and she prefer it in the open air. It happen just so. She was right below me, spread flat out, when I notice that she wasn't movin' no more, an' the groan she used to give was comin' low. Then it stops comin' for good. I call out twice, but she didn't hear, an' the third time

I call the answer was clear. The old girl had done give up her ghost. I never look back. I run all the way, with that whip in one hand and my heart in the next. Scar Face rob the purse all right but the owner was dead. Done dead.

Teeton observes Potaro's silence, and is sure he knows Chaca-Chacare's account of the Belvedere case. What doesn't Potaro know?

SANTA CLARA: I suppose the law would call that murder by consent.
CHACA-CHACARE: I could never confess. There was something 'bout my performing which make me shy. It was only after Scar Face hang that I lose my shame. Ever since I feel I been livin' his life.
POTARO: Scar Face was a police informer.
CHACA-CHACARE: Makes no difference. His life was a real life, an' he lose it on a false charge. To hear 'bout injustice is one thing, to see it live and see it at work in the Belvedere case is a next. I lose whatever obedience I had for the law.
POTARO: Sometimes I think you go too harsh.
CHACA-CHACARE: You can learn to be that way. A man is what he do, an' there ain't no limit to what he will try.
SANTA CLARA: You sound like the Judge Capildeo when he get in a rage.
CHACA-CHACARE: It was he send Scar Face to his grave.
SANTA CLARA: He would send his own son if he cross the law.

Potaro looks up, observes that Teeton is withdrawing into his silence. He knows of Teeton's friendship with Judge Capildeo's son, and tries to curb any further reference to the law.

"But the son too had to make his escape," Teeton says, as though some other loyalty forces him suddenly to honour his relationship with the Judge's son. Potaro nods and follows his attention back to the bundle of notes on the table.

"The rich can produce some strange offspring," Potaro observes.

SANTA CLARA: Young Capildeo still making music?

Teeton nods yes.

CHACA-CHACARE: But he live on such a low scale in this town.
SANTA CLARA: Poverty is like an epidemic with some people I say.

Teeton makes no comment. Beyond the secret world of the Gathering and the basement room he has kept his friends in their own compartment; and he must keep them there. The code of the Gathering demands that they must be kept in the dark about his departure which is so near. Potaro's smile attracts his glance; and Teeton tries to avoid the rival claims of need and duty which force the Old Dowager on his attention. He must find a way to let her know that he is going home. After six years in her care, she assumes a priority that makes her different. She inhabits a compartment that is all her own, as though she has earned a brief exemption from all codes. He knows he will let her know that he is going home. 'And not a word,' he smiles, as he watches Potaro's hands shuffle the English notes, 'she's never said a word about that night. How it was my error which made us meet. Not a word.'

"Money will serve any master," Potaro declares, as though he has made a new discovery. "But I think I hear someone come."

There is a rattle in the keyhole. A draught shakes the lamp shade, and the light starts a dance of shadows on the table. The whole room rejoices at the long embrace which shakes Potaro's arms. Fola of Forest Reserve has arrived. She is the only woman who shares the secrets of the Gathering.

"October first," Potaro says as they settle down. "Two weeks from today. Just two weeks from today."

2

One

Anyone could tell from the state of his hands that Roger might have been in some kind of trouble. The fingers were stiff as pegs. The palms were frozen white. He didn't recognise them as his own although he kept a faultless vigilance over their movement above the bottles. He counted the empty quarts again, and the total came to six.

"Six at fourpence each," he said, and consulted his fingers for advice. In moments of crisis he found the simplest language of arithmetic more treacherous than any foreign tongue.

"Six at fourpence is two shillings," he said.

But something must have gone wrong. A pint bottle had suddenly appeared among the quarts. It stared up at Roger like a dwarf forcing its way into view. It had avoided his count; should now have been given some welcome. Instead, he had begun to curse it for being there. He had never bought a pint of beer to take away. The bottle seemed to watch him, bearing witness that a robbery had taken place. Someone must have stolen into the room and exchanged the pint for one of his quarts.

In bad times the rooming house had the nervous, hectic atmosphere of certain banks. Beer bottles were the only currency available, a recognised rate of exchange. It was common to borrow a couple of quarts when cash was short. Each floor had its own vault where the empties were held in reserve. It could be serious if these deposits were tampered with. And Roger had already started to name his roll of suspects. Would it be O'Donnell who shared the top floor with the architect. Or Derek? But he had to give it up. Each had been acquitted at the very sound of his name. Except the girls who lived in the room opposite his. But he had scarcely thought of the charge before he felt ashamed. The girls would never have gone into his room when he was away. Poverty made for a very mean imagination. He was scolding himself, hating this tendency to accuse. It was a stigma which he must have inherited from his father who was a judge, and famous in San Cristobal for his austerity. Roger looked at the bottle again; and his resentment soon gave way to a new discovery. Include the pint and the total now went up by twopence.

"So that would be two shillings and twopence," he was saying. "Which shall it be?"

One pack of cigarettes and half a pint of bitter. It was his habit to think of them as one item. But new obstacles were coming between him and his appetite. Cigarettes cost one shilling and ninepence; and the beer was ninepence. The tyranny of arithmetic was about to crush his hopes.

"It doesn't sound right," he kept saying; and appealed to his fingers for an answer in his favour. But arithmetic was slowly proving its point.

"Another quart would just do it." His voice was barely audible. "Whoever took my quart."

He had to find some hint of optimism; and he started the count all over again. This thirst was quite normal for Roger at this time of day. It was a habit he had served for years. He had no fears of addiction; had never attracted any scandal of drunkenness. Half a pint of bitter. It was part of the routine of comradeship; the afternoon sacrament which he would sip at leisure in the Mona; grateful that his imagination was still alive even though his fortunes had been in such a state of decline. He had always kept this part of him aloof from the commerce of friendships which he didn't want to cultivate.

'Half a bitter and a pack of Weights.'

He heard them calling; but there was a difference in the way his thirst was making itself felt. It seemed to attack him. It was forcing him to be in need of a drink. He listened for some stir of life on the other floors; but there was no sound anywhere in the house. The silence had come like a warning that he had to be quick. He had to find someone who might come to his help. He started to collect the bottles. He selected one at a time, noted the brewers' label, and deposited them like eggs into the carrier bag. He made one hand secure under the bag, and raised it shoulder high to test their safety.

"Six at fourpence each. And one half pint."

He was muttering precautions as he cradled the bottles gently back to the floor. It was getting at him again: this need to have a drink. So that he seemed to forget the price of everything.

'Half a pint and a pack of fags.'

It looked as though he might have to choose between one need and another. But he had always heard them as a single item.

He felt some relief when he got into the street; but there was no sign that it would last. He had seen Derek. He stooped to put the sack of bottles on the pavement. He thought the light was making him a little dizzy. Derek must have thought so too.

"Can you lend me a pound?" Roger asked. "Please."

Derek looked as though he was struggling to dislodge a bone. He had made a sudden clutch at his throat, and tried to ask some question through this sudden violence of coughing.

"A quid, you say?" Derek was trying to enquire. "A whole one?" He paused, as though he needed time to grasp the novelty of this request. The coughing had delayed him; he reflected on the awesome burden of men who had to manage vast economies.

"Would you mean the one that comes to twenty shillings, Roger?" The word had become such an improbable idea among old friends.

"So when did I enter the diamond trade?" Derek concluded.

He couldn't have been more oppressive in his expression of dismay. He had relaxed the grip on his throat and was blessing the air with a noisy sound of sucking into his lungs.

"Could you make it fourpence?" Roger said quietly. A note of panic had emerged in his voice.

Derek was relieved when the talk came back to normal; but he had noticed Roger's agitated glances passing from him to the sack of bottles.

"You don't look too well," Derek said.

"Can you spare it or not?"

"The fourpence?"

"Could you let me have it now?" Roger was insisting. "This minute?"

"What for? What's up?"

"Telephone," said Roger. "I could probably get it off Teeton."

"But suppose he isn't in?"

"He's always in at this time."

"I say suppose," Derek insisted. He was scraping the edge of a coin in his pocket. "It's the Old Dowager who always takes the phone. That'll be fourpence lost if he isn't at home."

Roger was considering the chance that Derek might be right; but his optimism was beyond control. Half a pint and a pack of Weights; and he heard them call as a single item. He couldn't tell which was the more severe. Now it was his thirst; soon it became his need to smoke.

"Couldn't you walk?"

But Roger didn't answer, and Derek had already withdrawn the suggestion. No one called on Teeton without warning. The Old Dowager would never have let them get past.

"I'm expecting Nicole in the Mona at two," said Roger.

"She will wait," said Derek.

"I don't believe she is going to come," Roger said. "But I want to prove something."

He was aware of Derek's alarm, and he gave him no chance to speak.

"Don't ask me why."

But Derek had already done so.

"Why doesn't she want to come?" he asked again.

Roger gave his attention to the sack of bottles. He was trying to avoid an answer; but he knew it would be difficult to make it work with Derek. He was renewing his plea for the loan.

"Couldn't you risk the fourpence?"

"Can't afford it," said Derek, and thought there shouldn't be any need to argue. There was very little which they kept a secret, and certainly not money.

Roger was biting at his nails. He looked up at the sky, and then down at the wide sweep of windows in the houses opposite. His expression had grown sullen. Derek's humour had deserted him.

"Isn't there any justice in the place?" Roger's voice was full of complaint. It was a strange aberration from his normal habit.

"What's fourpence got to do with justice?" The complaint was real; and it made Derek a little angry.

"Think how many bastards spent four pounds in the last five minutes," Roger said, and he noticed Derek's surprise at this trait of envy.

"You should be more careful," said Derek. He was resisting the urge to scold. "I saw you spend half a crown last night on that cattle driver from Highgate. What did you do that for?"

"He had bought me a round," said Roger.

"You didn't ask him."

"But you know the type." Roger was quick with his own defence. "If you're dirty and dispossessed, they think you're not up to the game."

"So that's why you spent half a crown on him?" Derek's voice was sharp with scorn. "And you know what he said when he got home?"

Derek had felt a momentary relief. He was finding a role: the cattle driver recording an evening out.

"I think he was a little surprised," said Roger. "Didn't expect I would offer anything like whisky."

"Surprised my arse," said Derek, and he had started his turn of the cattle driver at home. "Scruffy little rump I met last night (now hear the oxen groan) artist type. Could see it was all he had." Derek was getting overwrought. He had found his own voice. "That type can tell when you hold a penny how familiar your hand is with a pound. They've got imagination too, you know."

Roger wasn't amused. His eyes had gone dark with fear. They heard the church clock strike two.

"I should have been there," said Roger. He was talking to himself.

"You talk as though the Mona is a mile away." Derek was calmer; a hint of reconciliation was in the air.

"I haven't got enough for drinks," said Roger.

"Perhaps Nicole has enough for both of you."

"Impossible," said Roger. "I don't want to ask any favours of her."

Derek was silent. He couldn't quite follow what he had heard.

"Favours?" he was asking. "Of Nicole?"

"I know she is my wife," Roger snapped. "You don't have to tell me that."

Derek had turned away. He might have decided to go into the house. But Roger had come close after him. He had never seen Roger under such strain.

"All right, all right," he was accusing. "You're getting as mean as the City men."

Derek realised that something terrible must have upset him. He was astonished by the charge; yet he felt no urge to retaliate. He had walked back to the end of the fence where Roger had left the bottles.

"But why, why do you say that?"

"It's not just the fourpence," Roger continued with his protest, "but other things. It's the way you calculate. Others have started to notice it."

"Notice what?" Derek tried to intervene. Yet he felt no emotion except alarm.

"You weren't like that," Roger went on.

"Like what?"

"Sort of ... you know."

"Sort of what?" And Derek's voice had suddenly risen to a shout.

"Well, to put it blunt," Roger shouted back. "You're getting mean. That's what. And it's not like you to be mean."

Roger couldn't bear the tension he had provoked. He glanced down at the carrier bag; but he wasn't quite sure why it was there. He was afraid what Derek would do.

"Listen," said Derek, and waited to make sure that Roger had heard. Everything seemed so obscure. "I've got an idea. Let's go to the Kings Arms instead."

"And what about Nicole?" Roger's answer came, but it was too automatic to be his own. "Suppose Nicole is waiting at the Mona."

Derek paid no attention.

"I'll help you with the bottles," he said.

But Roger was alert to the offer, and insisted on carrying the sack himself. He had offered no resistance at all. He could only hear his thirst calling: six at fourpence. And half a pint. And the cigarettes reminded him that they were one item. Half a pint and a pack of fags. He had always heard them as one item.

They walked slowly down the Hamden road. Soon they would turn right over the small wooden bridge and follow the course of the stream which made a frontier between the houses and the heath. This was familiar ground: a parade of dogs and children in the morning; a hunt for sex in the summer night. Now it had been taken over by a picnic crowd. A school of children were running wild. People lay on the grass, munching at sandwiches, grazing on fruit. There was a small market of ice-cream vans. A hot-dog stall was under the noisy siege of hands. An odour of onions filled the air.

Derek had given himself time to reflect; but it wasn't easy to invite Roger to talk. He was walking there; but his mind might have been an ocean away. Derek wondered whether there might have been trouble at home. There had been so much rumour coming out of San Cristobal, the discovery of plots, secret preparations for a major revolt. Roger's father would have been at the centre of these events.

And here it might have started: Roger's conflict with Nicole. She had never given up her efforts to bring them together, at least by letter. But Roger was adamant in his refusal. He had left that part of his life behind him; and that's where it would stay. Derek had often witnessed the most furious rows tear them apart on that issue. But Nicole would soon give way. In the end, it was always Roger's wish which won; which she wanted to win.

But the force of Roger's charge had struck him again: 'Mean, to think me mean'. It didn't hurt. It was too absurd to do any damage, and Roger would have known that too. But Derek now saw it as a cruel manifestation of Roger's fear; a savage defence against his state of panic. And this was new. He couldn't imagine what crisis might have reduced Roger to this nervous state. Roger looked as though he would have taken flight; gone into refuge anywhere. Or it might have been a question of his work. Derek hadn't noticed it before; but there had been no sound of the piano for over a week. And this was strange. Roger had a mania for work. He couldn't help it. The neighbours had grown used to the noise he made. They had been full of complaints in the early days; but this was a battle which Nicole had won; which she was determined to win. She was amiable as a dove; ferocious as the jungle cat if she had to strike in Roger's defence. It could have been some new crisis in his work. And that was the flaw in his relation to work.

Derek thought he had always detected this weakness in Roger. He had cultivated such an absolute dependence on work. He was indifferent to the future of what he did; and it seemed there was so little future for anything these days; but he had to be doing. This was no longer a matter of discipline with Roger. People thought of it as a virtue. It might even have contributed to the tolerance of the neighbours who were being disturbed. But Derek thought otherwise. This furious industry had ceased to be a virtue. It had become routine, a necessary property of Roger's existence. Life would have been a disaster if this daily fuel had been withdrawn. And this is what must have been coming. Derek thought he had always seen it threaten. He had always wondered what Roger would do if some illness made it impossible for him to work. It's true Nicole would be there; but he couldn't imagine what she would have to endure.

And now Derek was shaken by a sudden fright. He hadn't seen Nicole in the past few days. He was rehearsing the dates, counting forward from the last evening he could remember. This too was new. Everything was beginning to feel so different. Her absence would have seemed normal at any other time.

Nicole and Roger had all their meals in Roger's room in the Hamden Road. But they didn't sleep there. In the evening they transferred to Nicole's room which was a short walk away. It was simply a matter of convenience. The piano had made Roger's room too cramped. She didn't want to be breathing down his neck in the day. It made him so irritable when things went wrong. They had both agreed on this arrangement for the extra room; but there was nothing vacant in the rooming house where Roger lived. It suited them well. They lived happily together in separate rooms. They would leave for Nicole's room at night; and Roger returned to his first thing in the morning. It was the same every day, except on weekends when the arrangement was reversed. Nicole would abandon her place on the Friday afternoon and remain at Roger's until the following Monday. 'We have a nice little flat,' Roger would often say, 'but you'll have to take a threepenny ride from one room to the next.' Like his mania for work, it was an arrangement which had become routine.

They were leaving the sun worshippers behind. Roger knew it wouldn't be long before Derek started making enquiries about Nicole. He expected it to happen any minute; and it seemed to make him more depressed. He would hold him off.

But Derek didn't speak. He was glad for a moment's distraction from his fear. He was encouraging an unreasonable interest in the heath. It lay soft and warm around them, a temporary solace of countryside in this eccentric suburb of London. Couples were twisting about each other. They stretched close and hot over the crumbling sheets of fallen leaves. Derek could see the children, swift and mad as birds, swinging their hands up from the water. The pond was an ocean of fists.

They were approaching the street. A family of pigeons had rocketed down in front of the Kings Arms. There was a small fountain opposite. A man with a stockbroker's face was letting the water spray his clothes. The pigeons were dancing round him, eating birdseed out of his hands. They were making a cage of his bowler hat. He was their sole benefactor; and Derek thought it was good to see him there. He must have taken the afternoon off. The sun had chosen him for a rendezvous with nature; had granted him a reprieve from the rigours of commerce.

Derek watched the pigeons squat on the crown of the man's bowler hat. It might have been a ledge of scaffolding they were tripping over. Derek could have watched him all afternoon. He enjoyed this kind of spectacle. It made him forget he was out of work. And so did the Kings Arms with its face of a prison. He had never gone there before. But they had arrived. It was time to negotiate. But Derek had little more than souvenirs in his pocket, his small collection of foreign coins. He didn't know why the hell he carried them everywhere. Then he heard Roger say six at fourpence and a pack of fags. He was carrying the sack of bottles like a hump on his back.

Two

'Gently does it,' said Derek to himself, 'go easy with this gangster.'

The barman had taken the empty bottles away. He had slapped the change on the counter and gone off. Now he saw them waiting. He was coming back. He moved very slowly. There might have been some fearful weight planted in his crutch; something that could explode. He came so slowly forward; a hurricane was gathering in his eye. They could feel the grumble in his gaze. But Derek was calm as the summer sky. 'Gently does it', he went on saying to himself. Until the barman was there. He had got as far as the counter, and looked surprised that he couldn't go further. A great ship of a man, fat and windy as a cloud.

Derek never smoked; yet it was the cigarettes which he ordered first. The barman didn't move; but he had sent his hand for the pack. They saw his arm travel in an arc over his shoulder. Then his open sleeve was sailing it back. The box fell on the counter.

"That'll be one and ninepence," the barman's voice had bugled.

Derek smiled and looked as though he wanted to say it was a fair price, an honest enough warning. He was picking the right coins from among his souvenirs. He paid for the cigarettes; then passed the box to Roger. 'Gently does it', he heard himself say.

"And could we have half a pint?" Derek said.

"Two halves?" the barman's bugle was calling out.

"One half," said Derek, "and two glasses. If it's not too much to ask."

The bugle wanted to be heard; but it had lost its wind. The hurricane was swelling in the barman's eye. A girl had come up with the two halves of bitter. Derek took one. He was busy with the change which remained on the counter, segregating the halfpennies from their better half. The barman watched Derek's hands playing draughts with the sixpences. He was shovelling the price of the beer across the bar.

"If you could spare the extra glass," said Derek.

The barman didn't move; but he helped the other hand under the counter. It went without his consent. It came up so slowly, suspending the glass in the air. Derek took it gently away. The barman watched them divide the beer; one half pint in two glasses. The barman's bugle must have lost its sound. Derek gave Roger the rest of the change, and bowed to the barman as he reversed. They were sitting down. It seemed a long time before they had taken a sip of the beer; but they were sitting. That's all the barman could be sure his eye had seen. They were sitting. Half a pint and two glasses. He had never heard a case like it before. But there they were. Sitting down. He wouldn't have shown the least surprise if they had started to fly. Half a pint and two glasses. Soon they would fly.

The Kings Arms had the face of a prison. The doors were difficult to swing. They had the solid, leaden feel of gates that closed you in or shut you firmly out. There was a clown's head of John Bull grinning from the wall: a thick red foam of lips; the dead stump of a cigar was slipping from its teeth. There was a smell of iron;

the shades of rust were crumbling from the walls. And mirrors everywhere. The naked crown of a head began to shake in the saloon bar. A worker's goitre was boiling with talk in the public bar. The mirrors were like a cinema show. Reflections entered and melted swiftly from the glass.

An old couple were sitting at opposite tables in the private bar. They had looked up to see who had joined them; brought a silence to their talk, like a token of respect for the dead; and then continued as though no one else had come in.

Derek guessed that they would soon be gone. The barman lingered as though something unexpected might happen. He would be ready to intercede.

"You see what I mean, Jim?" the old woman was saying, and Jim's head began its feeble dance. He was nodding. "You see what I mean, Jim?" the old woman said again. The man tried to light his pipe while the nod went on. His head was rocking like a doll on springs. "See what I mean?" And the hinges ordered the old man's head to nod. It looked as though he had been making this answer all his life. The pipe was lit. The head was rocking gently to a rest. But the old woman was summoning his attention once more. "She died in her sleep," the old woman said. The old man's head awoke. "Best way to get out o' this life," he said. It was the only time he spoke. The old woman got up. "Died in her sleep," she said and started for the door. "Best way to get out," the old man agreed, and followed after her.

Roger looked as though he was about to faint.

"Are you feeling all right?" Derek asked.

"Fine," he said. But he was still hearing the old man's voice as though there were some magic in their decrepitude which cast its spell over him. Derek had paid more attention to the woman. She looked older than the man; but there was still a sharpness of vinegar in her tongue. He wondered where they came from; where they would go next. And Roger kept thinking that he had seen his future in the old man's eyes. Derek noticed the sign of panic coming back. Roger had reached for the glass.

"We're not all down on our luck," said Derek. "There's still Teeton."

Roger had swallowed quickly as though the beer had made a lump of ice in his throat.

"What about Teeton?" he asked.

"I never thought he would bother to have an exhibition," Derek said.

"I hear he's given the paintings away," Roger said. "Not quite, but almost."

"Who told you that?"

"That's what he told *her*," said Roger, and turned to the glass again.

Derek felt his caution take over. It must have been serious for Roger to refer to Nicole as *her*. Derek was trying to judge what he should ask.

"That's what he told Nicole?"

"You heard me," Roger answered; and there was the hint of curtness in his voice. He was trying to build some guard around his trouble; but it was not easy for him to do so with Derek.

"Didn't he take any money?" Derek asked, now keeping clear of Nicole's name.

"I suppose they paid him something," said Roger, trying to declare his lack of interest. "Don't ask me how much."

Now he was trying to concentrate on what Teeton might have done. Teeton and the old couple who had gone. He was inviting them to occupy his mind; to protect him from concern about Nicole. 'Best way to get out of life', the old man had said. It seemed such a positive way to speak of dying; of something you really couldn't do. Like Teeton who had decided to get out of painting. Why would he have wanted to make this break with the only force which had really kept him alive since he fled from home? But you couldn't get Teeton to talk about this. He had a way of keeping himself apart. Even in friendship he seemed to make that distance a condition. Unlike Derek who could convert any feeling into some form of partnership. That's why he was so afraid of being here with Derek. He knew he would have to talk.

"Do you think he'll ever go back?" Roger asked.

Derek wasn't paying attention. He had been conducting his own speculations on Nicole. He looked at Roger, and quickly turned his attention to the beer.

"What did you say?"

"Teeton, I was thinking about Teeton," Roger said. "Why has he stopped painting?"

"He's never told anyone." Derek seemed to show little interest in the matter. But he noticed that Roger was still waiting for an answer. It seemed he needed to hear something different; something that might come to his support.

"He never talks about his wife," said Roger.

Derek agreed; but he made no comment.

"Did you know Randa?" Roger went on; as though he needed some firm commitment from Derek who had become almost careless in his replies.

"I suppose so," he said. "In a way."

"They were together before the trouble in San Souci," said Roger.

Derek agreed; but his lips were already on the glass. He didn't speak.

"Why didn't she join him here?" Roger persisted. His curiosity was now beyond control. It seemed he had to find an ally in someone else's marital defeat. "She could have come if she wanted to."

"If Teeton wanted her to come," said Derek. He was on the point of turning the interrogation back on Roger. "Do you know what happened between the two of them?"

"No," Roger said quickly, almost hopefully.

"Nor do I," said Derek, retreating from this bait of gossip. "And we can't get anywhere if we don't know what's what. Can we?"

Derek had let his caution slip; and Roger knew he couldn't hold him off much longer. But he was going to resist. He felt it was a matter of his own survival to keep this trouble with Nicole strictly to himself. But Derek was preparing his bait again.

"Why were you going to ask Teeton for a whole pound?" Derek asked. "Are the bailiffs after you?"

"I wanted to entertain her," said Roger.

It was plain that his meaning had escaped Derek who had suddenly brought his hand to a halt, delaying with the rim of the glass under his lip. He was breathing heavily on to the beer.

"Are you feeling all right?" Derek asked.

"Just fine," said Roger, trying to distract attention from himself.

"I don't follow," Derek went on. He had returned the glass to the table without drinking. "To entertain Nicole?"

"Let me handle this myself," said Roger. "There are things each man has to handle himself."

"For example?" Derek's voice now seemed ripe for argument.

"Close as we are," said Roger, "there's still a little room for privacy."

Derek looked stung by this rebuke; but he was just as eager to deny Roger's claims to such a private life. They had always shared in the mutual gossip about their own affairs. Roger's attempt at secrecy now had the force of a betrayal; and Derek was never slow to detect any vice which might put a strain on their friendship. Such fear always brought a casual obscenity to his rescue.

"Privacy my arse," said Derek, inspecting the bar over his shoulder, "either you want to talk or you don't want to talk. But don't come giving me this privacy shit."

"OK," said Roger. "I don't want to talk."

Derek made a move for his glass, considered how much beer remained, and decided there wasn't enough to survive an argument. They still had half an hour before closing time.

The barman had come into view. He was not only there; but he was letting himself be seen: an enormous and attentive guardian of the brewers' daily fortunes. He looked up at the clock; and then across at Derek's table. Roger's glass was already empty. There was nothing but a ledge of foam slipping down the bottom of the glass. The barman was reading the clock hands again with a slow, scholarly deliberation; and when he turned to check again the measure of Roger's glass, Derek leaned forward, very low over the table and dribbled half of his beer into Roger's glass.

And then it seemed a miracle had happened in the Kings Arms bar. They hadn't seen the barman coming. They might have forgotten that he was there. But the lid of the counter had been pushed up; and the enormous waist was struggling to bring the man on the other side of the bar. He had got through at last. The hurricane had retreated from his eye. The summer must have done something to make him glad. They didn't know. But they thought they saw him smile. It was impossible to tell whom he was after. They were the only people left in the bar. He was standing at the table. They didn't know how to welcome him; but the air had suddenly lost its fist of iron.

The barman put the pint of beer on the table. It was done very quickly, and without a word. The miracle was there, plain as day. It was theirs. But the barman didn't make a sound. He was gone. They watched his body labouring back to the counter. The lid went up; and his shoulders were rowing him through to the other side. In a minute it was over. He saw them staring at him. He did a kind of handshake with his ears; and the bush on his eyebrows quickly jumped up and down. Then he walked to the saloon bar, and out of their view.

The barman's gesture had produced an effect of appeasement; for Derek had suddenly become less truculent with his queries about Nicole. Indeed, it seemed that he had resigned himself to the status of a stranger. He would be content to bear witness when it was allowed.

"I suppose it's not my business," he said, "but I was never too happy about you and Nicole taking separate rooms." He raised the glass to acknowledge the barman's generosity. "Everything seemed so right the way it was before. Even if the one room was a bit on the small side for two."

For the first time Roger looked composed. He was massaging his hands up and down his thighs; putting his fingers through a nimble exercise, knuckling his fists to crack the joints; and all the while he weighed the meaning of what Derek had said. He wanted to agree; but he was also careful to protect his own judgement from any out-side influence. Grateful to Derek for this mild concession, he also felt an overwhelming need to be in absolute control of his decisions.

"It was her idea," he said, and interrupted his thinking by giving his attention to the drink.

Derek held a different view, but he was reluctant to encourage any conflict. If Nicole had suggested the change, it was really Roger who had created the situation which led her to offer. During previous discussion of this matter, this was the version which Derek had accepted. But it wouldn't have been prudent, at this moment, to challenge Roger with such a denial. For a moment Derek felt he was betraying Nicole by his failure to disagree. And in her absence!

"Not that the change made any difference," he said, groping his way round Roger's defences.

Roger was preoccupied with his hands, craning the glass up slowly from the table. He noticed that it was a matter of five minutes to closing time; and the earlier fears came over him. What was the future of this afternoon? He had retreated from his promise to meet Nicole at the Mona. The lights had started to warn of closing time in the Kings Arms. The barman had started a noise with the empty glasses which he shovelled into the warm water. Voices were making arrangements for vague reunions in the evening. It was activity which gave Roger a moment's respite from his obligations. He drained his glass, and gave Derek warning of his departure. But it was all in the nature of preparation. He had no notion what he would do; or the direction he would choose when they left the pub.

"We didn't do too badly," said Derek, indicating a penny on the table. "As I say you never know what's waiting at the end of the road."

"Where do you go from here?" Roger asked.

Derek pondered the question; then said: "Hadn't thought of it. But I suppose you'll have to find Nicole."

"Listen," said Roger, "if it will put you at ease. The truth is I don't want to find Nicole."

"Don't get me wrong," said Derek, "I'm not interfering."

"All the same, you might as well know," said Roger. He had broken into a stammer. The quiver of the upper lip was sharp as wire. And Derek watched him, waiting. There was a look of peril in Roger's eyes.

"Know what?" Derek asked.

"Nicole has found herself a man," said Roger. "That's all."

Derek was uncertain how he should react. This news made no impact on him except to recall Roger's agitation when they met.

"Who told you that?" he said. His voice was negligent, almost dismissive. He was still far from feeling the reality of what Roger had said.

"She is pregnant," Roger said gravely, "that's how I know."

He had pushed himself up from the chair.

"Nicole's pregnant?" Derek repeated.

"That's why we were to meet at the Mona," said Roger. He

was halfway to the door; then waited to make sure that Derek was following. "So now you know."

They stood outside the door, waiting to see who would be the next to speak. 'I'd better not leave him alone', Derek thought.

"Let's go," he said. "Let's go back to my room."

Three

Their friendship had also acquired a quality of routine. It had grown without effort. Neither could have said with any certainty how it had started. There had always been respect; and there was also an element of admiration. Each had come to regard the other's adversity as his own. All these things would have been true in their relation to Teeton; yet there was a difference. Whenever they spoke of Teeton in his absence, they would recognise some force of intimacy which never got beyond themselves. Somehow it didn't reach out to include Teeton. Teeton knew this was so; but it had never been a cause for envy. In a way which he couldn't be bothered to explain, Teeton admired this exclusiveness in their relationship; and there were times when he gave the impression that he enjoyed it. Sometimes Teeton would withdraw from their company as though some instinct made him anticipate that Roger and Derek would soon want to be alone. It would be wrong to say that they would have preferred him to go. Their need would have been too subtle to name. It existed below the level of choice. But Teeton would know that it was there; and he would go. They would scarcely be aware that he had gone. It might have been a duty he was glad to perform. He would leave them alone.

That's how he would have found them now in Derek's room. It seemed they had survived the turbulence of the Kings Arms bar. The afternoon was a stranger which loitered outside. They had come back to the security of a home. Roger sat in the chair he called his pew. It was an austere piece of furniture. The back came straight up, hard and high against his neck. The seat was like concrete. But he might have been sitting in clover. He was paddling a spoon through the sugar, crushing wet lumps of crystal against the side of the bowl. Now he was turning the handle round, working it like a plough over the bottom of the bowl.

Derek sat away from the table in the low arm chair. He said he thought it would rain. A cloud was making new shadows outside the window. The air had gathered weight. There was a feeling of damp descending from the ceiling. The light wasn't bad; but it might have been brighter for this time of day.

"You must think me a real bastard," Roger said, taking his hand away from the bowl. "I didn't even ask you how it went today."

Derek gave an idle glance to the table and shrugged his shoulder. "Not bad enough," he said, "there's the usual bit part going."

"You're not going to play a corpse again."

"It's the body again," said Derek. He was getting ready to laugh. "It's the body or nothing."

But Roger didn't want to be amused. He didn't like sharing in Derek's mockery of himself. His loyalties were about to get the better of his judgement.

"You think the agent plays you fair?"

"It's difficult to tell," said Derek. "He doesn't write the plays, so I can't accuse him of keeping me out. I don't fit the parts that come his way."

It was difficult to challenge this argument. The agent was simply an agent. He couldn't order parts that would fit Derek. But Roger had lost his taste for reason. He thought of the agent with a slight disgust. The odour of the merchant put a shiver in his smell.

"I think you ought to change him," he said.

"They're much the same," Derek reminded him. "He's about the third I've had."

"Still think you ought to change him."

"From the corpse to the grave?" Derek was laughing. "That's some consolation."

"Doesn't he even offer any advice?"

"He doesn't say it," Derek said, "perhaps he thinks I ought to get out of the business altogether."

"The bastard."

"He might just have a point."

"But that's impossible."

Roger raised the cup and finished the cold remains of the tea. He saw the agent's skeleton under the leaves.

"I'd give him a wide berth," he said.

Derek was considering the alternatives he might have had. But he had gone through all this before. He had trained himself to go on waiting.

"There's only one reason I'd want to change," Derek said. "He looks so bloody hurt when he has to tell me the truth. It's not so easy for him to go on saying no, nothing doing. It's a bore. Absolute torture for him."

Roger was going after the agent again, but he withheld his attack. Derek's composure was quite beyond him. It was almost too easy to be true: this serenity of feeling which Derek showed when he talked about the agent's failure to find him work. Roger felt something like envy when he reflected on these fruitless journeys which Derek had been making in and out of agents' offices. It had given Roger a strange admiration for actors. He didn't really care how good they were. It made no difference whether they were successful. He thought of them as the most extraordinary of all the people he had known. They wore like iron. In all weathers, after the harshest decline, they'd still keep bobbing up, patient as stone the way they waited.

Roger had taken the spoon again. He was steering it gently round the rim of the bowl. He was forgetting his disgust with agents. It was the actors' occupation which haunted his thinking. So utterly dependent on others! And when they were out of work! He had been close to Derek, but it was still difficult for him to understand the nature of this joblessness, the menace of an actor's inactivity. It had very special rigours for them. There was nothing they could do when there wasn't anything for them to do. He thought of Teeton and the life of painters he knew. This was a different kind of isolation. Like his own, it could always be kept active. His services might not be required; but he always had work to do. The meanest occasion could fertilise Teeton's mind, drive his hands to invent a form he had never seen before. And it was the same in his own experience of making music. He had come to think of instruments as something of a bore. He had no great passion for the concert performance. He could do without them while he struggled and searched through the darkest corners of his mind to build a score. He lived and flourished in a ferment of silence. And he was alone. Always it had to be done alone.

But an actor out of work was a fish out of water, a man who was literally deprived of his calling. He had to fortify his resistance to defeat by practising the art of being idle. And yet there was nothing about Derek to suggest that he was ever idle. When you heard him singing in the morning, it was as though he had found some cause for celebration. It was the same when you saw him strolling over the heath. The earth might have selected his stride for special welcome. He gave you that feeling. And it was there now. He might have been in the agent's office, hearing his future announce that he would never be discovered as a corpse again. Roger heard him laughing. He couldn't understand why Derek found this waste of gift so funny.

"But it's true," Derek was saying as he sank under his laughter into the hollow of the chair. "Death is my bank. It brings what little grub I get."

"Don't be an ass," Roger was trying to protest.

"But it's true," Derek went on. "Take the last five jobs. In each play I was the body that was found. Once it fell from the loft in the middle of a lunch. Then I was the body they found in His Lordship's chamber. It has brought disaster to at least three dinners. That's me, Roger. My corpse may be found anywhere, but it turns up especially at eating time. What a career!"

Roger had got up from the table. He could barely hear Derek's voice chase after him as he looked out from the window.

"And I rehearse," said Derek. "You can't be found dead without proper rehearsal. Every corpse has its own angle, its own way of going stiff."

The clouds had started on a slow retreat, breaking formation as they moved away, unfolding lazily against the distant fall of sky, like bolts of cloth. There was a dazzle of sunlight, searching briefly over the face of the window pane. Roger was watching the slow collapse of shadows slipping down the trees. A squirrel was investigating the black scab of bark which opened like an old wound over the root of the cherry tree. Its body was a shiver from nose tip to the tail. Roger saw its eyes dart everywhere, two flaming beads that set their own gaze on fire. Roger watched the squirrel leap forward and as quickly land again. The lean neck stretched, a cord of elastic that could bend and swing to meet any warning of sound. There was an air of meekness and terror in its vigilance. It had detected signals of danger everywhere. It nibbled at the air; the eyes blinked, reading the rustle of leaves, reporting on every rumour of the wind. There were enemies everywhere. The nearest neighbour was a cause of fear, an honourable reason for flight.

"More tea?" Derek asked, shaking the empty kettle.

Roger turned from the window and listened to the sound of gas hissing from the burner. There was a spurt of flame; and then the ring of fire came on. Derek sat the kettle down over the blaze.

"You know something?" he started.

"Yes," said Roger, "I think I know."

"Hold on," Derek chided him, "I'm not trying to meddle in your business."

"I didn't think you were."

"I was only going to say," Derek resumed.

"That it's seven years since we left," Roger broke in.

Derek smiled. He thought of teasing with a denial; then chuckled, and raised his hands as though he were going to applaud.

"How did you guess?" he asked.

"Just felt it coming," said Roger, as he heard the first wheezing of the kettle.

They had travelled together from the torrid island of San Cristobal into the surprising bleakness of an English spring. They had spoken kindly of the cold; admired the elusive lustre of their first snow. The rain came, paused and came again. Summer was in the habit of deceiving them: rash bursts of sunshine would soon disappear behind the sullen brooding of the city's spires. The weather displayed its malice in various ways; but it had acquired the privilege of history. It was inconvenient and forgivable.

They were young and devoted; the most eager of candidates for adoption, indifferent to the simple demands that nagged the social herd. They had invested all their virtues in the rigorous struggle of being artists. They had discovered a style of difficulty that promised to free them from the insecurities of their origin. More important, they had escaped the cruelties of neglect. Whatever indignities the foreign city might impose, it had achieved a most vital claim on their affection.

They had come from a land where loyalties were fragile, and confidence in scarce supply. Something was forever threatening to give way. Each day smelt of catastrophe; threatened to tear the fabric of their lives apart. The poor cursed their deprivation; and the wealthy grieved drunkenly over their lack of power. There was no evidence of comfort anywhere. The climate was a brothel, sordid with pleasures. From the earliest discovery of ambition they had realised that their future would have to be found elsewhere. Childhood was a warning; and school was further proof. From the beginning they had been educated for escape. This city had chosen them the moment they discovered their ambitions. Now the kettle had perfected a music which was their substitute for the sea. They had consumed oceans of tea; seen the islands daily at breakfast whenever they broke an egg and pondered the fragile beauty of its shell.

But time had begun to put a strain on their refuge. The islands were no longer behind them, on some other side of the ocean. New cargoes of men had crossed the sky; and San Cristobal had started to multiply in the heart of England. Their gifts had remained steadfast; but events had begun to alter the nature of their vocation. They were conscious of pressure where, formerly, they had detected simply the necessary emergence of challenge. Once a black man had stopped Roger on the street, and attacked him with the simple question: "Tell me, sir, what do you do in this man' town?"

"Music," Roger had greeted him. "I'm a composer."

And the man's answer was a rude awakening: "I say there must be a stop to that. All dancing done. Is men like you make niggers think with their feet. Give me a law and I amputate every dancin' nigger from his legs. An' singin' likewise. I against all that activity what make niggers swap play for power."

Roger, recovering from the thought of these fearful punishments, had tried mildly to protest. "But all races have music."

"But niggers get a surplus far in excess," the man had replied. "I would ban it from every meeting place. School an' chapel. If 'tis musical instruments niggers need they must learn the gun. That makes a sound to some real purpose. You follow me, sir?"

Roger had no intention of following him; but when they were about to separate, the man had taken Roger's shoulder and brought his face close, inspecting him like a passport. "Ain't you Judge Capildeo's son?"

And Roger had answered with a nod that he was. And the man

began to smile, kindly and perplexed. "Can't understand your type o' people at all."

Roger would never have engaged in argument with such a man. He would never waste his time in controversy which he regarded as fruitless. Nor would he have encouraged the man out of curiosity to learn more about him. Such interest would have struck him as an idle and fraudulent exercise. Learning was not a game you should play with people who had no real meaning for you. It was an attitude which had isolated him from his own place of birth; for Roger could never recognise any links between him and San Cristobal. It seemed that history had amputated his root from some other human soil, and deposited him, by chance, in a region of time which was called an island. He had never really experienced the island as place, a society of people.

San Cristobal had no antiquity; no magic of remoteness; no trail which led to some prize of ruins that might be waiting for discovery. It was always a kind of embarrassment for Roger that the island could not say 'before the birth of Christ' and go on to trace its memory forward to his own time.

He had never heard any music stir in his hands when he climbed the rocks in the Cockpit country. There was only sound; a fury of noise conferred on the landscape from outside. That's how he had always thought of his childhood. It lacked some melody that was native to the rocks. He couldn't trust the rhythms of nature which had given this landscape its music: the rivers in their torrential bursts of passion in the morning; or the melodies of the mountain breeze at night. His father had often taken him to see the waterfall at the Kaiteur pass; but it had aroused no sentiment in him. The water simply fell, a waste of energy which could only shout its echoes through the forest, increasing their noise until they fell in deadly confusion on the aimless coastland. He had grown afraid of the landscape; afraid of the sudden, early descent of the nights; the quality of darkness which seemed to be secreted at the heart of daylight. Everyone around seemed to take a mad delight in celebrating the impure; so that he had inherited this horror of impurity. He had always wanted to get away; to be gone from the chaos of his childhood.

"It was always more difficult for you," Derek was saying. "You'd so much opposition to cope with. And from the very start."

"Not any more than you." Roger had grown more patient with the past; and he resisted any explanations that might be offered on his behalf.

"I didn't have your kind of father," said Derek; and paused as though some shadow of foreboding had drifted back from his childhood.

"That's true," Roger conceded. "That was the greatest opposition of all. I must have hated him from the very start."

But it was a difficult kind of hatred to resolve; for his father, the only man of civilised tastes in his own profession, had been the first to recognise Roger's gift for music. He had taught him the piano himself and continued to supervise his progress long after he had ceased to be anyone's pupil. But there was some deep conflict of spirit; some subtle and bitter antagonism in their needs, which had set father and son apart.

"I don't think he ever realised it, you know."

"It can happen that way," said Derek. "The biggest offer of help makes for the greatest obstacle in your way."

"It was only after I got away," said Roger, "that I realised what was wrong. He had nothing he could call his own, nothing at all. Everything he had he got from learning. Everything was like the law he'd been taught. Even when he was angry you could see he was simply practising what he had learnt. It wasn't really his. And when he smiled it was much the same. He was simply doing what he learnt. But it wasn't really his. Not even his smile."

Roger showed no sign of emotion when he spoke. A meeting with his father would not have been a very friendly affair; yet he had come to think there was some change in his attitude. It was one of the many benefits which had rewarded his life in London. He had been freed from the tribal irritations which were natural to the status of such a family. Yet he knew he could never accept any offer to return to their protection. It was the most certain conviction which had grown with his separation from the island. But it made him a little sad at times: the certainty of it; and the sense of finality which it signified. That he should have trained his feeling to be forever out of reach of his father's generosity.

"It's a terrible thing," he was advising Derek, "not to be able to accept what's honestly given."

"I don't suppose you'd ever touch the old judge for a loan?" Derek looked a little grieved that it should be so; but he didn't want to return too soon to the question of Nicole. Or he would have suggested calling on the help of the old Judge. He would have given Roger and his wife any house which their happiness could buy.

"Of course," Derek went on, trying to hide his meaning under cover of a joke. "It wouldn't be against my virtue to touch him on your behalf."

"I wish I could approve," said Roger, "just for your virtue's sake."

Everything was so clear to them that the reference to Derek's virtue had evoked the same response. They were both laughing, although Derek looked a little ambiguous all the while.

"I don't suppose I'll ever change," Derek said, "but the influence on me was just as strong. You don't know how powerful a chapel education can be. And from infancy."

"Honesty is," said Roger, bringing his mockery to an end, "how does it go. Something to do with policy."

"The best," said Derek with absolute lack of humour. "Your old man might make use of it in the Court. But in my chapel it was like the first meal of the day. For the pastors it was literally true."

Roger listened without further comment on this familiar difference between them. They had been nourished on much the same kind of belief, but Derek's obstacles of poverty were easier to overcome. At any rate they had no power to threaten his future; for he had inherited no kind of privilege which he couldn't with a good conscience betray. Roger's father was a comparatively wealthy man, whose ambition was to build his name into a monument of statues and impressive family tombs. The future was like a bailiff who kept one step ahead of Roger all the way from his birth until he lost his trail in the anonymous haven of London life.

"And when the call comes," said Derek, recalling the fearful prophecies of the chapel, "where shall you be? How stands it with you, sinner man?"

He was looking for ways to impersonate his answer. "To be honest with you," came his reply, "we have lost our feet. For the moment, that is. We are flat out on what was made for sitting. But only for the moment." He was talking to the ceiling, but Roger couldn't resist making the answer his.

"It's been a long moment," he said.

"Are you complaining?" Derek looked up, half in rebuke. "What's behind should not be brought forward. It's against the rule."

"You sound like the noble Moor," said Roger. "Or don't you remember?"

He was getting up from the table.

"God, all that attention made me dizzy," said Derek.

Roger was drawing his attention to the photographs, to souvenirs of a more recent past.

"We enjoyed it," said Roger. He had got up to take a closer look of the photograph over the mantelpiece. It was the scene in which Othello meets Desdemona after the first rumour of her infidelity. Roger was playing his fingers up and down the smooth, dark grain of the wood. It was a huge frame, almost two feet in length, and made all the more impressive by the sombre shades of olive gold which covered the surface. The light made a neat division of Derek's face so that the left cheek shimmered under a haze of starlight as though the camera had caught a moment of lightning that threatened to explode the massive obscurity of the head. Desdemona appeared under a veil of shadows, clean and nervous as a bird: her hands, slender and trembling, forever engaged in the act of offering.

"I didn't think you did a bad job," said Roger.

"Terrible. It was terrible." Derek's voice was distant as though he had to detach himself from all active feelings about this phase of his career. Roger refused to support this severity. He had grown used to Derek's tendency to be in doubt about the excellence of anything he did.

"You're always hard on yourself," he said, ignoring Derek's effort to protest.

"It's better than fooling yourself," said Derek.

"Not always," Roger was arguing. "Self-criticism can work like sabotage. I've known some people with an abundance of gifts who won't ever get anything done. They keep too sharp an eye on every move they make. Every slightest flaw gets looked at as a failure. The only way to avoid failure is to avoid flaws. Which is just a way of saying that you won't do anything at all."

73

"Thus spake the prophet," Derek was jeering. More serious now, he added: "You just can't go into things blind. You know that. A man must know what he is doing."

"Sometimes you have to go blind," Roger argued. "It's the only chance of discovering what you have to do."

"You put a great value on ignorance."

"Enormous," Roger broke in. He had become passionate in his defence. "It has a value all its own."

"You talk like people back home," Derek chided him. "They take such pride in not knowing."

"I'd say it's you who won't get rid of home," Roger returned. "They think it's really a crime not to be right."

For a while they kept up this ardent struggle to extol the virtues of a different point of view. It would become spirited, almost combative in its sharpness of exchange; for it was a measure of their friendship that they allowed no secrecy of feeling in such moments of attack. In moments of anger, or prolonged frustration, their judgements might hurt; but they left no poisoning wounds. They had achieved a kind of comradeship which made them free from the fear of malice. There were no debts of apology in their account.

They had transferred their attention to the other frames: portraits of famous actors whom Derek admired; shots of the National Theatre stage; a foreign company in rehearsal. But the supreme memory would always be Derek's season as the Moor at Stratford-on-Avon. Roger had paused to admire the portrait of themselves. He was on the left, short and slightly bent with a hint of dilapidation in his clothes. He was wearing a pair of blue corduroy trousers which floated at the knees. The pullover sagged about him like a pillow case. He was laughing. Derek was on the right, tall, and neat in his white T-shirt. His body displayed that suppleness of muscle which recalled his days as an athlete. He wore blue jeans which had acquired the prim dignity of an evening suit. Teeton occupied the middle place. His hair was the first thing you saw, and it never allowed you to look elsewhere. It had grown berserk, thick and long and wild like some vine or vegetable root which had lost its natural rhythm of growth. He was staring directly at the camera, his eyes open in alarm as though he was about to bring this game of recording faces to an end. His arms were stretched wide and lost from sight until the

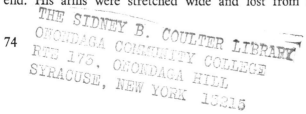

hands emerged on either side of the other two. One arm supported Derek round the waist while the other finished in a grip of Roger's shoulder. These were halcyon days. Derek was paraded like a hit song with Roger and Teeton as his chorus. Stratford was like a dream that would never end.

"You never take credit for it," said Roger, "the way you got us in on that."

But Derek was quick to detach himself from this offer of gratitude. Roger had got a small commission for the music which accompanied the revelling scene; and Teeton was apprenticed to the designer who had provided the sets. It was the only opportunity they had ever had to collaborate on a single project. But Teeton could barely survive the tensions which had grown between him and the producer. Neither allowed the other a single opportunity for toleration. And Teeton would certainly have left if he hadn't considered the possible dangers which an abusive row would have had for Derek's career. Perhaps he had no temperament for the stage. There was a frenzy of emotion which seemed to swamp everything the people around him had to do. They were always in a sweat of passion. It seemed their frequent changes of face had put them beyond any ordinary act of recognition. They seemed to live too much inside each other's disasters; they were always exchanging personal miseries. They made Teeton feel like a spy.

Derek appeared to lose interest in the photograph. He was trying to resist the temptation of drawing attention to himself. He didn't trust the subtle briberies by which the past could lead you on; seduce you into a state of irrational delight; provide you with a mortgage of excuses for every decline of judgement that plunged you hopelessly into the future. Roger was still engrossed with the photograph as though he wanted to identify every moment of feeling which he had experienced that day.

"Yes," he shouted, "now I've got it." Derek barely looked up to acknowledge his excitement. "We had just got back from that lunch. First time I ever had a sandwich without bread. Was chicken and strawberries. You remember? And Teeton was laughing all the time. Just look at the chicken and he was laughing like a lunatic. It was he who decided to do away with the bread. Just have a chicken sandwich with the strawberries as bread."

"And you drank a bottle of champagne each," Derek said coldly. "I've never since seen strawberries that size," said Roger. "Some were large as tomatoes."

Roger walked away from the photograph, slightly dizzy with his memory of the afternoon. He observed Derek's reticence. There was such a calm over the room. Roger resisted the urge to talk; he wanted to see how long it would last; who would be the first to break this spell of reverie which had invaded the atmosphere. Any image of home was now utterly absent from his mind. There was something remote and imperturbable about this tranquil mood that had come over him. He was observing the room; admiring the incredible order to which it had been submitted. Everything was modest, and perfect: the shelves of books erect in their celluloid jackets, supported by chiselled slabs of white stone; the dancing curtains of white gauze; the huge bamboo mats that looked like enormous rims of hats spread out in circles over the floor. Above him the lamp shade opened in the shape of a cage with strips of paper that looked like ribbon twisted round the bars of wire.

Roger was about to break the silence. He was going to make some comment on the lamp shade when he heard voices ascending from the landing below. The low, secret throttle of giggles soon broke free into scandalous bursts of laughter. The girl tenants had arrived. Derek turned to face the door. He was going to call out to the girls to be quiet; but they had already locked themselves out of hearing. It was always the same at this hour. A clatter of heels gave notice of their coming; then an interval of whispering, and the final crescendo of their laugh announced they were well and safely home. Soon the church clock would strike five; and Roger started to anticipate the arrival of the others.

The day had suddenly changed mood. Roger felt the room stir with his apprehension for the hours ahead. He was feeling a mild regret about the way he had spent the afternoon. It might have been wiser to keep his engagement with Nicole. If she had refused to come, then he would have been fortified by the knowledge that he wasn't afraid to let her know what he was going to do. But what was he going to do? He looked towards the window where the first evidence of the darkness was appearing. Now there seemed little doubt that it would rain.

Derek had sensed his difficulty. He knew that Roger was probably trying to make up his mind where he should sleep. Whenever he had quarrelled with Nicole, it was the normal custom for him to break their domestic rule by sleeping in his room. But this was not a quarrel, Derek thought. It was a wholly new stage of crisis that couldn't very well be kept within the ordinary limit of their rules. He was fond of Nicole; had come to feel this fondness inseparable from his friendship with Roger. It would be impossible to abstain from all participation in their future. Whatever they decided to do, he would be involved in the result. But he couldn't bring himself to give any importance to what Roger had said. About her pregnancy, yes. That was natural, though contrary to their intentions. But another man? The suspicion was quite beyond belief. No one would have accepted it, not even if Nicole herself had said so. And yet there must have been some basis for Roger's charge. Derek felt a stab of shame as he tried to speculate who it could be. Certainly no one they knew? And what extremity of revenge would drive Nicole to such an act of deception against herself?

Each question seemed more absurd than the one it had given rise to. But he had seen Roger's agitation earlier in the afternoon; and there was nothing absurd in his behaviour. Nor was his sullen brooding any less real now. For Roger's terror had returned. Perhaps he should try to call Teeton who was always brisk and brutal in his decisions on matters in which he wasn't directly involved. Then he remembered that Teeton might have been away. According to the Old Dowager, Teeton had been gone for two days. He had left no word when he would return. But Derek didn't believe her. The Old Dowager had appointed herself Teeton's guardian and thought it her duty to keep the world at bay. She was always postponing delivery of his calls. She didn't think Teeton was in. She didn't think Teeton was awake. She didn't think Teeton would approve. She kept eternal guard against all efforts at intrusion. Derek was getting carried away by his angry recollections of the Old Dowager; so that she appeared, for a moment, to be an obstacle to any comfort which he might have provided for Roger and Nicole.

"I think I'll call Teeton," he said; as though it were just a way of making himself heard.

"Teeton isn't back," said Roger.

"But how do you know?"

"He isn't, I say."

"But this afternoon you were insisting ..."

"Just panic," said Roger. "It was just my way of wishing that he was."

Derek showed a moment's surprise; then settled quietly for his explanation. It was reasonable. Panic was really what he had seen when Roger was trying to borrow a pound; but he hadn't felt any warning of disaster at the time. He had only seen it there in his excessive care for the bottles; and the incoherent gaze he would turn on the old couple in the Kings Arms bar.

Derek was growing tired of the effort to restrain himself. He couldn't postpone his curiosity any longer. He looked across at Roger, determined to argue, and prepared for any kind of rebuke if that was how it had to be.

He said: "Tell me, Roger. Is it really true about Nicole?"

"I think so," said Roger. He was calm, almost docile in his readiness to reply. "Nicole is pregnant."

"But is it true about another man?"

Derek had to wait for the reply. Roger might not have heard him. He was threading his fingers in and out.

"What other man?" Derek asked again.

And now Roger was swift and sharp with his answer: "You should ask Nicole yourself."

"She told you she is pregnant by another man?"

"Please, Derek, leave it alone." Roger got up to relieve the tension; but he sensed that Derek was not in a mood to be ignored.

"What do you mean leave it alone?" Derek too was on his feet.

"Just leave it alone," Roger repeated.

"But I won't," Derek said. "I can't. I just can't."

"You will," Roger returned, "because the child won't be mine. The child will not be mine."

Suddenly they both looked at each other, embarrassed. Someone was knocking at the door; and Derek had a feeling they had been overheard. The message was for Roger. He was wanted on the phone. Neither made a move until they heard the last footfall give the cue that the girl had gone. Then Roger went out to the phone on the landing. He didn't close the door. Derek could hear his replies; but they gave no help.

"No ... Yes, yes ... Yes."

That was all Roger said before descending the stairs at a trot into his room.

Four

Roger sat all evening in his room and tried to imagine how the future might be lived without Nicole. It seemed that every vein of feeling had gone dead in his hands. He would scrape his nails over the leather rest, observing the tracks his hands were making. A quandary of lines chased in all directions. The chair had composed itself about him like a prison cell. He was grateful for Derek's company; but he couldn't take the risk of talking. Every sound would have led them back to Nicole. It was inevitable. And he had to have some respite from thinking about her. He needed time to consider what he was doing; what he would do.

But she was there, more powerful in her absence. He looked at the piano, and her shadow was walking towards him through the light. The keys were visible; delicate white bones now laid at rest over the board; but he could hear her voice. He knew every chord of her feeling. Clean, it was always a clean feeling which had put him in her debt. It was debt, the admission of debt which he wanted to resist. But he couldn't find a quarrel here; could find no cause for resistance when he tried to think himself into her debt. Yet his resistance was there; a pressure and a challenge which he had allowed to build up inside him; intangible and more oppressive than the claims of jealousy.

He might have been relieved if she had suddenly come through the door. He could have endured whatever punishment she chose to inflict. Even this pregnancy. For a moment he had the conviction it was so; that it would have to be so. She had achieved all the conditions for his surrender. Every moment of their past would confirm it. Derek was a witness; Teeton was a witness. There would have been no moment of conflict in their verdict on Nicole. Yes, they had always agreed, and would in this very moment agree that she had found Roger; she had met and discovered him in some desolate region of himself which he had never visited before; had never dared to explore. Some arid soil—maybe his father's doing—where the richest spaces of his desire had somehow gone to desert. Vulnerable, afraid, he might have gone dead in his pride if Nicole had not arrived. And she had found him at the very height of danger; when he hated the world around him; knew all of it to be in conspiracy against him; had come to see an agent of malice in every face he met. Merchants for his soul who might have been in league with the spirit of his father; hunting him down, tempting him with bribes that would inevitably force him back into captivity. And when his resistance seemed to work, he saw the enemies make a sudden change in strategy. They left him alone; left him with his pride and the harsh consolation of their neglect. Soon he would even be without the instinct to complain; as though they knew the very moment he would begin to rot.

And then Nicole arrived. After one night of madness when he had let the pig in him trample over his pride, suddenly released from his habits of caution; when his host decided he had gone too far; when they had to expel him from their company. Gentle as frost on the pavement, they had laid him down in the night. And some time after that she arrived. Natural and unknown as magic, Nicole had come into his life. And it seemed that she was always there.

Now he watched the piano and it was only her shadow which he could see. But he knew she wasn't coming. She had made that clear on the telephone. He would have to find her as he had always done at this hour. But his resistance was now so strong. It seemed to gather strength from some part of him he had forgotten. It was holding him to the chair. And he held on. A word from Derek might have come as a relief; but his caution was the same. Derek didn't want to take any risk. He sensed some unfamiliar danger stalking them. Everything had become delicate, too fragile. It would have been dangerous to offer advice. Any gesture might have come as an intrusion. Even the virtue of his silence seemed to be an offence. Until Roger spoke. The voice might have been the end of an echo coming from outside.

"I'm sorry about this afternoon," Roger said. "But if you can help, I'd be grateful. If you want to. I'd be glad."

Derek had heard him; but he didn't answer. It seemed the best way to accept his request. It struck him as the safest way to reply. And he wasn't wrong. Roger said nothing more. And Derek knew he was right.

3

One

Teeton was conscious of waiting; but he had given his eyes some useful occupation. An old habit had come back to haunt him. He was uncovering another shrimp, spilling it gently out of its shell, when he noticed the shaven slope of the publican's profile. His skin was exactly the colour of the empty shell: a glazed pink, bright and clean as polished glass. Teeton watched the publican sideways; he glanced at the shrimp hanging from his hand, and let the likeness delight his eye. Exactly the same texture, his eye was singing. This old habit kept him company while he waited.

His eye had become an ear which heard the sound of colour. It had begun to hum with these vivid similarities which converted the publican into a shrimp. Teeton's eye was arranging the slow, tedious harmonies which had evolved the shrimp into the stature of a man. His eye could hear the ancient dance of fish liberating the publican from his species. He shook the last grains of shrimp out from the shell and stared at the arc of white flesh on the plate. And his eyes returned the publican's tonsils swimming through a tangle of sand and saliva: pink ribbons of meat waltzing up from the sea into the still, closed circus of the publican's face.

It was an old habit of seeing which had now surprised him, as he waited in the Mona. Each face gave some evidence of its specific animal clan; some ancestry of insect or bird. Teeton always had to discover the right ancestral creature before his eye could hear the noise which a face was making. Sometimes it was the only way Teeton could remember some people's faces, or the circumstances in which he had met them. His eyes had gone wild with the music of the publican's face. He wanted to hear it more clearly.

"Let's check it," Teeton said, and he went over to the bar.

But there was such a rivalry of voices. The noise had brought him back to the normal environment of the saloon bar. He took the chance to look at the clock. It was struggling towards eight. The Mona was dreamy with light and the slow, rising swell of talk.

A group of men were talking commerce at one end of the bar. The Old Dowager sat at the other end swivelling a pick in her gin and tonic. She greeted Teeton with her eyebrows which he acknowledged with a similar movement of his cheek. It seemed that he and the Old Dowager were agreed on this technique of concealed greeting: a certain anonymity of welcome.

The men went on talking in chorus; a rehearsal of inherited attitudes about smoking, boxing, spending. The publican had seen Teeton, but he didn't hurry to serve him. It was his way of reminding some customers where they stood on his list of priorities. It didn't really matter who you were, he would finish his anecdote before he asked what you wanted. According to their importance, the men would take part in this delay.

Teeton listened to the men, and thought: Yes, I like the publican. He knows his mind, his priorities, his end. And Teeton had a great respect for consistency: the hard core of belief which guided a man through the most novel circumstances. It was a quality which he associated with the Gathering. He had worked hard to achieve this. He saw the publican as a standard of reference. The other men were common speculators in friendship. Their tastes in drink and friends were no more than a calculated diplomacy whose end was approval both at work and in their private lives. Gross and cruel as the publican might have been, he was a man of formidable independence. He knew that the ace of spades was black and no less useful when it served its purpose.

"I often wonder how you do it," the man was saying, as he added a tail to his signature. "Christ I couldn't."

"And sometimes the sums aren't that small," the other said, memorising the amount which was written on the cheque.

They were paying homage to the publican's astuteness. He could tell the proper size of an income from the weight of the writing on the cheque.

"And you've never had any bounce?" the fat man was asking.

They were alarmed at the publican's reply.

"Once," he said. He was smiling. "Only that once."

He would have to relate the exception; but his eyes had finally found Teeton. He was back on the job again. His smile was making rapid progress as he came forward to serve Teeton. He had a vivid memory for the slightest transaction; and a glance at the table made him wonder what Teeton wanted. In a matter of seconds the publican had noticed Teeton's glass of beer, and the plate where one shrimp had not yet been touched. He had already bought cigarettes. So it had to be matches. But the publican would never anticipate an order. It was always bad business.

"What can I do for you?" he asked.

"I'd like some more shrimps," said Teeton.

"Another one?"

"No," said Teeton, "could I have seven?"

The publican's smile had vanished, but he showed no awareness of the order. He had a gift for reducing any novelty to a state of ordinariness. He slid the glass partition across the case and paddled the shrimps with a wooden knife on to the plate.

"That'll be seven shillings," he said in a voice which seemed almost cheerful.

Teeton took his change and returned to the table. The men hadn't noticed the order for shrimps; and the publican returned to tell about the cheque which was an exception. He was smiling: a wide, gay carnival of teeth which told his strength.

"Three, four years ago," he said, "decent sort o' bloke, came in one morning with his missis ... bought a pack o' cigarettes and bottle of whisky for his missis ... then signed for a tenner ... and I never saw him nor the missis again ... but a week later the bloody cheque came back with the bank manager's signature: Drawer deceased! ... Never saw the bugger again ..."

The men were in hysterics. They started a round of questions about the legality of the situation. Couldn't the publican get it after all? And what about the missis? The publican was casual as his smile.

" 'Course you could always make a claim," he said, "but it wasn't worth it, waiting for intestate and all that ... and the poor bugger was dead anyway."

The men were still laughing; for the publican related such episodes with great assurance. He had a dry irony, clear and hard as bone.

"Drawer deceased," the fat man repeated and tried to explode with laughter. "Never heard of it before."

With astonishing precision the publican had turned away. He walked towards the small bar where a woman was waiting with a sack of Charrington bottles.

"Won't be a second," he said to the woman and went to find the extraordinary cheque. He always kept these things as a kind of evidence; an expert in conserving important trivialities.

Teeton got up again, trying for a view of the clock in the Mona. The heads had congregated without notice. It was Wednesday and just on eight o'clock; but there was going to be a crowd in the saloon. The Old Dowager's predictions had gone wrong for a change. He sat alone at the table near the empty fireplace; but he had put the evening paper on the chair directly opposite him. He wanted it to be known that this table was going to be occupied. Now and again he would exchange a glance with the Old Dowager; but it might have been an arrangement to stay discreetly apart.

She had given him the message that morning. Jeremy Rexnol Vassen-Jerme was the name. She thought it was a trade mark, some kind of weed-killer. Man from the San Cristobal Embassy; but he called it Mission, the Old Dowager had remembered. Cultural attaché was the name he gave to his business. Said he was a friend, the Old Dowager apologised. She had kept the man guessing what to do, because she didn't make his enquiries welcome. But he said it was urgent, and his occupation had made that sound true. She gave no indication when Teeton would be at home; said she never knew. But it was possible, and with a pinch of luck, that Teeton might be found at the Mona bar. She couldn't say what time. The man said he would be there; not sooner than eight, and certainly not after nine. She was a little suspicious when the man gave it as an opinion that Teeton wasn't likely to call him at the Mission. But he had left the number, just in case. It was really intended for the Old Dowager to verify that the Mission was not an excuse. By the most devious route of enquiry, the Old Dowager had checked. And there he was. She was relieved to see that Teeton had come.

Teeton looked at the clock again; and heard the heartless grin of the publican's voice: "Drawer deceased". It had taken him a long time to decide what he should do. His first instinct was to avoid any meeting with Jeremy. Teeton had a natural apprehension about the Embassy's interest in his whereabouts. They would certainly have known where he lived; but he couldn't do anything about that. A meeting with one of their representatives was a different matter. And they had chosen with exquisite care. He had known Jeremy a long time before the events at San Souci; and well enough for his visit to be a private affair. But he also knew that Jeremy had an acute sense of danger; and a private meeting with Teeton would have struck the Embassy as a foolish mistake for Jeremy to make. They would have known when and where it had taken place.

It seemed a lapse of judgement in Teeton to accept. This was only a way of saying that he was already here, and he felt it was now too late to go away. But it was also his suspicion which had influenced him to stay. Had they discovered something about the Gathering? This was his immediate worry; and the reason he had come. There was a chance that Jeremy might let something slip; a chance which seemed too slim for comfort. But that was how it had to be. For the rest of the night he would have to be on guard.

The indecent applause of the fat man's voice rose again: "Drawer deceased. Never heard it before."

Two

Teeton watched Jeremy slide his way past the men. Flexible as a worm, he seemed to penetrate the narrowest spaces, emerging through the crowd of shoulders with barely more contact than a falling curl of hair. But it was impossible for them to ignore him. Had he slipped in, unseen, his presence would soon have brought itself to their attention. He had that kind of head; small, almost tiny for his height, but distinctive and eccentric in its composition. There was hardly any backside to his skull; as though the crown, sloping gently from his brow, seemed to undergo a precipitous collapse before it plunged into the valley of his neck.

Jeremy was staring up at the feudal decor in the Mona saloon; and his head had become a crown of fierce red hair. He was barbered with elaborate care. His hair was short and fine and coiled like the springs of a watch. His eyes were intelligent, restless, elusive, smouldering with a latent flash of temper. His skin looked delicate as cream; a curious mixture of complexions that always startled and deceived those who were seeing him for the first time. It was an odd compound of tangerine and dry ginger. It was probably this enigma of colour which had promoted Jeremy's assertiveness of manner, as though he needed courage to present his face, and did so finally with a flourish of conviction. It was there for everyone to see as he came slowly towards Teeton's table. Teeton couldn't keep his eyes away. He admired Jeremy's authority. Jeremy had seen him; but he was giving the Mona the first sample of his attention. And Teeton recalled that he had always brought method and style to the most casual of his engagements. But Teeton's guard was up. It didn't let his admiration linger. There was nothing casual in a meeting with someone from the Mission.

"May I sit at your table?" Jeremy asked as though his presence were an act of blasphemy.

Teeton nodded and pointed to the chair.

"Are you going to have a drink?" he asked.

"I'll get it myself," said Jeremy; but he didn't move.

The publican had stopped listening to the men at the bar. He was keeping a close watch on Jeremy whose clothes might have been a gentleman's disguise. The publican thought he might have been a thief in the act of preparing some enormous raid. Jeremy followed every movement of Teeton's hands as he slipped the shrimps into his mouth.

"Why are you eating so many shrimps?" he asked.

"I bought them," said Teeton, "and it would be a pity to waste them."

Jeremy looked elated. He was trying to corner Teeton into some sort of dialogue. It didn't matter very much if it led nowhere.

"I've spent a week trying to trace you," he said.

"And now?" Teeton asked, realising that Jeremy was up to something devious. That statement could not have been true.

"I'd like to begin exactly where we left off."

Teeton made a heap with the shells and looked towards the bar.

"I've given up thinking aloud," he said.

"You mean you refuse to talk?"

"I talk," said Teeton, "but certain things must be said in silence."

"For example?"

"The kind of thing you want to discuss," said Teeton.

"So I've wasted my time trying to renew our friendship," said Jeremy.

He was pretending to look angry.

"I'm glad to see you again," said Teeton, and immediately regretted what he had said.

Jeremy had studied the shells and watched Teeton eat the last shrimp.

"You didn't really want to eat those shrimps."

"Not all of them," said Teeton.

"But why did you buy them?"

"I wanted to have them."

"Are you working on something to do with the sea?"

"I've given up painting," said Teeton.

Jeremy looked astonished. It was as though a healthy pair of eyes had asked to be made blind.

"You've given up," said Jeremy.

"I said painting," Teeton replied.

"And what next?"

"I don't know," said Teeton, "I'm just waiting."

"What for?"

Teeton considered the pile of shells on the small plate. He was giving way to Jeremy's wish to talk; but the guard was warning against indulgence.

"I'm not waiting for anything," he said, and drained his glass.

Jeremy chewed his teeth in silence, and timed the moment he would launch an opinion. But Teeton got up.

"I'm going to have another drink," he said, "what about you?"

"I'll get my own," said Jeremy.

They both walked towards the bar, and the publican was now in a hurry to serve them. His attention was cautious and prompt.

Teeton ordered another pint of bitter.

"And you, sir?" the publican asked.

"I want a glass of soda water," said Jeremy.

He made it sound extravagant and rare. The publican seemed unsure of himself.

"Bottle o' plain soda?"

"No," said Jeremy, "I want what I asked for. A glass of soda water from that."

He pointed to a siphon on the bar. The publican pushed it towards him, and shoved a whisky glass behind it.

"Could I have a large glass?" Jeremy asked.

He siphoned the soda water into a half pint mug and put a shilling on the bar.

"That won't cost you anything," the publican said, waking up his executioner's smile.

"Oh no, I want to pay for it," Jeremy insisted.

"It's not done here," said the publican, "that's always on the house."

"I'm going to pay for that," Jeremy insisted, pointing to the siphon.

The publican tightened his jaw and half turned to look at the men.

"You would be better off elsewhere," he said.

Jeremy hesitated. There was an obvious show of national pride in his obstinacy. He was proud of everything which distinguished him from the publican. He was determined to spend his money according to his taste.

"What's the price of bottled soda water?" he asked.

"Sixpence."

"Could you open one?"

The publican reached to the shelf for the soda. He opened the bottle and passed it to Jeremy. Teeton had returned to the table, but he watched this little drama which would probably grow into an enormous row. The publican had squeezed the lid off the bottle. Jeremy passed him the shilling, waited for his change, and then walked back to the table with the half pint mug.

"You've left the soda," one of the men said.

"I know," said Jeremy, "I only wanted to pay for this."

He raised the mug to remind the publican what he had originally asked for. The publican tried to ignore the open bottle on the bar. He was wondering whether he should have asked Jeremy to leave; but the whole incident was too subtle, too lacking in demonstration to warrant such an action. He turned towards the men and whispered his abuse.

Jeremy seemed utterly indifferent to the effect he might have had on the group of men who watched him from behind their shoulders. Teeton was uncertain how he felt. He enjoyed the publican's indecision, but he could never be part of any alliance with Jeremy.

"The English are very strange," said Jeremy and looked at Teeton for agreement.

"In what way?" Teeton asked.

"They don't understand simple things," said Jeremy.

"They understand what is customary," said Teeton, "and that's true of everybody."

Jeremy paused. He was perplexed by this novel conversion in Teeton.

"You like them?" he said.

"That's neither here nor there," said Teeton.

"But what do you say to a man who looks so startled about something so simple as paying for what one wants?"

"It is not the custom to pay for that," Teeton repeated.

"Am I as strange as he thinks?" Jeremy asked.

"I don't know what he thinks," said Teeton.

"What do *you* think?"

"About what?" Teeton parried.

"About me being strange?"

Teeton rubbed the glass against his mouth before he answered.

"I don't think you're all that strange," he said.

"You don't?"

"That's what I've said."

"And why does the publican think I am?"

"I don't know what he thinks," said Teeton, "but there's no reason the publican and I should think alike."

"There is *every* reason why you shouldn't," said Jeremy.

"Perhaps, I don't know."

"But you agree there's nothing strange about me?" Jeremy asked.

"It's not a question of agreeing," said Teeton, "I simply state that you're not strange to me. You do things which create a difficult atmosphere, but your relation to them is not at all strange."

"You think I like to shock people?"

"I don't know," said Teeton. "It is possible that you are trying to shock yourself."

Jeremy put his glass on the table and stared at Teeton. He was chewing his teeth again, and now he looked almost fierce in that mood of intense vigilance.

"Do you think I'll ever shock myself?"

"It depends," said Teeton, "it might mean having to do something very simple."

"Go on ..."

"Some people have lost the capacity to be surprised," said Teeton. "I think that's bad."

"Go on ..."

"That makes any kind of shock impossible," said Teeton. "Any crime acceptable."

Jeremy had forgotten his soda water.

Teeton had come to the defence of the English with surprising ease. Jeremy watched him; studied him; tried to get the measure of this departure from normal practice. A most unpredictable departure, it seemed. He hadn't seen Teeton in many years; but he couldn't imagine any change which might have brought the English in for Teeton's praise.

"Perhaps it's true," said Jeremy, "the climate does something to an emigré. Cools his judgement, you might say."

Teeton looked as though he might have applauded. He would be more at ease if he thought Jeremy would settle for this view. But Teeton's caution was like armour. He wouldn't let it slip; and he heard the questions knocking inside his skull: why has he come here? what is he after?

Jeremy was admiring the background of voices in the Mona bar. A fresh sample had arrived; lively, articulate, the product of a superior legacy. Gossip was passing gracefully from the desolation of the suburbs to afternoons spent with the famous who were now dead.

"No wonder," Jeremy began, and paused. He didn't want to provoke Teeton to anger. That wasn't his reason for coming here. "My professor of history was quite right. You're abroad because London offers a richer pasture in which to graze."

"The professor ought to know," said Teeton, "he was among the first of the goats to get away."

Jeremy was about to take his glass, but he brought the movement to a sudden halt. He didn't approve of Teeton's reference to the goat. He was deeply conscious of his debt to the professor.

"His generation had no alternative," Jeremy said, "and what's important is that he came back. That's where he is. He is where he ought to be."

"He doesn't think the home pasture is so green," said Teeton, "not from all I hear."

"It may not be too green," Jeremy countered, "but it's good grass. Much better than this."

He had taken his glass again, making a vague signal where the voices rose behind him. He admired the atmosphere; but there was an element of resentment in his admiration. Teeton knew he would have been at home here. He was a man of the quick exchange, his memory ever so fertile with quotations. The appropriate text was always waiting like a layer of bile over his tongue.

"Do you think these people can ever understand," Jeremy started, expelling the benefits of the Mona from his praise. "How could they understand what you and the few like you could mean to us back home? How could they?"

Teeton was familiar with this theme: it was a tropical variation on the treason of the clerks. Of course his own departure was a little more complicated, as Jeremy would have known. But the welcome had already been extended to come back. Teeton was slow to intervene; for he had the feeling they might now be approaching the fire. Is this why Jeremy had come? Who was now behind these exploratory visits? Teeton was still waiting for a clue. The emigré theme could only be the prologue to what was to come.

"Take the other two," Jeremy was saying, "what kind of a life is that? A man and his wife are together, yet he beds down one place and she in another." He had noticed the change creeping over Teeton; and he thought it might be better to modify his statement. "But you know it's true. That's no life for a man like Roger."

"How many lives have you for sale?" Teeton's voice was almost a drawl.

Jeremy might not have heard.

"I see nothing wrong with being poor," Jeremy allowed, "but what is he doing? There has never been a musical gift like his in San Cristobal. And he was appreciated, wasn't he? Have you ever known a concert of Roger's with one seat vacant? Now have you? Ever? No. Never. Yet what does he do? He abuses his family and packs his bags. For what?" Jeremy had come to a rest, as though the answer couldn't bear a moment's reason. It was so utterly beyond comprehension.

"Tell me honestly," he returned, "what does Roger do here? What in heaven's name is he doing here?"

"He lives here," said Teeton. "In his own name."

"Be clever if you want to," Jeremy rebuked him, "but you know what I mean. He copies scores, that's what he does. Composes incidental noises for newsreels he never sees. And even that hardly comes his way more than once a year. But copying scores! Why, he might have been a common mercenary. A man like Roger! Can you imagine that? Who knows him here?"

"At home," said Teeton, "we have a monument to the unknown slave."

Jeremy looked as though he had run out of passion. He was listening to the voices in the Mona bar, so near, yet utterly remote from his own preoccupations. What could they really care what was happening to Teeton or Roger? He had omitted himself from a share in this momentary reflection. He observed the bubbles that floated over his soda water; and studied the glass, inviting it to join in his indignation. A monument to the unknown slave. It was hardly an occasion for jocular comment. Slave was the name of a unique predicament. Like time, it signified every kind of moment; grew echoes in every corner of his own history.

He was burying the word in meditation. And he watched Teeton; but Jeremy knew how to organise a glance. It alighted; it crawled. It could strike direct as an arrow; or descend like a diver in slow motion. There were times when his glance seemed to travel round its target: a mysterious circumnavigation of the eye. Teeton sat quiet, like an audience in some doubt about what they are hearing. They know the details; but they can't quite follow where the subject is going; where it will lead them.

"And in case you forget," Teeton said, "there's Derek who is still learning how to die."

Jeremy hadn't forgotten. The theatre was going to be his next port of complaint but Teeton had taken the sting out of his contempt. Jeremy wasn't himself an addict of theatre although he would always have argued its importance in the habits of a largely illiterate nation.

"By the way," it was a moment for imparting information, "we've got the Arts Centre."

"I didn't know," said Teeton, "but the Americans aren't without a sense of gratitude. That I ought to know."

Jeremy was using the arrow's glance. It went fast, straight, and was soon swallowed up in space. He didn't want to encourage any comment here. Not yet, at any rate. It seemed much too soon; for Teeton hadn't yet put away his caution.

"It could be a chance for someone like Derek," Jeremy said, "whatever the limitations. He wouldn't have to go on playing a corpse."

"True," said Teeton briskly. "For once the corpse could be real. Really his own."

"You make a luxury of despair," said Jeremy.

"I've read it," said Teeton. "Flamingo in his essay on Being Away. But they've never quite understood what that peasant was saying."

"I've never read Flamingo," Jeremy objected. "He thinks words should be used like bullets. And there's no future in that kind of battle. Not for a writer who wants to last."

"He must be dead by now," said Teeton.

"He is still there. But he's getting on. He thinks the Thirties were yesterday."

"He also thinks the slave is very much with us today," Teeton replied.

And Jeremy was observing the glass. Slave was a kind of bait which Teeton wanted him to bite. He hadn't come here to engage in conflict. His business was of a more serious kind; of a more urgent and melancholy nature. He looked across at Teeton as though he might be asking his advice.

"I believe you know Roger's wife," he said. "Is she American?"

"Yes," Teeton replied, "and not a trace of nigger in her blood. Absolute, pure white."

Jeremy found his glass; hugged it for a while. His eyes had started on the crawl.

"Wouldn't she want to live in San Cristobal?" he asked. "We have no complications of skin there."

"And so say all of us," Teeton was trying to sing.

"Wouldn't she?" Jeremy pressed him.

Teeton was going to direct him to Nicole for an answer; to tell him he should find out from her direct. But his caution suddenly struck him into silence. Perhaps they wanted to get at Nicole. An American was an American was an American.

"She wants to be where Roger is," Teeton said. "Of that I am sure."

Jeremy announced that he would be candid.

"Couldn't she persuade Roger to come home?" he asked.

'So it's the Judge who sent him', Teeton was thinking. 'It's Roger he might be pursuing, after all. Me first, via Nicole, and on to the target his mission had really chosen.'

"At least they'd be able to live under one roof," said Jeremy.

"Whose roof?"

"A roof of their own," Jeremy assured him. "His father has never cut him off."

"I think he prefers it here," Teeton said. "So you need not work on his wife."

Jeremy was arranging for a retreat. He thought for a moment about Nicole. Soon he was offering to be candid again.

"It's really you I'm thinking of," he said. "Wouldn't you return if the others did?"

"I see." Teeton was showing signs of applause once more; but the guard was firm, a censor in charge of his lips.

"It's me the old Judge is after."

But Jeremy had intervened with assurances that this wasn't so.

"It was Capildeo who handled the San Souci affair," he said, "but he was only doing a job."

"I would agree," said Teeton, almost without trace of recollection. "Every man must do his job."

And the pause had begun to stretch into an interval. Perhaps we're coming into the very last stretch, Teeton was thinking. He couldn't really harness his recollections now. They came free, full of warnings, more numerous than he had bargained for. He felt his body come taut under Jeremy's glance. There was such stillness in that glance; a subtle, invisible crawl of spiders stretched over the web of his eyes.

"You've never kept in touch with home," said Jeremy.

"Oh yes, I have."

Jeremy was guarded. He searched his memory; fled through the long record of conversations for some evidence of this. No one, he was sure, had ever heard from Teeton since he left. Was there some flaw in their supervision of the exiles' correspondence; some strategy which had escaped their attention? He had come near to telling Teeton that it wasn't true. But it would have been too great a risk to show his confidence.

"You never wrote me," he said.

"That's true."

Jeremy was engaged in a private battle to restrain his curiosity.

"I never met anyone who heard from you," he said.

"That's true."

Teeton didn't venture beyond this brief, enigmatic admission.

"Did you write anyone?"

"No."

Jeremy was relieved. At least there had been no failure in his surveillance. He was encouraging his optimism. Elaborate preparations for a smile were building up, prodding the corners of his mouth.

"But you said you kept in touch with home," he offered.

"That's true," Teeton hadn't abandoned his preference for brevity.

"I was thinking of San Cristobal," said Jeremy. "Isn't that your home?"

Teeton was appealing to the mug to support his resentment; to extinguish any spark of conciliation from his interest in Jeremy.

"Home is where I am," he said; and offered a glance across the bar where the Old Dowager had been sitting. But he caught the publican's eyes.

"You think of London as home?"

"It's where I am."

"Do you mean?" Jeremy interrupted himself to take a sip from the glass of soda. "You've decided to stay."

"I'm here."

"Permanent?"

"The future makes its own arrangements," said Teeton.

"But you must have thought of it?"

"My business is now," said Teeton. He saw the level of his beer fall by an inch.

Soon he will try his hand at resurrecting the past, Teeton thought, and that's more difficult to evade. He could hear his own thought, like a pulse beating out the charge of desertion. It couldn't be long before Jeremy offered his own witness in Teeton's defence. And what could be worse? To be protected from an injustice by those who were destined to be the agents of your destruction?

But Jeremy had surprised him by a sudden reversal of tactic. "You shouldn't have left," he said. "Not then, at any rate."

"I see." This was the most convenient exit Teeton could seize on. He had been caught siding with the wrong option. So there was still some remnant of prestige left to him, since Jeremy had disapproved of his going. He too had joined the voices which had announced this act as an example of desertion. It was a bitter charge; now made more bearable by the fact that it was also Jeremy's charge. He had found a source of relief, however fitful, in Jeremy's opposition. So he, too, thinks it was desertion, Teeton was musing.

He said, appealing to Jeremy for moral counsel, "You don't think I should have left?"

"No," Jeremy retorted briskly. "Not then."

"Not then?" Teeton was weighing what hope he could extract from this reservation. "When should I have left?"

Jeremy had accepted his role. He was presiding over the gravest of moral issues: how to be responsible to others without any servile abdication of interest in oneself. He had no praise for those who had made courage an act of demolishing the individual self. These men were no better than common mercenaries; always a target for his contempt: these mercenaries of the soul. A fatal deficiency in most political converts; poisoned by the vapours of sacrifice. Self-sacrifice was the most fatal narcotic of the soul.

"When should you have left?" Jeremy was still turning the question over. He was giving scrupulous attention to all the ambiguities which a just answer must satisfy. He took a certain pride in this lack of certainty.

He said: "Perhaps never. Perhaps you should never have left."

"I see."

Teeton was barely audible. For a moment he thought of the Old Dowager and her belief in the future of words: the mysterious durability of their sound. For it seemed that he hadn't really spoken; but a voice, unmistakably his own, had escaped from some other circumstance and place to come between himself and Jeremy. It was some minutes before he could disengage himself from this distraction.

"Of course, you know why I left," he said.

"I know *what* made you leave," said Jeremy. "But why? That's not so easy."

Jeremy looked supremely confident again; sniffing for the early stages of doubt which such a distinction might have started in Teeton. His doubt was there; an obscure, dormant growth of fungus that would soon find the soil which made it flourish. Jeremy was willing to help it ripen. In fact, it was his duty to nurture this distinction with all the knowledge which he had; so that Teeton would come to recognise what he should have known; what, in the depths of an honest solitude, he must have known. His situation was beyond solution. His departure had been futile; just as his youthful ardour had led him to commit crimes of conscience which others had to pay for long after he had escaped.

Do you see (Jeremy was rehearsing the preliminary stages of some future argument) that it would have been better to concede that your own difficulty was insoluble? The word had been given a special flavour. Insoluble. He let it unfold; slide round and over; a strange mellowness cuddled his tongue. He knew this distinction would strike a blow at Teeton's solidity. He would open up a weasel crack in that remote, impenetrable fortress that was his privacy. It was like an oath of chastity in nearly all Teeton's relations.

"I don't think the other prisoners ever knew what happened," Jeremy said. He noticed the wincing of Teeton's eyelid; a brief, frantic pulsing of the skin over his cheek.

But Teeton had trained the oldest of his habits to be of service. To protect himself, he now appeared to abandon all interest in his own safety. So that's why he had been trying to find me. This was his latest assignment: to assure me that the other prisoners didn't know what happened; that they had, in fact, rejoiced to hear that I had got away. The news would have come as a shock; but it would also have contributed another promise to their faith. 'So the other prisoners didn't know.' And of course, the query about writing home had now found its niche in this circuitous puzzle. The question had suffered a slight loss in subtlety. Teeton hadn't kept in touch; didn't feel it in the interest of his general prestige to take this risk; for he would have had to shed some light on his getting out.

"Of course," said Teeton, "some of the prisoners knew what happened." He was going to play it bold.

Jeremy considered the fizzy surface of the soda water; but declined to cool his thirst. There was a point of heat stoking the pit of his throat. He wanted to say something utterly pointless; too ordinary and useless to be of relevance to anything they were talking about. But his curiosity had a special greed; it resisted all efforts to prolong the moment of discovery. 'So some of the prisoners knew', Jeremy was thinking. Teeton looked safe enough behind his fortress. Perhaps he had changed; the big city had encouraged him to expel his normal traits of secrecy. It was seven years; time enough to shield himself against the indiscretions of his youth.

"You say some of the prisoners knew *why* you left?"

"They knew what happened," said Teeton.

"But did they know *why* you left?"

Teeton let himself yield to this challenge. He seemed content to open himself to any inconvenience which might arise from this distinction. His eyes were sober; almost proud to be so; and his voice struck Jeremy as a little frigid. He might have been giving notice of his lack of interest in the past.

Teeton said: "Could be."

"You are not sure?" Jeremy was betraying a new urgency.

"I'm sure they knew it was the American Embassy which authorised my release." Teeton paused; he was eager to offer some correction. "Perhaps it would be more accurate to say the Americans suggested that I be released."

Jeremy seemed a bit impatient. Teeton was almost frivolous in his insistence on making the correction. He was taunting Jeremy with these imitations of the official's obsession for precision.

"Or was it the Germans?" Teeton threw in. "The German Embassy had a great interest in the native cultures of San Cristobal."

"They also had a great interest in the Americans," Jeremy said.

"Did they?" Teeton's manner infuriated. "Of course you were fairly close to the German ambassador at the time."

Jeremy felt a rawness of nails in Teeton's voice.

"Quite a nice man," said Jeremy.

Teeton began to hum very softly: "And so say all of us."

This was the first real note of rancour which had made itself felt. It had carried with even greater thrust than Teeton intended. An effective parody was about as much damage as he had hoped to give warning of; but he had, in fact, ploughed deeper into Jeremy's defences. Teeton was astonished by his own triumph as he saw Jeremy's face go slack around the mouth; and his eyes colour as though from sudden bloodshot. They looked a vivid red, moist and richly grained, like birds' eggs prematurely taken. But Teeton didn't trust these signs of inconvenience. Not with Jeremy whose discomfort might prove to be the most effective of all his snares. He was, in Teeton's recollection of those days, a really dangerous type. Smooth as alabaster in his charm; secret and sure as a reptile when he strikes. Now Jeremy's silence was like an interval of unspoken regrets that fall upon old comrades who rarely meet.

Teeton glanced at the soda water; then inspected the bottom of his mug. He would soon have to decide whether he was going to refill it; to decide whether he would prolong this meeting with Jeremy who seemed to drift slowly further away from Teeton's thinking. 'The other prisoners didn't know/they knew/I see. I see.' Teeton had been guiding his mind towards other matters; forward from the disastrous episodes preceding his departure to the ambiguous delights of his life in London. His reflections had gone off like birds migrating to more favourable seasons; to the warm cave that was his room: 'you must tell the Old Dowager you're going home. You must tell her soon.' This duty had become more pressing than any menace which Jeremy's presence might have threatened.

Yet Teeton felt some tendency to return to Jeremy; to probe the reason for this meeting. For Jeremy wasn't a man who spent time without some calculation of its profit. He used it, always, to some purpose unforeseen by others. But Jeremy had taken cover behind a sullen and strangely troubled reticence. The noises of the pub rose everywhere; fell and were washed away by rival argument like a waste of rain. Jeremy had grown impervious to its strident impact. Teeton listened; switched off, as though at will, and soon would be alerted by some comment that had strayed his way. Teeton's hearing walked around, as it were, inspecting those items which might be collected for later meditation. The Old Dowager's theory of sound was calling to him again; and in the same instant he was arrested by a feeling which warned him not to let the Old Dowager down. You must tell her you're going. You must tell her soon.

Jeremy had emerged out of his profound seclusion. His eyes retained their vegetable sadness; yet the pupils seemed to breathe an air of menace; a meek and dangerous look of hunger. But his voice was curiously winning; soft and devoid of subterfuge. The hint of pleading was barely suppressed.

Jeremy said: "It wasn't true what they said about the German ambassador and me."

Teeton looked perplexed. He had to make an effort to find his bearings; for it seemed that Jeremy had suddenly changed course. Teeton hadn't yet worked out what this return to the German ambassador would be in aid of. He didn't trust himself to get it right. But Jeremy seemed determined to spare him this worry. He wanted Teeton to dismiss the rumours he might have heard.

"It was nearly true," he said, fixing Teeton with his stare, "but it never happened. Nearly but never."

The pearl was about to find its owner. Teeton heard some previous knowledge return; and recognised, for the first time, the echoes of sexual torment he had aroused by hinting at an intimacy which Jeremy had shared with the German ambassador. Teeton felt a trifle embarrassed.

"It's none of my business," he said. It was the most he could offer by way of a truth. "The German ambassador is no business of mine."

"True," said Jeremy; and he kept repeating the word like a man who was practising a foreign language. "True, true. But the American is your business. Or rather was your business. Perhaps it doesn't matter any longer."

Teeton wasn't inclined to hear him further. Ever since he had mentioned the American ambassador, Teeton had been struggling, in vain, to bring his rage under control. But it had got the better of him; and again he seemed to plan his safety by squandering all the means of self-defence.

"You're bloody well right," said Teeton, now prompted to order another drink. "It doesn't matter any longer."

He had scarcely paid any attention to Jeremy's reaction. But Jeremy witnessed every change of mood which now came over Teeton. It was the beginning of his own recovery; he was recovering his taste for the motives which had sent him in search of Teeton. He hadn't really come to see Teeton in connection with the politics of San

Cristobal. It was really a private matter. But was it to satisfy his own curiosity? Or was it really out of respect for Teeton that he had risked this meeting?

"I didn't come here to insult you," said Jeremy.

"Impossible," Teeton shouted; and his voice had penetrated the noise around them. He was indifferent to the curiosity of those who had turned to see what was happening. "Insult me?" Teeton repeated. His tone was back to normal. "And how would that be possible? After seven years! How the hell can I care what my wife did then? What the hell do I care what she is doing now?"

"Randa," said Jeremy, taking advantage of the pause. But Teeton had pounced on the name.

"Yes, I know. By now everyone must know," said Teeton. "Randa slept with the American ambassador; fornicated with him every night of my internment. I know that. Offered to become his mistress if it were possible to get me off the island. And of course anything was possible for the American. He made Judge Rivera destroy the evidence of the security officers. Made them drop every charge. Randa kept her end of the bargain. And so did the ambassador. I couldn't have had a safer sponsor. He kept every word of the contract he made with Randa."

Teeton was giving himself a pause. He was like an athlete marking the interval when he should take the pressure off himself.

"So you've come to remind me why I left," Teeton went on. "Now isn't that so? Isn't Randa the crux of your little distinction between the *what* and the *why* of my going. Isn't that what you mean? I let a personal whim—isn't that what you'd call it—a whim about my wife's infidelity tear me away from men who must have known similar insults from the authorities. But they had to suffer tortures which I escaped; which the American ambassador saw to it that I would be spared. God bless America. Bless all ambassadors." He waited. "So the German ambassador was fucking you too?"

Teeton was laughing: that strident, uncensored burst of elation which the Mona always recognised as a call to scandal. There must have been a marvellous catch in the news. But Jeremy realised he had cornered his man.

Jeremy remained on the defensive. He could find no way, it seemed, of claiming a right to be heard. Teeton's revelations fell on

his ears in a tide of controlled abuse. But Teeton was never too far
gone to check the moment his knowledge might be of use to Jeremy.
The discipline of his partnership with the Gathering was at work.
Like an echo of trumpets cutting across his own words, he could
hear the Gathering warn not to tangle with this type; whatever his
sympathies, never swap a virtue with this type. Jeremy waited. He
decided that he would wait until Teeton could afford to be quiet.
For it seemed that talk was absolutely necessary to Teeton, a passion
which he was, in duty, bound to spend while he was caught in the
treacherous currents of Jeremy's interest. Each word struck like an
oar that was steering him to safety.

"You're right, it matters no longer," Teeton was saying. He was
about to add that these events had never mattered at any time; but
he had managed a timely restraint on this thought. He wanted to
avoid any argument with himself; to freeze up all doubt about his
life with Randa.

"Of course," he said, seeking to confer a compliment on Jeremy,
"you had a soft spot for Randa."

"Yes," Jeremy said quickly, "I always admired Randa."

"I'm sure."

"Even after what happened," Jeremy hurried on, making the most
of Teeton's pause. "She had no interest whatsoever in the ambassador.
She didn't even hate him. But she got word what they were going
to do to you."

"I'm sure she did."

"You wouldn't have been alive today."

"Thanks to Randa."

"Had it not been for Randa," Jeremy said firmly.

Now Teeton was returning to his earlier posture of defence. The
heat had gone out of his resentment; had gone out of everything
that had to do with Jeremy. Teeton watched him; inspected him;
turned every syllable over; weighed every item that was of interest.
But Teeton was now free of feeling; he was loitering in a museum
of remote antiquities; everything was of interest; yet nothing had
the power to quicken his attachment to what he saw. Seven years
had worked a lasting burial of all these events which were the basis
of Jeremy's life, his work. The whole kingdom of his mind was

populated by these notorious ghosts of foreign commerce and local whoring.

So that's why he had come, Teeton was sure. To find out where I stand on the central issues of that time: between the *what* and the *why*? But it was too late. He had left this excursion much too late. The season of neat distinctions was now over. Teeton had already taken his decision to avoid these speculations; for they were never without some attraction for him: the bait offered by ingenuity; the comfort that came from a pride of skill.

He had decided to refill his glass; to reward Jeremy with some gesture of benevolence.

"Is it to be soda water again?" Teeton asked, his shoulders up and bent in a hump over the table.

Jeremy had declined.

"That's better," said Teeton, "let's have a proper drink."

Jeremy said no.

"Nothing at all?" Teeton continued.

Jeremy rose from the chair. He had taken Teeton by the shoulders with both hands, forcing him gently back to his seat. Amid the noise and drunken traffic of the pub, Jeremy's departure was about to pass without notice. It was exclusively a moment for Teeton's witness.

"As you say," Jeremy's voice was making a tunnel through the noise, "these matters are no longer of interest."

"Quite." Teeton was hearing him clearly; hearing him as though the pub was already empty.

"I came because I had to see you," Jeremy said.

"Had to?"

"Yes, I had to. It may not matter any longer, but I thought you ought to know ..."

"Confidential Jeremy?" Teeton smiled.

"That Randa died ..."

"Randa!" Teeton went deaf.

"This morning."

"Dead?" Pipes were bursting in Teeton's ears.

"Suicide," Jeremy concluded on a note of brutal triumph.

He didn't wait a moment longer; so that Teeton, recovering his sight after the momentary blindness brought on by the pressure of his hands, was startled to discover that he was alone. He was staring across the table, and down at the empty chair which Jeremy had vacated even before he broke the news. Teeton continued to stare at the crowd; with half an expectation that Jeremy might be there. His absence had a uniquely frightening effect on Teeton, who was still trying to recognise the emotions he felt. He could find no name for the spreading congestion at the top of his skull: a gradual wave of heat that went in circles round his head; sucking in his brain, forcing a pressure of air out from his temples. His brain had the soft, sinking feel of sponge. Teeton didn't shift once in the chair; but his eyes were busy, searching for some sign of Jeremy. The pub noise had imprisoned his thinking; made him incapable of reflection. His memory could find no exit for escape. It was as though his memory was a carriage whose occupants had all fled; an innocent train surprised by the sudden end of the rail. Teeton sat still. He saw the little white beads of froth at the bottom of the mug, the pink shells emptied of shrimp; crushed petals that seemed to float on the echoes of the publican's voice now ordering everyone to go.

It was closing time.

4

"Last orders, please! Come along, last orders!"

The publican's voice had acquired a genuine tone of command. Those words were like a directive intended for Teeton.

"Last orders, please. Come along, last orders!"

As he walked down the pavement and turned right along East Heath Road he could hear the publican's accent fall, each syllable sliding into the general silence of the night. No sound now but the three words which had survived the distance.

"Last orders ... come! Orders ... come ... Last orders ... come!"

That voice had been invested with a message from some divinity which had chosen this moment to remind Teeton of his doom. It was good to pause, let patience immobilise all ambition until you had learnt your own desires from the start. But he had waited too long for the unknown visitor. He had almost forgotten why he was waiting. Until tonight!

The heath lay black and dead under a purple shadow which came from the city lights. The trees wore a soft red veil. The grass was damp. He stooped and collected the dew. It felt cool and fresh as spirit over his hands. He was going to taste it for the sheer need of feeling some intimacy with the earth. He put out his tongue in the dark, and suddenly withdrew it in a shudder. He had been repelled by the thought of other bodies which might have sojourned here on the grass. The moisture stung his hands. For he was sure this dew was diluted with urine. How many pints of piss had rained down on this acre of grass. Bladders from all parts of the world and of every sex must have made an ocean over this acre of grass. The earth had drunk it all up. Baked dry by the day, it was sweating another kind of moisture for the night. He wanted to wash his hands. Perhaps they were clean; but he couldn't resist the snobbery which ordered his hands to be clean. There was nothing like the disgust of feeling another person's offal cling to your own body. He ran towards the pond. He had stepped forward, slapping his hands free of the grass, then returning them to the water.

He couldn't walk much further. He had heard a splash of water from the pond; but the heath seemed utterly deserted. Now the grass felt good where he stood. He had let his weariness pull him down. He could hear the clap of hands coming up from the floor of the pond. Then a march of feet moving in slow procession across the water. Candles started to blossom, waving like lilies as the petals of yellow flame were blown across the night. The wind came hard like the midnight sound of the ocean washing over his sleep. His memory was wide awake. His eyes were stalking through the marble images of the family graves. He was standing there, under the sobbing illumination of the candles, mourning the villages of his childhood.

Every year they would come: these mourners who by native custom had to settle their final account with the dead. The cemetery was a parable of leaves and water. It was familiar as the sun at morning: this annual parliament of the dead. Saragasso. The name was bread and wine to his childhood. A faith that could make the mountains of San Cristobal crumble at the whisper of a voice coming up from these graves. It was here the living came to submit their charges; to hear the dead answer in forgiveness or rebuke.

Every year they came to this Ceremony of the Souls. That's where he had met Randa. She was then a girl, much the same age as himself.

Teeton could get no further. His memory wouldn't take him forward; held him where he now seemed to be shut up in sleep. He was hearing the water shake with pebbles, and the distant clap of hands. The procession was coming nearer. He could hear them almost inside the cave of his ear. He could identify one face; but the water suddenly rose and covered it over. And then it came again like the return of the dead to hold its forum. It was Jeremy. He could see him clearly; but the enigma of skin had disappeared. It was Jeremy's head, the same delicate line of bone. Rexnol Vassen-Jerme to be sure! But the face was now black as tropical dirt; it glistened like mountain soil in the rainy season. It was Jeremy, hovering like doom over the pond. He saw his final judgement there.

The what and the why of his going!

When Teeton opened his eyes he couldn't see anything but an absolute blanket of night; and beyond what must have been the first row of houses he detected the flare of a street lamp. He wasn't sure where he was. He had forgotten where he had been all evening.

It gave him a fright; this sudden intimation that his memory might have gone completely. It was not a new fear. It always threatened when there was some crisis that involved a death. But it was a long time since it had come over him. He kept his eyes on the little fist of light that shook in the distance. It might just provide him with a landmark. Then he heard a woman's voice. But he couldn't recall hearing anyone approach; and the voice seemed so near. He wasn't quite sure what he ought to do; but he was relieved to know that someone was there. It was good to hear someone speak. Her voice had shaken him out of his sleep. Now he was sober as daybreak.

She was searching the pockets of her macintosh. Teeton felt like reaching towards her, not from a desire for contact, but rather because he wanted to be sure someone was there. The voice was light, casual, flawless in its composure. But he didn't touch her. She had turned her head away. He saw a yellow flame briefly impaled on the night, then a whiff of smoke dissolved. She kept her head away from him, concealing her identity; and dragged long and leisurely at the cigarette.

"It's hardly the right night for bathing," Teeton said.

She didn't answer. There was a movement of feet over the grass behind them; and Teeton waited until the noise had passed. A torch flashed briefly towards the pond. There was a pause in the traffic of feet over the heath, and then the stride continued, louder and more hurried. But it was moving further away.

"Were you waiting here long?" the woman asked.

"I don't remember," said Teeton. "I must have been asleep. I wanted to be alone."

"Why didn't you leave when you heard me?" she asked.

"I didn't think it would matter since I can't see you anyway."

"Perhaps you expected to find I was a woman."

"I never thought about it," said Teeton.

"And suppose I had turned out to be a man," she asked, "would you have stayed?"

"I think so," said Teeton, "but I wouldn't have spoken to you."

"Why?"

Teeton didn't answer. Jeremy's voice had started to pursue him.

"Why?" she asked again.

"They might be police or men whom the police are looking for."

"Are you afraid of the police?"

"Not afraid," said Teeton, "but I prefer to avoid them if the circumstances could arouse suspicion."

"You could always explain."

"I have a feeling that the law never pays attention," he said, "and I don't like talking to officials about private matters."

"He would only have asked your name and address ..."

"And what I was doing," Teeton added.

The woman lay still; the cigarette was making a red hole in the night. The noise was passing behind them again. The woman waited to hear where it would end. It came nearer; but the torch flashed in the opposite direction, and the noise followed the light, until the boots had lost all sound.

"Don't you have a place to sleep?" the woman was asking.

But Teeton's interest had gone astray. Jeremy's voice was taking over.

The what and the why? So that's why he came. There was a sharpness of salt in Teeton's eyes. Jeremy was probing a fear he couldn't deny. The what and the why? It was Jeremy's malice which had brought him to judgement; but Randa's suicide had given the distinction a formidable power. The question had come back, renewing its attack with every fresh thrust of Jeremy's voice announcing the facts of his desertion. He thought there should be some other name, some other word that might reduce the sting of these accusations. But I did leave. You took up the offer to get away. It was not even escape. I might have stayed. It was your duty to stay. Whatever the consequences, he had a duty to honour his promise to the men he had left behind. Your courage was then a promise which required no oath. There was a chance you would have died. It happened to some you left behind. You knew it was more than a chance. Your commitment had accepted such a certainty. Was it, then, his fear? Was it your fear of death which, after all, is soon over? It was his fear of knowing that he would have to die. He would have had to bear witness to his dying. You would have been condemned for life to the spectacle of yourself about to die. They would have made him inactive. That's true. We would certainly have made it impossible for you to function. But this doesn't justify your decision to go. Was your safety more important than your allegiance to the men you left behind? Was it so simple? A choice between your own salvation and their doom? Were you more important than what they were trying to do? Is this why he really left? Was this the reason behind your desertion? Then the bargain was a loss, an act of robbery against yourself. You told me that much in the Mona bar. What has the escape brought you now? There is no service for you to perform. You have given up painting. I had heard it before; but you made it known to me yourself. So there are no fruits to be gathered from this freedom you had chosen. You are no more active than you might have been in the prison of the island you left behind. There is no service which can compensate for your desertion; no service the men themselves will recognise as honourable compensation. In fact, you have done nothing at all to promote any further interest in you. I know why you can't go back. Or is it Randa? That's why I came in search of you. I could see that it wasn't her death, but the manner of her dying which made you tremble. I saw you get ready to crack. I had always been wanting to see you crack. He couldn't resist the dangers now lurking in any charge which might relate him to the cause of Randa's suicide. There was a feeling of dread before this lack of foresight. His hatred of Jeremy couldn't obscure what he had already known. Did you really know how much she loved you? Randa had not, in any important sense, betrayed her love for you. He was lingering on this knowledge; hoping, it seemed, to bring some sceptical intelligence to his aid. You will think well of Randa now she is dead. He had to preserve some confidence in his judgement. Her suicide had made San Cristobal more than a place of birth. The island was a nerve his exile couldn't kill. The what and the why. Would he ever be rescued from the tyranny of these distinctions?

Teeton heard himself giving these answers. But the woman was coming to his rescue. He had begun to recognise where he was. Not by sight. He would have liked to get a look at the woman; yet he felt no special interest in seeing her. He was crowded by his own misgivings. But there was a fragrance in the air which told him where he was. The woman's voice was baiting him again.

"Do you like sharing things?" she asked.

Teeton felt some muscle propel him forward. He was astonished by the directness in her voice. There seemed a strange lack of prudence in her question. Her tone had become familiar, even confidential. He wondered what she was expecting to hear; what she would have liked him to say.

"Or don't you?" she asked again; and stunned him into reply.

"What sort of things?"

"Anything," she said, "provided it's really yours."

"I share what I can afford," he said.

"And what's that?"

"Friendship, company." He thought of the Gathering and the recent sale of his paintings; then added: "And money when I have enough."

"And that's all?"

"I don't list these things," said Teeton, a little puzzled by her insistence. "But they happen and sometimes I remember."

But it seemed her passion for enquiry knew no limit. She hadn't heard enough.

"What have you shared recently that you would always want to remember?"

Was it his loneliness or the news of Randa's suicide which made him yield to these interrogations? For the woman had found some way of making the most improbable encounter seem so real. She had given him the feeling that it was his duty to reply. Different kinds of answer were offering their service. The woman let him prolong his delay; and Teeton wondered what need was driving her to extract these accounts of himself. There was no warning of frivolity in her questions. The voice was earnest, occasionally desperate in its need for certainty.

It had taken him a long time to reply. 'Something shared which you would always want to remember?' Now he was reflecting on his association with the Gathering; but this answer had quickly fled. He didn't think the Gathering would provide the answer which he wanted to give; to give the woman and himself. Above all, it had to be an answer for himself.

"You can't recall anything?" she asked.

"I remember quite well," said Teeton, "although it's not so recent. Three years ago when I met a girl for the very first time. I gave her the best painting I had ever done. It was a gift I was sharing. I wanted it to be a souvenir of that evening."

The woman noticed the change in his voice. It was softer, less formal, almost emotional at times.

"You are a painter?" she said, prodding his memory to deliver whatever he might have been trying to conceal.

"And what I remember was the way she accepted," he said. "She accepted as though it was the most natural thing that could happen."

Teeton had stopped. He realised how abrupt this pause might appear.

"Why did you choose her?" the woman was probing.

"I liked her," Teeton said quickly.

"Was that all?"

Now he hesitated, and the woman's silence, like his own delay, seemed a little too urgent. The woman was still waiting for him to find his reasons. He knew what he had to say; but he would have to put a limit on his disclosures. The painting was a portrait of Randa; but he didn't want to mention her name.

"Was the girl beautiful?" the woman asked.

"Yes," he said. "But that wasn't the reason. I think I was rewarding her for something I had seldom seen. Something I had lost."

The woman had felt a slight shudder at the mention of some loss, but she said nothing to betray this momentary discomfort.

"The girl," she said. "What was there so special?"

"I couldn't name it," said Teeton. "It's the kind of recognition which comes sudden."

"Have you seen her since?"

"I see her," he said, "but it's always the first evening which I see. That first evening we met her."

It's only then, he was thinking, only under the spell of such a moment that I have been able to recognise some possibility in myself; some real potential for any act that would really connect me to what we ordinarily call living. Nicole's presence dominated his memory.

Where had she come from? What strange order of accidents had brought her to this party? He didn't know; and he had felt no desire to make such enquiries. But she had suddenly freed him from the banalities of that room: the effervescence, the transitory and graceless noises that passed for communion between those cattle, grazing on their voices, mowing their praises; passing out their counterfeit cards of welcome, inviting everyone to get aboard, to catch a ride to some palace of joy. What a leprosy afflicts these occasions: the

Cocktail Party; the Reception which assembles these professional vultures. There was food enough for the armies of the world; and drink enough to keep weddings going through eternity. And there was Roger who knew he had every possession except fame. He was declaring war on the furniture. He had struck out as though he were going to smash every face; was turning the wine bowls into sewerage canals. Now he would threaten to rape every royal virgin to celebrate the martyrdom of his kind. He had become a poor, stunted plebeian soul whose tongue had got all its vowel sounds wrong. Roger had become a blabbering curse, ranting until his memory ran short of crimes committed against his kind; and finally he collapsed like a parcel that had burst. And nothing, it seemed, had happened. The citizens shovelled him gently into a coat; and his body was deposited outside the door. A plastic voice was proclaiming judgement: unmitigated disaster. And there was a round of applause. Now the train could get back on its wheels. The celebrants resumed their cattle noise. The party had been restored. Nothing had happened. Except this strange discovery which he had made. Nicole had come with him to look for the expelled man whom she hadn't known. But Roger had disappeared. They stood on the pavement, and her whole body was beating like a pulse beside him. But he couldn't get her to talk. And yet he felt; knew, like the famous visitations that come over some converts, that in that suburban cattleshed where brain and art and the prostitutes of the tongue were on display, there was one anonymous heart: anonymous and hurt and terribly alive. And for years he had remembered nothing of that night except Nicole's voice, choking like a child from tears when she was able to speak.

'He has too great a sense of injustice,' she said of Roger. 'It will kill his heart.'

Teeton couldn't quite recover from the spell of that evening. It seemed he would have liked to delay his attention there; to let it linger for a moment over the strange conflict of meaning it held for him. He had often tried to trace his change of attitude to painting back to that evening. He could never find any absolute proof that this was true; but some warning of danger had pursued him ever since. His skill, the circumstances of its function, the whole context in which it had to work and make itself known, was not with-

out the menace of those vultures. They could put him on the trail.
He had already taken up the offer to pasture with these cattle; to
nurture the fruits of his exile from their manure. Suddenly he heard
the woman's voice remind him that she was still there.

"Suppose you came to realise that the girl didn't really deserve
the painting," she was asking, "would it matter very much to you?"

"Not really," said Teeton, exploiting the certainty of his knowledge about Nicole.

"You wouldn't feel hurt that your judgement had failed you?"

"I think not," said Teeton. "I don't like to be wrong, but I'm
never ashamed of making mistakes, particularly about people."

"You wouldn't mind if they came to think of you as a bad judge of
character?"

"I don't ever want to be a judge of character," said Teeton, "good or
bad, it makes no difference."

"But there are people you like and people you don't like."

"Of course."

"And you must have reasons."

"I'm sure there are always reasons," he said, "but I don't separate
what I like from why I like it. My reason is only a part of my feeling...."

"You really believe that?" she asked.

"Believe what?"

"That it's your feeling which comes first with everything?"

"Not only first," said Teeton, "it comes at the very beginning and
at the end and it runs right through the middle."

"And your reason?"

"They aren't separate," Teeton said, "at least I don't feel that way.
If I like you, then all the reasons are already in the feeling which
tells me that I like you. The same is true if I dislike you...."

"And don't you ever try to analyse this feeling?"

"It's a waste of time," said Teeton.

"But why?"

"It analyses itself," said Teeton.

"And you're not interested in finding out more about it?"

"Of course I want to find out more and more about my own
emotions," he said, "but I won't set to work trying to do so."

"How then can you find out?"

"Through my behaviour, I suppose," he said. "Every day I do something, I say something, and what I do or say belongs to me."

He was suddenly astonished by the sound of his own voice. He felt there was something static, unspeakably dead about these replies. They might have been right as the signals which indicated his feeling. They might have given some idea of his needs, of a desire which could be quickened into life, into the very principle of his living. Now he heard his answers remind him of what might, in fact, have been possible. But the words had begun to stagger. They went out from him; took up their positions about him like a defeated army. The moment the words fell from his mouth, it seemed they had become exhausted by their service. He didn't feel what was inside them. He couldn't recognise their meaning in the way he saw, had so vividly seen what Nicole's presence had given to him that evening.

There was the scratch of a match, but the flame had died when he turned his head towards the woman.

"You don't feel much guilt?" she had asked.

"I have regrets," said Teeton, now doubtful and nervous with his answer. "But I have never let myself nurse my regrets."

He heard the slow turn of the woman's body as though she was moving farther away.

"Have you ever murdered anyone?"

"What?"

"I don't mean a literal killing," she hurried. "But sometimes it happens. The other person never recovers from what you've done. Can never come back to life after what one has done."

For a moment he seemed afraid to risk any answer. The echoes of Jeremy's voice were in his ears again. What would Randa have said if she were here, lying where the woman was? What would have been her verdict on those seven years of spiteful silence? He was gazing up at the sky which wasn't really there; since no eye could detect where this darkness began or where it came to an end. He was seized by an effort to imagine what Randa might have felt before she died, what stages of premeditation her agony had gone through.

"You see what I mean?" the woman was asking again.

"Yes, I do," he said, slowly, cautiously, feeling his way towards an answer that would protect him. "How can you ever tell whether you've done so or not?"

"By the evidence of the other person's life," she said. "You have the person you found alive and whole, and you have the person whom you've left dead."

Teeton was thinking again of Randa's portrait which had become his gift to Nicole.

"You see what I mean," the woman said again.

"Yes, I do," said Teeton, "but I still can't see how you can tell. Sometimes a person may want to die on your hands. You become the perfect excuse for their refusal to be alive."

"Is that true?"

"I've had friends with that kind of trouble," he said, "and some of them have stayed together all through it."

The movement of feet was passing again. It came towards them, and the torch flashed up at the trees, but the woman paid no attention. She was thinking out her questions, and wondering: who was this man? She couldn't see him in the dark; and suddenly she wondered what he looked like: the colour of his hair; was he short or medium height? How tall, and what sort of walk did he have? A momentary fear made her ask herself whether he might have had a limp, one arm. Or was he blind in one eye? The possibilities were innumerable. Suddenly she turned round. She was looking directly where his head should be. Teeton was curious about the occasional noise of feet in the distance.

"Tell me something," she said, "but not if you think you shouldn't." Her voice came abrupt and final into the silence.

"I shan't if I don't want to," said Teeton.

"I'll understand," she said and paused; then added: "Have you ever been in love?"

Teeton felt a sudden shudder: like being spied on or caught in the act of spying. He didn't answer, and he made it seem that the noise of leaves nearby was the reason for his delay. The torch flashed again above their heads. Someone knew they were there, and was watching for some movement. The woman sat up.

"You wouldn't have heard of the Ceremony of the Souls," Teeton said.

"Some kind of religion?"

"A religion of some kind," he said.

And Teeton felt a certain reluctance to go on. It seemed too great an effort to find the right words; to hit on an opening that would lead her straight to his meaning. Perhaps he should have said that Randa was dead; that she was his wife; that her death had now deprived him of any chance to know what their future might have been; to know what their past could really have meant. But Teeton couldn't bring himself to speak Randa's name. How could he begin to tell the woman who Randa was? He knew what he would have said; knew so much better since Jeremy's news what he had to say. But the obstacles had arisen. Where should he begin? Yet he knew the beginning; but the simplest task was proving to be the most difficult to achieve. And who, after all, was this strange woman beside him? Why was she here? What did she want?

"This ceremony," she began; and Teeton was struck by the lack of effort in her voice. She might have been calling attention to some familiar trifle that had slipped from her memory.

"It's to do with the dead," said Teeton.

"The dead?" Her voice had suddenly taken on a peculiar force.

"Yes, the dead," Teeton repeated, "and the living as well." He paused as though he wanted to give her an opportunity to interrupt; to say that it wasn't a matter that might interest her. "It's a family occasion, really. It's for the relatives of the dead, that is. It's mainly their business."

But there wasn't any interference from the woman; no sign of apprehension. She was quiet; so utterly calm as she waited for him to go on. Teeton was growing used to this quality in her attention: this curious probing which showed no trace of hurry, always kept in check by a sombre gift of patience. She was still waiting; yet she didn't seem to treat the intervals as waiting. She was simply there.

"The relatives gather," said Teeton. "Every eight years or so according to custom. In one place. And when the Priest has found his powers, the dead come forward. You don't see them; but they will be there, and you can hear them. They speak about all the things that had never been said when they were alive. They are now free to accuse, and free to pardon. And the living must reply. Always through the Priest.

Sometimes they argue all through the night. For hours. The living and the dead. It will go on until they reach a point of reconciliation. Then you know it's the end. The end of all complaint from the dead; the end of all retribution for the living. The dead depart, and the relatives are free at last to go home."

Teeton had become conscious again of her silence. For a while he had almost forgotten she was there. She might have gone without his notice. Then he heard her; the voice had become a familiar signal.

"Have you ever spoken with the dead?" she asked.

"No. No." His answer was no more than a reflex action, a surprise awakening to his surroundings. Everything seemed so ominous and yet full of welcome.

"But I would like to."

And the moment he made this admission he felt unusually relaxed; an infinite calm fell on everything he touched. The grass was asleep under his body. The strange woman had become more than a voice; she seemed to be there in a wholly new way; a presence which had been waiting to be known; someone with whom there would soon be the mutual arrangement for further acquaintance; a revelation of identities. He felt this promise like a message that was on its way; but he wasn't conscious of promoting it. He had even put an end to his guessing who she was.

"Would you really?" she asked; as though she had suddenly escaped from some total absorption with herself.

"Would I?"

"Would you really want to speak to the dead?"

Teeton felt a slight embarrassment; and wondered for a moment why it had happened. Was he afraid of the answer? Was he worried how she would judge his answer? But even this fear was premature; for he hadn't yet found any answer until the thought of Randa provided him with one. And now it was more difficult to reply; for the answer would be yes. But he didn't want to risk any further enquiries about his relations to the dead.

An echo of the clocks was hurrying over the heath. One strike only; but Teeton couldn't tell which hour was halfway. The woman was quiet. Her silence was like sleep. He heard her breathing come near, and he wished she would speak. He wasn't sure what he would have liked her to say; but it would have been enough just to hear her voice distract him from the Ceremony of the Souls. Soon he might have to struggle against the intrusions of Jeremy's voice. He thought he had discovered some element of luck in his meeting with Jeremy. The news had driven him out on to the deserted heath; but its timing had brought him to the curious solace of this strange woman's company. He didn't know how he would have borne these hours alone. He wanted to thank her; but it might have struck her as absurd. She too must have had her reason for being here. But his curiosity had gone dead. He had nothing to offer her.

"I'll make you an offer," she said.

"What's that?"

"Let's separate now. But you can answer my question tomorrow."

"Tomorrow," Teeton was musing. His memory was striving to find the name of the day.

"And where do you go from here?" he asked.

"I don't want to say," she said. The voice seemed more friendly.

"I see," said Teeton, and wavered in his acceptance. "What time tomorrow?"

"About the same time," she said. "Right here. That street light is my landmark."

"What time is it now?" Teeton asked.

"I don't know," she said, "but I'll be here half an hour after closing time. I'll wait until the clock strikes twelve. If you're not here by five past, I'll assume you changed your mind."

"Shouldn't I take you where you live?"

"No."

"But why?"

"For one thing I prefer to be alone now," she said, "and also I prefer, for the time being, not to see what you look like."

"Have you any ideas?"

"None at all."

"Make a guess."

"I don't want to guess," she said. "Let's leave it at that."

"Very well," said Teeton.

He wanted to take her hand; but he could not see; and it would have been silly to search for it and miss. She had got up.

"Goodbye," he said.

"Until tomorrow night," the woman answered, and walked off towards the horizon of the houses now rising like trees where the heath ran into the street.

5

One

"Should never, never, never...."

Nicole had been crying ever since she came through the west door of the church. She had been kneeling for an hour or more; ever since she charged in, tottering through the oppressive silence of the church, to offer her body to this pew. Soon she would have to rest her knees. She tried to give all her attention to the altar which appeared far away. It was barely visible behind the columns of mist which were floating down from the blue panels of glasswork above.

It seemed that an age had passed since she left Derek. She had run all the way down the main Heath street and come stumbling like a drunk into the refuge of the church. Derek didn't go after her. He didn't know whether it was fear or shame which had held him to the spot. He had stood there and watched her galloping down the main Heath road as though her heels had caught fire. But he felt no shadow of a doubt that he had done the right thing. Nicole had known him long enough to allow this liberty. He didn't believe Roger's story that there was some other man. He despised all relationships which could only survive when someone was kept in the dark. Nicole must have recognised this to be an obsession with him. Whatever was worth having could be brought, without fear of loss, into the light. But her silence had wounded him. He had wanted to rid himself of any speculation that might put the slightest doubt on Nicole. He had done the right thing.

"Should never, never, never."

Nicole couldn't restrain her sobbing. It came without sound, like the noiseless crackle twisting through her hands. She had wrung them until there was no feeling left anywhere. Only in her knees which felt like spears of bone piercing her flesh.

"Should never, never, never."

The words came from her mouth in quick, sharp gasps of breathing; bubbles of sound which were gone before she could recognise their meaning. She couldn't be sure whether they were intended for Derek. She felt no change in her affection for Derek; but she might have wished that he had spared her this revelation. Or was it Roger? She couldn't quite focus her attention on Roger. There was something too ominous, too utterly beyond her power to grasp. Whenever she thought of Roger, this grim warning of something perilous came over her.

Her life had been safe and simple until she met Roger. She had never ventured beyond the difficulties which she had inherited from her family. They were ordinary as any artisans she had known in her small midwest town, fundamentalist in all their notions of decency. There might have been some streak of the rebel in her father, but her mother had watched over his ambitions without provoking his resentment. They were uncomplicated folk. Their expectations on earth were modest. But their faith was beyond measure. She must have seen some portion of her father's spirit in Roger. There was a similar fervour in their attack on work. It was a punishment, and the source of all their pride.

It was an entire lifetime since she had last made such a visit to any church; but she hadn't forgotten how to pray. Her small town childhood had provided her with faith for a thousand years. The gospel was a food which descended on her town like air; the air that was free; which no breathing could avoid. She had savoured every possible flavour of prayer; a miracle of nourishment which started the day.

Now she felt ashamed; felt every wish, the merest whisper of a need, rise in contempt; as though she had come with the sole intention of abusing a generosity she didn't deserve. She was blaspheming against a grace she could no longer hope to receive.

"I love him, love him, love," she was crying, "but never, never I should never ..."

And again it seemed too awful to go on; to give sound to her rebuke. Abortion was murder; and she had already committed a murder for his sake. She couldn't go over that ground again. He didn't know that she had already killed some part of herself so that her life with him might continue. She had lived for him. She had asked no other reward than his recognition that this was so. And he knew it was so; he couldn't have failed to see; to smell; to tell by every sense, every nerve that made for knowing, that it was so.

"Why? But why, why, why...."

The sobbing had cut her off again; as though it might be better for her to grieve in silence; to spare herself the agony of hearing her own voice join against her. She was thinking herself in circles; plodding through a territory of mind which was clearly hers, and where she had become an utter stranger. Every ghost from her childhood seemed to come alive; every smile was making ready to turn a mockery on her. She couldn't find any way around Roger's lack of reason; couldn't grasp any particle of sense in his experiment to disgrace her; to persuade his closest friends to disown her. Why should he wish such an abominable infidelity against her? For so it seemed to Nicole, taking refuge behind her lack of worldliness. It would have been a wickedness beyond human forgiving: to use him as father to another man's child.

"But he isn't, Roger isn't, isn't a wicked man, isn't."

Now she found herself coming to his defence; struggling to find him some exemption from the momentary bitterness which she was feeling. It seemed her own safety, her innocence, depended on him; on whether she could find a way to provide him pardon.

She was trying to pray; but it was no good. She took the weight off her knees, and sat back on the pew. Now she felt like an ordinary trespasser who had found this house a good enough place to take a rest; to gain a little privacy from the democracy of the street. It was free as a park and more quiet; enclosed against traffic, and absolutely safe from rain. No place like it if your feet were in trouble. A good place to recuperate; difficult for anyone to eject you if your sin was no more than exhaustion.

She was too ashamed to smile; or too tired. It would have been impossible for her to tell which feeling made her go sour at the memory of these pleasantries. She sat further back; so that her knees gained height and came forward to support her hands. She could feel her flesh come warm again. A little tide of movement was coursing up her thighs. She felt an ache startle her knees as though a clamour of nerves was pounding against the cap of bone. She would soon be in the street; but she felt no instinct to resist.

She got up. It gave her a shock to discover that she was still able to carry her weight. She looked surprised that her strength had come back. She was walking down the steps that led from the west door to the street. She took them one at a time as though she felt her feet might go astray. She was reflecting on her meeting with Derek. His voice was overtaking her again. Now she was sorry that she had run away. The pavement showed her what she was feeling. She was alone. And suddenly she thought of Teeton. She should have gone in search of Teeton. They hadn't spoken with Teeton. He knew nothing about Roger's story; and this exclusion made her feel some greater confidence in Teeton. Perhaps he could tell her what she ought to do. But she had called at the Old Dowager's in the morning; and he wasn't there. At least the Old Dowager had said that he wasn't there. She thought she might try again. She would avoid the Old Dowager this time. She knew the secret entry Teeton used through the garden gate. It seemed there was no one else left. After three years of marriage she hadn't trespassed far beyond the world of these three. It was as though they had always chosen each other's friends.

"Should never, never, never."

Nicole was surprised to find that she hadn't moved beyond the first stride of pavement. She was standing there, her body half collapsed against the wall. The church clock began to strike; and suddenly she could recognise the street again. The clock was pounding its leaden blows over the heath.

She had started to count, but her attention lapsed after the third stroke. But it had to be after five since the lights were on in the Railway Arms. She followed the road until it forked; then waited to watch the bus take the bend which straightened out towards the Mona. It rose like a ship's hull over the first stage of the hill.

Nicole thought it was the traffic which had made her stop; but the street was now clear; and suddenly she was embarrassed by the reason for her delay. She didn't know where she ought to go. The streets seemed to stretch in more directions than they could really offer. Each rose, uncurving like an arm to greet her. It might have been easier to choose if she had been a stranger here, but she knew this portion of the Village like the back of her hand. Yet she couldn't move. She felt paralysed by her knowledge of the houses; the gaping welcome of the cinema behind her. The crackle of chips in paper wafted around her. She felt utterly alone, as though there had been a conspiracy to forsake her; to keep her shut out. She felt, as she had never known it before, the overwhelming separateness that could descend on a foreigner. Every face seemed to announce its right to be different from her own; and to claim, without shame, the abiding privilege of its distinction.

She knew where she couldn't go. The Mona was definitely out. She didn't want to meet Roger when there were others around. She couldn't endure the effort of having to apologise for her presence. For that was how Derek's interrogation had made her feel. She hadn't the slightest doubt about his motive in telling her what Roger had said. It was the duty of affection which had forced him to do so. He had to clear the air; to make sure that he hadn't misplaced a trust; and it was precisely this candour which made her feel some lack of completeness in herself. For there must have been the fear—however vague—in Derek's mind that Roger might have been right. Not right, perhaps, but not entirely wrong. It was this shadow of a reservation which made her feel reduced in her own eyes. She had found it so difficult to reply, so utterly impossible to make her denial; as though there would have been, in denial itself, some mild concession to the charge. So reduced in feeling now, she didn't dare take the risk of having to acquit herself by argument. She opted for retreat; told Derek how grateful she was for his concern, but she had nothing to say; would never have anything to say until she had spoken with Roger. The Mona was out of bounds. She felt she could never again meet Roger there; not in the company of his friends.

But it seemed strange, incredibly difficult to bring into focus, this feeling of isolation which had overpowered her, making her speechless, deprived of any purpose for being there, a solitary loiterer, rooted to the stones which showed their worn backs over the cobbled pavement. Nicole couldn't move. She felt, for a moment, that it must have been a mistake to leave the church. Her shame and confusion were not so absolute in their warmth, so harsh and chilling as this loneliness which threatened to break her in pieces; to scatter her like fragments of garbage across the street. She felt safer inside the church, restless and torn by the conflicts which had now become the sharpest ache of her pregnancy, but safer; she felt safer there.

"It would have to be the end, the very end of us."

She was barely conscious of her own proposals. She would go to Roger's room. She would wait for him there. She was no longer interested in matters of acquittal. Nor did she feel any urgency to press Roger into some admission, private or open, that he had told a lie against her. It seemed strange how this earlier sense of desolation was giving way to an extraordinary force of will; as though some fanatical stubbornness of temper now ruled over every current of her feeling.

"Not again," she was saying, as she started the first tentative stride past the sweetshop. "Never kill that part of me, never, never."

She paused under the light, and searched her bag for the pocket mirror. She would offer some apology to her face. Weeping had made an awful mess of her eyes. She would cheer them up with the news which she was about to release. The mirror sobered her. She looked at her hair, an unruly harvest of corn blown about her head. The once blond cheeks had gone pure scarlet. She decided to adjourn the moment for these small facial chores. It seemed there was too much to be done; or too little that was really worth doing. She decided she should give herself a little more time. She had to compose herself for a meeting with Roger. She went to rest in the Kings Arms bar.

Two

O'Donnell drank slowly, turning his head like a weathercock to learn the faces that were new to the Mona. The saloon was full of advertising men, red, plump, and articulate with achievement.

"Swine," said O'Donnell, and the beer spilt when he hammered his glass on to the counter.

He saw that Derek was anxious; but he hadn't yet told him that the news was good. He was busy counting sums of money that hadn't yet come into his possession. He was adding like a child in kindergarten: Stokes owes me five pounds, and Bobby Cunard seven or eight. The figure would have to be checked. He reflected on all the transactions he had had during the last month, and the sum increased. Rowden owes two pounds and Lotty Berwick had never paid off her balance. His assets had leapt to another two pounds ten shillings. He was searching his memory for debtors, convincing himself that the list was far from complete. Now he was ready to add Derek's name; but he hadn't settled on the fee for such an emergency.

"What are you going to have?" he asked.

Derek shook his head and refused the offer. But O'Donnell wasn't going to be denied.

"I'll take a sip of yours," said Derek, and guided the glass to his mouth.

He looked nervous; and his worry had made him incredibly formal. He thanked O'Donnell for the sip of beer. The architect bounced against him when he raised his glass; but Derek had hurried to apologise.

"Have a brandy," said O'Donnell.

"Would be wasted on me," said Derek. "Can't taste a thing."

"Take it easy," the architect said, making a casual gift of comfort.

"Do I look that bad?" Derek smiled.

"Not to worry," said O'Donnell, "you should be celebrating your escape."

Derek drew closer to O'Donnell in order to give some privacy to their business.

"Any luck?"

"Fixed," O'Donnell said, "it's absolutely fixed."

"Have you seen Teeton?" Derek asked.

O'Donnell was making a whisper over his glass; and Derek turned his head to get a look at the man who sat alone in the corner. Derek had never seen him before.

"Clean as they come," O'Donnell said, "and no questions asked."

"Did he say how much?" Derek asked.

"Fixed," said O'Donnell, "that's absolutely fixed."

Derek looked at the strange man again. His hands were small as a dog's paws. He kept his head down as though he was interrogating the contents of his glass.

"You've used him before?" Derek asked.

"And before that," said O'Donnell, as he snapped his fingers at the barmaid. "We all have your kind of trouble some time or other. But he's clean as they come. And no questions asked."

But Derek couldn't overcome his own suspicion that this was a dirty business. He had offered his loyalty to Roger again. This was natural. He would have come to his help at any time; but he was now giving his support to a wish that was bound to go wrong. Nicole had left him in no doubt that she would have her child. She didn't tell him that much; but he knew her well enough to reach his own conclusions about what she would do. And it made Roger's charge all the more outrageous.

She had made him feel like a worm when he probed her with questions about her loyalty to Roger. He didn't actually probe; but that's how it struck him now. She had realised what he was trying to say; and she didn't spare a moment in dragging his motives into the open. Is that what Roger says? Did Roger tell you that? Derek had little gift for deception; and Nicole had now made it impossible for him to deny it. He couldn't bring himself to inform her of their plans for the abortion. But he had kept his appointment with O'Donnell. It was too late to withdraw. It seemed that he had suddenly lost all sense of timing. There was a moment when he thought he should have persuaded Roger to drop these plans; but it was too late to make him change his mind. Roger had become so resolute in his conviction that he was not the father of the child. It was too deep a humiliation for anyone to accept.

But Derek had changed course after his meeting with Nicole. He was now on her side. No evidence could now alter his certainty that the child was Roger's. Yet he had kept the appointment with O'Donnell. It must have been his instinct to play it safe. It was no more than a precaution. There might just have been a chance that Nicole could be persuaded to have the abortion. It had happened before. Roger had argued his way out of becoming a father. But the reasons were different. They couldn't afford it; and Nicole had resisted her own wish to be a mother. Roger had persuaded her to accept that the circumstances were wrong. They could wait. But everything had now changed. Nicole had no intention of waiting any longer.

This must have been the reason for her absence from the house. Derek thought he had found the origin of her quarrel with Roger. She must have refused to wait any longer. It was quite in character. She would never desert Roger. Derek knew that; but she would resist him to the death in a matter which she thought to be in their interest. She needed the child because it was also part of her need for Roger. And Derek couldn't get over the feeling that he was giving his support to a dirty piece of business. But it was too late. He couldn't tell O'Donnell to call it off. That's what he would have liked to do. It was what he wanted to do before leaving the Mona. But he would have to talk with Roger. He would try to argue Roger out of this resistance to being a father. Their circumstances were not ideal, but Nicole would find a way of making them tolerable. He felt a little more relaxed. He would join forces with Nicole. Together they might be able to bring Roger to his senses. They would make him see that the child might be what he really needed.

Derek was looking at the abortionist again. He would have liked to introduce himself; to warn the man that they had wasted his time. His services would not be required. But O'Donnell was in expansive mood. He was arguing with the architect about the futility of living under the permanent menace of the bomb. There was a stampede of voices in the small bar. Derek wanted to go. He knew it was time he should leave. Every moment made him less sure what he should say to O'Donnell.

O'Donnell's voice was playing every note. Now it was low, an old man's grumble, grim with warning.

"Grab what cunt you can. But see that it makes no claims. He's a broken man who doesn't know how to refuse a throne. Disown, I say. Hit it and run. Hit it and hard, but keep on the run. Keep moving. On the move."

The architect was wasting his beer. It kept leaping over the glass whenever he laughed. His hands were laughing. His face had gone soft as a sponge. His nose was playing the clown to O'Donnell's giggle. His lips felt like tubes of air. They rubbed and suddenly exploded. He couldn't put an end to their laughing. O'Donnell was in the groove again. His voice was crystal. There was a clarinet sound coming up from the back of his throat.

"In for a penny and out for a crown. Don't wear it, I say. I'm all for weddings, but no marriage, I say. I've seen the best half of a generation go down. Ruined, finished. Couldn't steer the prick away from the cliff. Now they're caught. Like a rat. Toronto, Vancouver, even Regina. You can't smell nothing but husbands. Caught in the trap. Dead as rats, I tell you. Didn't know how to keep on the move. How to hit it and run."

He was washing his throat with beer. The large moon face went into eclipse when he threw his head back. The light had struck a shadow over one eye. He leaned his head forward, brought it low over the bar. The voice had gone velvet, grave and confidential in its new deliberations. He beckoned the architect to come near. He had recently discovered fresh booty, new spoils for the taking. Derek didn't hear what O'Donnell had found.

"You're kidding," the architect contested.

"But I'm telling you," O'Donnell said. He might have been trying to persuade a child out of its disbelief.

"No questions asked?" The architect was incredulous.

"Hardly a word spoken," O'Donnell replied. "She just lets you take it. Free plunder. No need to play pirate. No argument whatsoever, I tell you."

"On the heath?"

"Where else you think I'm talking about?" O'Donnell rebuked him. "Same place. Our heath. It's God's bedchamber."

"No argument?"

"Not even for the asking." There was a crackle of dry leaves in O'Donnell's voice. "Hardly a word is ever spoken, I tell you. It's just for the taking. I've hit it three, four times in the same night. Don't even know what she looks like."

"Crazy, absolutely crazy," the architect said.

O'Donnell was appealing to his hands for proof. He started to scratch his loins.

"Pity my prick can't talk," he protested. "We've hit it three, four times in the same night. She just wanders, I tell you. Not even up for sale. It's free. Just gives it away, she does."

The architect could feel his heels calling for spurs. He was ready for the hunt. O'Donnell must be mad, he thought; and then he judged that O'Donnell really wasn't mad. O'Donnell's fantasies always proved to be real. Now he had hit on a fortune.

"It's worth a visit, you say?" The architect was ready to go riding.

"Could be," said O'Donnell, "if you're there on time. Some butcher was on to it last night. I was on the prowl myself, but they beat me to it. Must have flogged his prick to a thread. I was back two, three hours later and the pirate was still packing it in. Must have a cock of iron. An absolute marathon of a beast he must be. Hours later, I tell you, and the butcher was still there. Sharpening his knife for another carving. You've got to be on time, that's all. Be on time."

The architect was dying of thirst. His eyes were swinging chains round the barmaid's throat. He was putting her in the stocks of his enormous thighs.

They had forgotten Derek who turned away as though he was ready to leave.

"Let's celebrate your escape," O'Donnell said.

"I'm off," said Derek, "I really must go."

He saw the abortionist get up and walk towards the bar; but the man didn't appear to recognise O'Donnell. Derek continued staring at the man, but O'Donnell quickly came between them. He had to explain.

"Not here," said O'Donnell, schooling Derek in the subtleties of his trade. "We have never seen each other before. You understand? No one could ever say we've met before. Just in case."

"I'll come back later," Derek said, relieving his arm of O'Donnell's grip.

"As you like," said O'Donnell, "but I'll be bringing him over."

"To the house?"

"Top floor," said O'Donnell, "my place. After closing time."

The barmaid had come into view.

"The same," said the architect, offering her the empty glass. "We'll have the same again. Just for the asking. Isn't that so, O'Donnell?"

"Not even up for sale," O'Donnell said, "it's just for the taking and no questions asked. Simply for the taking."

Three

Derek knew he couldn't loiter in the Mona this evening. He had forced his way through the militant crowd of voices piling up in the small bar. He could hear them outside as he waited on the kerb. They might have been poor, but they were eloquent and sure. They were predicting the end of the world, the birth of genius, the absurdity of the Second Coming. They would continue through the night, arguing as they walked from the urinal back to their drink. The beer would pour like rain into their empty glasses. Their only asset was to be alive. Talk was their investment in some future which might remain absent. But it was certain as their death.

Fixed, he was thinking, it's absolutely fixed. It was O'Donnell's warnings which delayed him now; the arid certainty of his advice. Grab it, grab what you can and keep on the move. It made him pause to reconsider his own relations with women. He was always on the move, it was true, but he had never seen this vagrancy as an example of what O'Donnell advised. It was rather some fear which made him avoid any permanent relationship with the women he had known. He had never had the courage to make any special claims on their devotion. He wasn't sure he could ever sustain this kind of permanence. But it was something he admired. He had seen it in Roger and Nicole. He thought of them as a kind of evidence, the absolute proof against O'Donnell's conviction that you had to be on the move.

He wondered whether O'Donnell could be right. It might be true. No man could ever really be sure. Perhaps it was this element of uncertainty which had given his own affairs their fugitive briefness. But he had always been careful to make his own attitude clear. He had never kept his motives in the dark; never laid his pleasures where they were likely to bring any harm. O'Donnell's voice was chasing after him as he climbed the Hamden road. You had to keep on the move.

He felt a prisoner of conscience; but it was the only way he could shield Roger and Nicole from the possible rumour that might follow. To offer himself up for O'Donnell's rescue. And it had worked. O'Donnell had asked no questions about the woman he had invented. He had heard Derek's story and it was familiar. Yet in all his experience of collaboration in these matters, each case bristled with a special aura of danger. In Derek's case, it was obvious reluctance to disclose any names which had made O'Donnell sharpen his wits. 'Anyone we know?' he had asked; and Derek, torn by twin necessities of deception and loyalty, had begged to decline. He just couldn't say. But O'Donnell had understood; for in his vast experience of rescue operations, this type of case was the most delicate, the one most fraught with actual danger. Immediately it had made him recognise his duty; he had to come to the aid of a comrade in peril. It would be arranged.

It might have been a moment of triumph for Derek; but he couldn't come to terms with his role. He had carried out Roger's wish. But he couldn't take any pleasure in his role; for it seemed that he had betrayed his own affection for Nicole. He didn't believe Roger's accusation against Nicole; yet he had given priority to Roger's wish for the abortion. Perhaps Nicole might have detected this; and that's why she had refused to talk. Her silence had wounded him. It was as though she wanted to abuse all his notions of bringing things into the light. Nothing had ever threatened this freedom of exchange before; not between him and Roger. He wanted to rid himself of any speculation which might cast doubt on Nicole.

Fixed, Derek was thinking, as he ambled down the last neck of road towards home. If he couldn't achieve a reconciliation between Roger and Nicole, at least he would have brought them some relief. And now the idea seemed to accompany him all the way towards Roger's room: that there might have been some other need than friendship which made him offer himself as the man who was on the hook. It was a hoax which seemed to convert itself slowly into some other reality, more powerful than a hoax, more convincing than his own efforts of deceiving O'Donnell. Suppose, he reflected, suppose it was true. Suppose he was, in fact, the man whom Roger had imagined to be Nicole's lover. And suddenly Derek was back to the days of *Othello* and the nights at Avon. Given his respect for Roger, why would he have wanted to burden himself with such a deceit; would he be able to carry, under the eyes of his friends, such a terrible load of duplicity? Would it have been possible for him to make it work? Now he was halted by the thought of Nicole; and the idea resumed its nature; had been promptly relegated to its content as a hoax. He didn't think it would have been possible for Nicole to support him in this role.

But it was his timidity which dominated his thinking. Was there some element of cowardice in his character? He had come a long way down; fallen deep into anonymity. Few people could remember anything about him now. But he had kept souvenirs of that Stratford summer. The paper clippings were still there. His room was a little, private museum of applause: the only evidence that he had known better days. Yet he was always reluctant to let this promise of his early days be known. And he wondered why he should have been so reticent about it. Why should he be ashamed to offer this brief moment in his career as example of what he had done; as some confirmation of what he knew he was still capable of doing?

Derek reflected on this shyness in his nature. It worked on him like an attack of cramp. It would strike him like a hammer on the inside, quick and clean in its effect. But it gave him warning. He always had some warning when it would strike. It didn't influence him in his relations with his friends. He would never know it in any argument with Roger or Teeton. Nor did it touch his boldness whenever his loyalties to them were aroused. He could speak up fiercely on their behalf. But he was dumb on his own account. He couldn't offer his gifts without making some gesture of apology.

Derek was smiling. He reflected on this modesty. It was like a virus which twisted his tongue; tied up his speech the moment he had been called on to say what he was worth. Derek was smiling at the thought of the Stratford season and Teeton's antagonism to the Moor. Whatever his virtues, Derek thought, the Moor didn't suffer this shyness. He knew his worth. He was eloquent and unfettered as any King when he called attention to his past, to the exotic splendour of his achievements, the incredible record of his adventures. He wished he had the Moor's gift for revealing his worth. It was this quality which Teeton detested in Othello; this facility of memory for what he had done. Teeton knew the Moor would come to grief. There was only one explanation for his sudden collapse into a murderous end. He had always been insecure, a hired foreigner among those men who accepted his command. They weren't fooled by his proof of bravery, the imperturbable eye in battle, the incredible armour of calm which he wore at the height of crisis. Teeton always said he would come to grief. Behind the granite countenance there was a squalid cesspool of insecurities. Something had been corroding inside the Moor.

Derek was now laughing. It was Teeton's resentment which made him laugh; the recollection of Teeton in brief, vitriolic exchanges with the young English producer at Stratford. He could hear Teeton again, withdrawing from his enemy's attention to nurse his fury against Othello: 'noble my arse, something wrong with a man who never gets scared, something rotten inside that kind of guy. Can't afford to get scared; a bad kind of shit inside such a fellow.'

Derek's laughter had attracted attention. He heard someone call out. There was a suggestion the police should enquire. Another nut was on the run. But it made him laugh a little louder; and suddenly he wished he could find Teeton. He felt a moment's anger turned on himself. He should have spent more time looking for Teeton. But the Old Dowager was getting worse than ever. It might have been better if she had given instructions forbidding telephone calls. Teeton was not in; was never in. She didn't know when he would be in.

He was approaching the end of the Hamden road. The night was beginning to settle down. There was a warning of autumn in the wind. There was the same smell of Avon in the air. He didn't imagine that he would ever be there again; but he couldn't rid himself of this attachment to his past. He thought he saw a light go on in O'Donnell's room.

He was covering the last neck of road. The house was there. It looked like scaffolding in the dark. He didn't know whether Roger was in; but he hoped he would be there. He tried to think of Roger and Nicole; and the suspicion began to dawn on Derek. There must have been some reason for Roger's charge. He didn't want to venture any further with these misgivings. He would have to wait. For the time being, he would try to find some consolation in his effort to come to their rescue. He would speak to Roger first about O'Donnell's arrangements.

But Derek had begun to feel some loss of freedom in his relation to Roger. Something kept warning that he would have to be careful. It was a new experience for him; that he should have to be on his guard with Roger. He would have to be cautious in his approach to Nicole. He didn't think he would find her there. But he had started to anticipate what he would do; how he should speak about the arrangements with O'Donnell. He would let Roger tell Nicole about this. But something had come to threaten his freedom; and he had never known this experience before.

Derek started to work his key into the front door lock. His mind was clear again. The door to Roger's room was ajar, as though someone had just gone in; or Roger might have been on his way out. Derek became strangely conscious that he was waiting. It seemed he could no longer be free in his relations with Roger and Nicole. What other reason could have given this delay such importance? Now he was trying to decide whether he should go to his room before he called on Roger. He wouldn't even bother to knock. He kicked the door gently back; and walked in.

Roger was there. He was alone, his hands wrapped round his legs, his knees propped high. He might have been a parcel in the leather chair. He looked relieved when he saw that it was Derek who had come in.

But Derek hadn't yet felt his confidence come back, and he

responded with the news he thought most likely to put them both at ease.

"It's fixed," he said.

"Fixed?"

"It's fixed," Derek said again and sat. "I saw O'Donnell."

Roger started to unwrap himself from the chair.

"Seen Nicole?" Derek asked.

Roger made a nod that he hadn't; then added, as though he had wished otherwise: "You seen her?"

"Yes," said Derek. "I had a little talk with her."

Roger brought himself to the edge of the chair.

"Does she agree?"

"I didn't let her know," said Derek, "not yet."

Roger was sliding back in the chair, as though some spark of comfort had suddenly gone out. Then it seemed to flare into life again when Derek spoke.

"I don't think it's true, you know."

"Not true?" Roger's eyes had begun to flash. "She isn't pregnant?"

"I'm sure she is," Derek said. "I mean about the other man."

Roger had suddenly vacated the chair. Derek couldn't quite decide what blunder he had made; but he had a curious warning from the quiver of his eyelid that some calamity was lurking where Roger stood, tense and frightened beside the table. It was the same stricken look Derek had noticed the afternoon he had met him with the bottles.

"Something wrong?" Derek asked.

"You didn't tell her about that?" Roger was doubtful whether he should turn to look at Derek.

"About what?" Derek asked, perplexed.

"About that," Roger insisted; and decided he ought to turn. "About the other man?"

"I raised it," said Derek.

"Raised it? What do you mean you raised it?"

"I tried to raise it with her," Derek said. "I thought it right to raise it with her."

Derek hadn't lost touch with his reason, but he found himself speaking in defence of it.

"You raised it," Roger said again, as though he found the wall a more reasonable audience. "What for? What did you do that for?"

Derek felt his voice fail; he was trying to talk, but he couldn't call any sound into his confusion.

"How do you mean?"

At last Derek had heard himself. But it seemed useless. His question made no impression on Roger who had turned again, making his futile appeal to the wall.

"He asks me what I mean." Roger seemed unsure how to divide his attention. He had glanced at Derek. "What for? Raised it with her? What for?"

Derek couldn't free himself from this stupor which was clinging to his senses. Some voice within was trying to prop him up; to convince him he was right; but it never got far enough in its support. It never came loud enough for Derek to be sure that he was not in danger. Of course, of course. The little voice, hidden somewhere inside his tongue, was hailing him. Of course it was right to raise it with Nicole; the most natural thing for him to do. But the most natural thing had become the least comprehensible to Roger. It seemed Roger's mind would grasp the secrets of the moon long before it could ever learn to understand what Derek had done. And Derek's small voice was still trying to put out its messages on his behalf; trying to break through the leaden weight of his tongue.

Derek stared down at the table and across at the wall; and it seemed so natural they should be there. What perversity of mind could make him ask them why they were there; could make him plead with them to go away? But the little voice couldn't make itself heard. Derek's tongue was sitting on it.

"I told you from the start," Roger began, and paused as though he had to be sure the proportions of his attack were exact. "I told you to leave this matter alone. It was none of your blasted business."

Derek's tongue had swept the little voice away. It seemed to hang, light as a feather, in his mouth. He had heard Roger; but it was not the same Roger. He didn't think it possible to identify this cold, savage rebuke with Roger's appeals for his help. Why did he make the abortion his business? Against his will and at the risk of making an enemy of Nicole?

"You made it my business," said Derek.

He felt an impulse to stand; but he was sure he would have continued through the door. And this accusation had to be answered.

"Always fucking right," Roger said, coming quickly to full voice, "you have to do the right thing. Must vet every fucking action, every omission to act. Like you live under some bloody threat of blackmail from your own conscience. Always fucking always you feel you have to look honourable. In your friends' eyes. In the enemy's eyes. You have to be honourable. In the eyes of every fucking living creature you pass by."

Roger should have stopped to cough; for there was a pond of saliva collecting under his tongue. It was about to flood his mouth, but he had managed to let his rage wade through.

"I didn't ask you to raise any matter with Nicole. Never."

"But you asked me to help arrange the abortion."

"That, yes. And don't shit your virtue on me now. What's wrong with that?"

Derek had found his tongue; but he couldn't focus his target. He was still suffering the disadvantages of his virtues. He couldn't quite free himself from this lumber of reservations which seemed to pile up to an astounding height around him. He had no warning how he would try to escape; but he knew he had to get out from under this weight which Roger had constructed with infinite malice for him. Each word fell like a brick; was shovelled into place; came to him like the last stroke of masonry which would complete the wall that closed in on him.

He decided to get up. It was as though this massive accumulation of rubble had dared him to shake himself free. He didn't think he had moved; yet he now found himself a breath away from Roger; as near, it seemed, as a shadow to the space which reflects it. Derek's words were coming from the cleanest tone of voice.

"Why don't you want Nicole to have *your* child?" Derek asked.

Everything now seemed to swell beyond normal size. The table and the piano could no longer hold within the room. The walls were going to burst from this sudden stampede of furniture. Everything was protesting for more space. And Roger felt only the glare of the light scouring his eyes.

"Do you know why?" Derek was asking; and his voice had suddenly gone soft and moist with some hint of pity or regret. "Perhaps you don't even know."

"Watchman," Roger intoned, "what of the night? When ordinary people are asleep you keep watch over every virtue. Report, watchman. Report your reason."

Roger could not have anticipated what he had heard; for his response had come from some deep and fearful cavern of his mind; lawless, unpredictable, untouched by any influence of a memory that might have restrained its violence. Roger had, it was possible, gone mad. His hands had scuttled all the contents of the table drawer: all but the knife which he had brought a blade away from Derek's throat. Derek couldn't move; he had no power of decision over any part of his body. But some force within was dragging him down towards the chair; and he saw the blade of the knife come inch by inch after his throat. The point was striking sparks of fire that burnt his eyes. He knew Roger was there; but he couldn't be sure that he was seeing him. It was Roger's arm like a bar of brass which blinded his eyes.

"Now talk up, little actor man," Roger was ordering, "stop wetting your pants and come clean, little actor man. Tell me again, I want to make sure I've got it."

The knife was making a quick sideways movement as though it was impatient to hear Derek speak and then get on with its business. And Derek, whose pride had now exorcised all his fear, could see the room again, and feel himself slide wilfully into the insult of the little actor man. He was transfigured by some magic as he prepared himself to repeat what he had said. He had to prepare, as though he were offering his final testament before suicide. He was going to be a corpse for real.

"Isn't that your fear?" said Derek, making his throat more welcome to the blade. "The child might be white; and you couldn't live with that; couldn't ever find comfort with Nicole again; because she had given you this white impurity. A bastard of any colour would be a blessing beside this white impurity. So you take cover in time, Roger, by passing the buck. You put up your defences before the floods break loose. The child isn't mine; wasn't mine; will not be mine; could never be mine. And that is how it is. But you should tell Nicole. Tell her now. Because there she is, behind you. There."

Derek's hand was making a flutter down his side as he tried to indicate the door. Nicole hadn't made any progress forward after she had witnessed this scene. And the knife! She stood by the door, stupefied, her terror alternating between the menace of the knife and the murdering impact of Derek's voice. She felt as though all her bowels were about to burst. Something was carving her up on the inside, spilling her life over the floor.

Roger didn't move. He didn't turn to see where she was. But he had a lucid moment which warned him that it was a trap which Derek was putting up; a last minute experiment to save his skin. Then the fear came over him that it might be true; that Nicole might have been there. And Roger was seized by a sudden panic, a sane, cold foreboding of the next minute and the minutes that would come after that. His body was now deceiving everyone. It showed the same strength, the same madness of purpose that supported his hand. But everything had gone slack on the inside. His limbs seemed to be going down, sinking slowly like the softening of tyres. But he kept his ground, waiting as though he expected someone to claim the knife, to come forward and take it from him. And the time was making a clock's noise in his head. He hadn't taken his eyes off Derek; but they stared as though they were doing a job for someone else. They weren't really serving Roger. The same was true of his hand which had lost all connection with the knife, but had to do its job by holding on.

Roger stood there like a porter waiting to be given some service to perform. There was a hell of expectation in every corner of the room, the silence of some terrible verdict which had to be put off; which could not, in the moment of hearing, be borne by those who had to listen.

Then Roger said, without the slightest shift of glance, "Get out." And holding the knife, without the slightest change of position, he continued to scream: "Out, out. Everybody! Get out!"

He must have known that Nicole was there. Yet he could hear nothing but his own voice ordering everybody to leave; and he never looked anywhere near the door which had remained open. It wasn't shut until the following morning.

6

"Are you there?"

And the woman's voice had surfaced with one syllable from this corner of the night.

"Here."

She was sitting on the macintosh. She listened to the noise of paper coming apart in her hands and waited for him to approach. Teeton's feet made a slow, dull drag over the grass; and then there was a sudden crush of leaves that turned to dirt under his hands. He sat on the edge of one buttock and hugged his left leg which was erect. But he didn't speak until he heard the rustle of paper which the wind was hoisting over the night.

"Well, I see you're here," said Teeton.

"You don't see," she said, "but I'm here as you say."

The correction had helped to put him at ease. Teeton wasn't afraid that trouble would come out of this meeting; but he wasn't altogether sure that some mild catastrophe might not arise from such a novel encounter.

"I brought you some chicken," she said, and put her hand out for him to find his share. His fingers recognised the flank and leg of the dripping carcass.

Daylight would have revealed at once the pleasure which brought his smile alive; but the night had made his thanks sound awkward.

"Thanks again," Teeton said; and felt that his insistence to be grateful was out of order. It was like a message of congratulations. She had realised Teeton's difficulties; but they didn't seem to merit her attention. She was busy severing the layer of flesh from the breast of the barbecued chicken. There was a veil of skin over her mouth when she spoke.

"Didn't you expect me to keep my word?" she asked.

"Yes," Teeton hurried; then put his answer under silent interrogation. He was sure it was true. "Yes, of course," he said again; and quickly offered to withdraw, 'of course'. He simply expected that she would come.

She was grinding her teeth through a shaft of bone, dispelling the splinters with her tongue. Teeton heard her tongue make a sound of kissing over her gums. The last particles of chicken were disappearing down her throat.

"Are you a slow eater?" she asked, wiping her hands over the grass.

"Yes," said Teeton, "and all the slower in the dark."

"I sprint," she said, "whatever the occasion."

"Food amuses me," he said.

"Amuses? You mean it amuses you to eat?"

"The sight of food," he said, "it always amuses me."

"That's a strange way to say that you like eating."

"Not eating," said Teeton. "I don't much care about eating." He waited until he was through with chewing the wing out of his way. "Not so much eating as I say. But food. The look of it."

"Amuses you?" she repeated; and there was a note of alarm in her voice.

"Yes."

"Now that surprises me," she concluded.

She pondered the meanings of amuse and thought that its meaning had slightly gone astray. She was trying to offer herself examples that were approximate to his meaning. She conceded there was something to be said for being amused by the sight of people in the act of eating. Faces could undergo considerable distortion; and it occurred to her that no two people ever suffered the same deformity of line when the exercise of chewing had begun. There was a nervous contraction of the jaws; the apologetic buttoning of a lip; some temples would suddenly sprout a row of tubes that threatened to burst at the slightest contact. She had seen a whole face balloon so that the eyes appeared to sink and the brow soften and fall to make an oval at the base of the chin. Teeton was alerted by her laugh. There was such a charge of excitement in her voice. She seemed unable to bring it under control.

"Are you all right?" he was asking her.

And each attempt at an answer was sabotaged by a strident renewal of her laugh. It was a strange outburst, like a sound released from some improbable region of sleep. A moment longer and Teeton's perplexity might have changed to a grave apprehension about her laugh.

Suddenly she said in the mildest tone: "Are you worried?"

"Almost," he said and guessed she must have sensed his doubt; but he refrained from any questions that might probe the cause of her outburst. He was more interested in her laugh. He wasn't prepared for this revelation, which contradicted his recollection of her the night before. Then she was earnest in her enquiries, almost a trifle rigid in her apparent need for exactness. There was a measure of distance, almost clinical, between her and the substance of her questions. Now there was some evidence of a feeling that roused her to gaiety. There was sparkle in her laugh and a promise of intimacy in her failure to control it.

"I enjoyed that," said Teeton, working a particle of bone from his teeth. A handkerchief rose from his hand and floated quietly down like a sail about to go out of sight. He was scrubbing his lips.

"Well," she said.

Her voice had come too sudden for any reasonable guess about her meaning.

"Well what?" he asked.

"Have you?"

"Have I?" Teeton went on, "have I? What do you mean have I?"

"Ever been in love?" she said; and her tone was that of a guide reminding the stranger of some direction he had taken before.

"I see," said Teeton, betraying his sense of error. There was a momentary shame in his failure to reply.

He wasn't in a hurry to produce an answer; and she gave no indication that time was important. His delay seemed natural. It might have been part of an agreement that each would have to wait for such answers to arrive. And she was patient as stone.

"Let's say I've known some moments," said Teeton, and felt a shudder seize his hands.

"Moments!" The response might have been addressed to herself until she added: "It never lasted?"

"In my memory," he said. "It's always there."

And Teeton was suddenly grateful for the night. It had deprived the woman of any chance of seeing what was now happening to his hands. They were clawing at the empty air. There was a violence of daggers in his eyes. The night was a forest vibrating with the sound of rapids which flogged the night with tides of blood. Suddenly he warned himself against any revelations of this fury. Here was a province of memory which he had sworn to tread alone. He hadn't shared the news of Randa's death. He knew he couldn't speak about her now. How could he speak about Randa without inviting the woman to discover his reasons for deserting. He was repenting the charge against himself. He heard a verdict which seemed to make any future effort just short of redemption. He was cut off; he had cut himself off by a fugitive act. 'But you are part of the Gathering,' he reflected as though such reflection might help him overcome the oppressive judgement of his memory. Teeton was still under the stupor of his brooding. He hadn't noticed that his body had put itself to rest. His head was cushioned by some nameless pillow of weed. There was a tickle of shrub behind his ear. A gathering of insects had found the slope of his neck. He had become aware of their progress towards the still, sharp precipice of his chin. They would never make it over the wet curve of his mouth. He brought his body forward, and heard his hands slowly clobber the itching side of his face.

"I am still here," Teeton said, trying to excuse his silence.

"It is difficult to return to some moments," the woman said.

Again he was struck by this habit of directness. He had observed it the night before. Now it was acquiring the severity of a custom. She was never slow to eliminate any preliminary noises which might otherwise have passed for talking. She delivered herself immediately to the matter in hand. It made for a certain ambiguity in Teeton's response. It tempted him to let himself be known; and in the same moment it warned him to be on his guard. But his caution prevailed. He wasn't going to speak about Randa nor how she had died.

"It was difficult for me too," she said, "but I came through. Not quite, perhaps. But through what you call those moments."

"You lost someone you loved?" Teeton said.

"Worse than that," she said, "it was a whole way of feeling that I lost. I think that's worse."

She was struggling to go on.

"I wonder," said Teeton, coming to her aid.

"That storm," she said in half a whisper.

Teeton had turned his head in her direction.

"You were in a storm?"

"Worse," she said, "I survived it."

Teeton was arrested by the sinister wish in her reply. There was no suggestion of despair in her quest for answers. He had judged her curiosity to be of a different kind. He had suddenly grown apprehensive about her laugh.

"What do you mean?" Teeton asked. "Wasn't it better to survive?"

Now he couldn't quite judge the purpose of her delay. But he didn't want to provoke answers that were different from the meaning she preferred to give; and he recalled her patience with his own lack of readiness in reply. She didn't intervene with gifts of consolation when he was at a loss for words. He yielded to this discipline of waiting.

"I couldn't answer without Father's evidence," she said, "and I haven't seen him since he died."

Teeton had become almost contrite. Her loss might have happened the day before. The change was abrupt.

"I was hardly three when we arrived on that island," she said. "Five thousand miles from home, and not a face that resembled our own. No native of intelligence to keep him company. Just the two of us. We lived alone until the day he died. The night the storm struck him down. We found his body in the lake next morning."

Teeton couldn't decide what he should say. He wanted to offer some word of condolence; yet he felt a reluctance to prolong the memory of her loss. He didn't want to tamper with the source of her grief. He felt an arbitrary urge to ask her name; but this was soon obliterated by her astonishing burst of eloquence.

"He taught me everything," she went on. "Nature was familiar as my own hands. The island had become my only home. I could name every plant, every flower. Not a single bird or beast could escape Father's curiosity. The rarest creature, the moment he saw it, would soon be subject to his learning. Never showed any interest in personal fortune. No taste at all for possession. He must have been a saint. The estate would have gone to ruin if it had not been for the care his servant lavished on him. He was the only school I had ever known. Until the day he died."

It seemed that the recollection of her father's death had liberated her into some perilous luxury of speech. She had become profligate with her gifts of personal history. Teeton had begun to find his way easily through the familiar names of her childhood. This shock of recognition had made him speechless. She continued to build, with elaborate strokes of memory, those massive generalities which revealed her relation to San Cristobal. Everything seemed to exist in the most vivid outline: the island, the inheritance conferred on her father in compensation for a robbery which he had borne gracefully and almost in utter silence. He confided in no one but his daughter, but he had always spared her any knowledge of the tragedy that had fallen upon his own ancestral fortunes.

In their mansion with its burning pillars of cedar and marble columns her father watched his exile through tearful meditation. Nature was the only presence which could arouse his respect. At noon, when the sun had made a furnace of the sky, and the earth was dying of thirst, he would listen to the clap of wind terrorise the leaves. The wind would swing great wheels of dust across the low, simmering plains of his sugar estate. He showed no interest at all in what happened there. There were rumours of others' existence beyond the opulent gates which protected his boundaries; but he had no energy for foreign needs. Only one person remained who was capable of thwarting his kindness—that was his servant, and overseer. Then his rage was barbarous. There was always murder in his language; and he had no equal in the arts of venomous abuse.

If the servant were a permanent thorn in his side, then his daughter was the only bliss that could distract him from his anguish. Innocent as she was in years, she had already learnt to sober him with applause. He would become an angel again under the spell of the little girl's admiration. She would have murdered to protect him against the will of heaven itself. She had continued to share his bed even when she was grown almost his equal in height. He couldn't resist the child's delight in answering to the wealth of his charms. And then the stranger from home arrived. And she learnt, for the first time, what was the origin of these fevers which had started to roast her body in sleep. Her father seemed kind as daylight to the man he introduced as his partner. He had come to help in the management of the estate. And she discovered what could happen when you were a woman. And she was happy.

"But your mother?" Teeton asked. "Where was she?"

It was less a question than a reaction to the vividness of her outline. He didn't even think that it was of importance.

146

"I don't know," she said. "Father never allowed any talk about her." Her voice seemed a trifle nervous, almost guilty in its sharp inflection. But it was a momentary flaw in her certainty. She said, without waiting for Teeton to satisfy his curiosity, "and it never bothered me."

"Wasn't she ever on the island?" Teeton asked.

"No. Not that I know of." It seemed her doubt was getting in the way, but she was quickly at ease, confident and conclusive in her tone of vague, almost indifferent speculation. "We've never met. I'll never know who she was."

Teeton showed little interest in this obscure aspect of her parenthood. It held little power of surprise, for he had endured a childhood's silence to questions about the absence of a father from his life. It was as though he was meeting her for the first time, and on that strange ground where the extreme circumstance had been converted by time into a process of growing that was normal.

Now it dawned on him that some new feeling had begun to stir in him. Normal as it should have been, it had adopted the power of something extreme. He was becoming fond of this strange woman. He was slipping voluntarily into the state of wanting to be with her. His interest had been enriched by this recent knowledge of her past. And his disappointment was sharp when he considered that she was only fourteen when her Father's partner came into her life. For a moment Teeton was amused to think that she might have aroused a feeling like jealousy in him.

She was there, beside him, near and yet safe in her lack of identity: a kind of absence which he couldn't take possession of. But her absence had begun to heighten the potential dangers of her body for him. Indeed, it was this very absence which seemed to stir a need in his appetite. The enticement was now greater than any visual knowledge of her body would have afforded. His curiosity had suddenly bullied him into frantic speculation about her life with the man who had achieved her father's approval.

"What happened after your father died?" Teeton began. "Did his friend take you away?"

"We left," she said, "but not together. I never saw him after he left the island."

"Weren't you in love with him?"

"I was in love with him," she said, "but I couldn't see him again. Not after what happened."

Teeton heard her voice fail. It seemed she was about to explain; but some memory was guiding her painfully back to a vision of the island she wouldn't be able to endure. Her silence was different; it seemed to give warning of a danger she didn't want to share. But Teeton had restrained his urge to hear her speak. Instead, his imagination was offering her in a variety of moods. Her face had become part of the rivers and the mountains which his maps had kept alive.

He wanted to look at her; to know her by sight; to learn by some slow and careful magnet of his gaze the most casual details of her face. There was a weight of hunger in his eyes. He leaned his head closer and stared blindly at the area of the night where her body was in recline. But something warned him not to trespass with his hands. It seemed premature. He might have run the risk of spoiling what now promised to be a perfect moment. He would abandon the ordinarily accepted role of masculine initiative. It was a foolish notion at any time; and especially in a circumstance which defied all notions of the ordinary. Now he was trying to imagine her in the greatest variety of light: at morning under the grey, dark lethargy of daybreak; what would happen to her eyes under the harsh, dry bars of sunlight. He was inventing her taking refuge under a shower of leaves, she was shielding her brow; a calm, amiable descent of rain was washing her hair out of her hands. Her mouth would be weeping rain; her ears were dripping with silver.

He judged it would be wrong to touch her now; to convert this sudden liberty of speech into some crude abuse of privilege. It was her privilege to stay as she was; to choose whether this was the moment she would make her body known. Would she have taken him in the dark? Taken him in all intimacy into her sex before they had ever seen each other? But knowing was a kind of seeing, Teeton thought. He wanted to diminish the special authority of the eyes; to reduce the claims of sight. Some moments should be sacred. The words made dumb circles before his eyes. To leave her body alone. Only by such voluntary self-denial could he have claimed, in all honesty claim, at some future date, that this night had achieved a sacred meeting. He was beginning to pass a mild condemnation on his own desire. The intention, so recklessly come over him, seemed almost as wicked as an actual assault. But he had to find a way to forgive his own misgiving; and he chose complicity. She, too, he thought. What was she thinking? Wouldn't she have also wished? Would she? Wouldn't she? But it was too late to bargain with these mute propositions.

"It's a difficult moment," she said, "to know that you must refuse the pleasures that are most natural."

Teeton was stupefied. It was as though he had rendered himself transparent; offered for her rebuke the squalid motives which had been haunting him. He was unsure how he would proceed. He had grown suddenly impatient of her delay. He was almost angry at this pause which seemed too long, as though she had already guessed his fear of waiting. He didn't trust himself to seek her meaning; and so he decided to invoke a calm. He would take cover under pretext of being patient. There could be no excess of waiting. There was no longer any need to see her. It was enough to know her as she was. A voice emerging at intervals from the dark.

'What pleasures?' Teeton wanted to ask; almost hopeful that the word might have come to redeem him from his own motives. For it seemed, and in his favour, that she, too, had been thinking of the pleasures which he had tried to defy. What other pleasures could carry, in this moment, the name of natural? And it was a point in his favour, a signal of encouragement, that she had spoken of refusal. But she couldn't have been a virgin. Could he tell from the music of a voice what was her possible experience of sex? Perhaps she was. He was thinking of his own wounds: the unspeakable treacheries that had threatened to break his life. Instead, he had tried to find some refuge in the virtues which he had always conferred on San Cristobal. He was feeling the loyalty of a patriot whose pride of country had become even greater during his long absence from home.

"But you loved the island," Teeton said.

Suddenly she felt a shudder of nerves opening out under her skin. It started with a tightening of muscles above her knees; then travelled up the inside of her thighs. A belt of steel had embraced her bowels. Her breasts had begun to thaw, as though the sweat had turned to sheets of frost spreading over her shoulders. There was a pressure of ice at the base of her skull, and a sound of glass crushing in her ears.

But she made no effort to stir until she heard Teeton's voice again.

"Didn't you love the island?"

"Until the night they came after me," she said.

"Who came after you?" Teeton was urging her to speak.

"The servant and his men."

"Came after you?" Teeton's voice had risen to a pitch of exclamation.

"I could only see the flames," she said, "like a million tongues licking and sucking up the night. That's how it was. They'd made a bonfire to celebrate their rape of me. Right there, in the open field, with the flames sizzling and spraying everything with heat. God! It was so hot. I'd never known such heat. And soon I couldn't tell any longer which was worse. That fire screaming and crackling about my ears, or the terrible pounding that started up inside me. There was only that tearing apart, like instruments opening up my insides. They found every crack in my body; operated through every opening in my body. I couldn't tell how many they were. But they seemed a whole army. Naked as wind they were. Not a rag to their skin. How many I don't know, nor how long. It seemed like eternity. They would rest and return, giving the interval over to the animals: Father's two hounds. It's as though they had trained the animals for this moment, put them through daily practice in this form of intercourse. They gave the animals the same privilege. Until I couldn't tell which body was the man's and which belonged to the beasts."

"Please, please, please!"

It was the only word Teeton seemed able to remember. He had heard enough; and yet there seemed no end to his curiosity. He experienced a violent conflict of tendencies. He wanted to hear. But he wanted to relieve her of talking. He felt his hands grow cold. Bramble was probing the flesh over his ankle. Suddenly it seemed that he wouldn't have been able to walk. There was a constriction around his feet. A clot of nerves had set up a dam inside his veins. The blood had gone dormant, still, depriving his leg of all sensation.

"Were you alone?" Teeton was trying to ask.

"No," she said. "Fernando hadn't left yet. He was there."

"But what did they do to him?"

"Nothing," she said. "They just tied him to Father's chair and made him watch."

Absurdly, as though deprived of hearing, Teeton could hear his stammer repeating his enquiries about the man.

"He was there, you say?"

"They made him their witness," she said again. "I believe it drove him mad."

"The servant and his friends!" Teeton began to shout. He was tortured by regret and guilt for what he had heard. For a moment he felt as though he had been the agent of these barbarities. His stammer continued with its irrelevant pleas for certainty.

"Yes," she said. "It was Father's servant who organised his friends. Perhaps he organised Father's death as well. We never knew what really happened that night."

Now she could feel the winter temperature of her body subside. The frost had cracked; and sweat was coursing freely over her shoulders. For a moment she felt she had made some escape from the dungeons her memory had built around her. Teeton's attention had come to her rescue. She had survived some unspeakable plague of silence. She felt she had outraged his hearing; and she knew it was the night which had given her this courage. Would she have taken the same liberty if she could see him? Now she felt a little fearful of the consequences. Would she want to see him now, to be known by him in daylight after she had delivered herself of the horrors which had been the climax of her torment on that island? They had driven her into a future where she would always be a vagrant, an empty port for anyone's pleasure; deprived forever of the delight which ordinary women found in sex.

She heard Teeton grow restless in the dark. He was exercising his legs, trying to stir some feeling into the flesh above his knees. She felt a soft weariness close her eyes, as she reflected on the muted noises which broke into the silence of the heath. She was exhausted; but there was also a feeling of relief. Her body was light; her hands had come into their normal weight again. She opened her eyes and saw the solitary light that framed a window on the far side of the heath. And she felt safe, as though she had suddenly discovered some novel promise of security from the presence of this stranger.

What more was there to tell him? What more could he want to hear? She was no longer apprehensive about the consequences of her disclosures. Revealed, they had now lost the power to silence her.

She could return to their former exchanges. It was like the night before. They had met for the first time then. An accident, yes. But it was too fruitful to be forgotten. Now she felt that they were about to meet afresh. Hidden from view, they were no longer wholly in the dark.

"Everything feels so different now," she said. The voice was casual, almost distant.

"Different?" Teeton wanted to resist any talk of change. He would have regretted any difference which made for an end to their meeting. He feared this was her meaning; but he felt no instinct to persuade her to act in his favour.

"Different?"

"Our meeting," she said. "It's like starting all over again. That's different from really starting. For the first time, I mean."

Teeton promised himself to talk with the greatest care. There was a difference for him; but it meant avoiding any mention of her rape. He had to avoid any talk which might put too great a strain on her wish to stay with him here. He couldn't afford an abrupt departure at this stage. 'The servant,' Teeton kept hearing her voice announce. 'The servant who organised his friends.'

"I don't suppose I can be of any help?" he begged. It seemed the safest way of showing his concern: to put himself in readiness for some future service.

"You have helped enough," she said.

"I've only listened."

"What else could you do?" she asked. "My past doesn't come under your control."

"True, perhaps," said Teeton, "but now. What about now?"

"Then you've helped," she said as though she was about to triumph in an argument which he had begun. "I am feeling fine. Now. This moment. That's help enough."

"For the time being," said Teeton, urging himself to prove his right to be of service. "What about later?"

"Later?"

"The future," he said quickly, "tomorrow. Will you be feeling fine tomorrow?"

"Let's settle for what I feel now," she said. "And now I feel fine."

Teeton restrained his urge to argue. He had come to accept that it was her privilege to choose whether she required his help, and how it was to be given. It might have been different if he hadn't heard her story. Or had it been a different story. Then he would have been free to challenge her right to choose on his behalf. But all privilege was entirely hers. He would never be able to challenge her with any wish that worked to his advantage. It was as though the content of her suffering had given her total authority to decide what he should mean to her.

"You're not sorry that I know what I do about you?" Teeton asked.

"Now you're off on the future," she laughed.

"Yes. It's the future I'm thinking of."

"You mustn't," she said.

"Mustn't?"

"Must not," she said firmly; and Teeton felt himself suddenly obey her warning. He couldn't bring himself to argue. He had conferred a privilege which now reduced all his instinct of rebellion to a whisper. He didn't agree; yet he felt it necessary, and in his interest, to refrain from any conflict that might displease her.

But she wasn't sure of her own warning. She was at war with her deepest wish. Yes, she was thinking, yes I should see him; and without any break in this pursuit of her desire, some other code of feeling which she called her conscience was shouting: no, no, you cannot see him; you can't let yourself be seen by him. She was tortured by a waste of passion. It grew fruitlessly within her; a sudden exaltation that bore her forward to the very edge of screaming. She wanted to shout; to call down the worst indecencies on her body; to blaspheme against the calm and tenderness of this stranger's yearning to know her. Didn't he understand? Didn't it make any difference that he had understood?

She was going to reach forward, half an arm away, and search for his hand; but only to mortify his hope. She would get a hold of his hand; imprison it in hers; and guide it slowly, cruelly into the barren grave of her cunt so that he might discover for himself the future of skeletons which he was now so eager to idolise. She would hold his hand to the very fullness of the fist and let her naked sex announce the only truth it had ever known: that nothing happens there, will ever happen there since the night her father's hounds played master over her body; sucked and pricked her privacy, and left her like a bone, clean, dead.

Didn't he understand? Couldn't he understand? The future? What innocence there was in his request! And as though she had recognised some power in his folly, she felt her rage yield; she could sense a softening towards him; and she was thinking again—and without any tendency to deceive—yes, I should see him; would like to be seen by him. Who was he? Who is he? But the code of feeling came back, prompt, stern, hard as flint in its opposition to her lack of judgement: No, you must not see him, must not let yourself be seen by him.

Teeton sat still, tame as the grass under his hands. She had given enough of herself. He had to grant her this privilege; this freedom to choose for herself; to choose against his wish. He would have to let her go unseen. At least tonight. Tonight, he was saying, weighing the danger it implied. Would there be other nights? Would she come again? But there were few nights left to him. He was on the eve of his departure. A week from tomorrow he would be on his way to San Cristobal. Who was she, really? What had these extravagant punishments done to her? Who is she? He was beyond himself with asking; but he accepted his private oath of discipline. He couldn't press her further with his questions. He was prepared to forgo the pleasure of seeing her. He started to coax himself into feeling that it was not necessary to see her. But she must promise that they would continue to meet. This was enough. Perhaps it was even better. This simple wish had grown with amazing speed into the certainty of conviction. It was better for them to meet, unseen. Sacred, some meetings should be sacred. The words had acquired their own holy rhythm. That's how it should be; that's how he really wanted it to be. Here, on this heath, under cover of night, they would meet like a legend of spirits, indifferent to the visible frivolities of daylight. The dark was their bond; the word their only necessary bridge.

And so Teeton decided that he should leave her now.

"Tonight," he said, hoping that the offer would confirm his wish, "it's my turn to go first."

"Yes, yes," she said.

There was no trace of a reservation in her reply, as though the terms of their ritual were now signed and complete.

"Tomorrow night?"

"Before midnight," she agreed.

"Goodbye."

"Go careful," she said.

And he was gone. She heard the noise of his stride racing over the fallen leaves. And then she saw the light of a torch come on. It had leapt in a flash from the pond; then started to probe the darkness where she lay.

7

One

Teeton was not at home; but he had given the Old Dowager her first assignment with the Press. She would know how to protect him from their intrusion. The day had begun with elaborate preparations for their afternoon tea. Alone, in the privacy of Teeton's room, the Old Dowager was going to celebrate his sale of the paintings. The exhibition would be formally opened at six.

When the door bell rang, the Old Dowager was prepared for the call. She coughed again, and gave her voice Teeton's last instructions. The sound came clear. The note was right for rebuke. But she knew she would have to make an effort to support this look of scorn which her eyes had started to rehearse. The call came again; but she checked with the mirror before leaving the bedroom. The hair net received her final enquiry.

When she opened the door, she drew her body smartly forward to fill the space. Her glance was sufficient warning that the men were not welcome. The reporter was wearily middle aged. The photographer must have recently begun his adolescence. His zeal might have been a cause of worry for the older man, who was calculating the first move he should make. He didn't like the temperature of the Old Dowager's gaze. The younger man was at a loss to understand what they had done. But his camera was urgent as a gun, cocked for action, and ready to capture his target for the day. The reporter had grown gentle and melancholy.

"With your permission," he said, "is the painter in?"

"It won't take long," the photographer intervened.

And the Old Dowager opened her first round of fire.

"What won't take long?" she enquired.

The reporter came to the rescue again.

"Just an interview," he said. "His exhibition opens tonight."

It seemed the Old Dowager had no knowledge to share. The photographer offered to say what he knew.

"But the painter is your tenant, isn't he?" he asked.

"What tenant?" the Old Dowager quickly demanded.

Her scorn was no longer improvised. It required no effort on her part. The camera had become an obscenity against her eyes.

The reporter was memorising a list of apologies. He was beginning to understand what had gone wrong. The lady might not have been on the best of terms with the painter. She must have had her reasons.

"They told us at the Mona that it was here," he said. "Dark gentleman. The publican thought it was the second floor."

"There are no tenants in this house," the Old Dowager said.

She took a step back; and it seemed she was about to close the door.

"Be a sport," the photographer was chiding her. "I can see you're a good sort."

"I say there are no tenants in this house," the Old Dowager reminded him.

It didn't seem that she would let them enter. But the reporter thought he noticed a change come into her voice. She might not have been so hostile to them as she had appeared. The photographer was prompting his cheeks to blush.

"You might at least tell us if he is in," the young man said.

"Do you have an appointment with someone here?" the Old Dowager asked.

The voice was forgetting its instructions. She didn't think she could rely on her frown much longer. Any moment her pleasure was likely to betray her. 'An appointment', she was asking herself, 'have you got an appointment with someone here?' The Old Dowager had recognised the reporter's indecision. Her question had kept them at bay.

"The appointment was made," the reporter conceded.

"He is expecting us," the photographer confirmed.

"Who is expecting you?" the Old Dowager challenged.

The reporter was getting angry; but he didn't want to risk the Old Dowager's wrath. Her scorn had resumed its service as she waited for an answer.

"You know whom we have come to see," the reporter said.

"And why don't I remember?" the Old Dowager asked, as though her innocence had been outraged.

"But the painter does live here, doesn't he?" the reporter was near the end of his patience.

The photographer was affected by the older man's tone of exhaustion. He was going to be reckless with his suspicions. He would offer the Old Dowager his allegiance.

"If you don't like this fellow, then you don't," the photographer said. "That's none of our business, and maybe you're right. But at least you can let him know we are here."

"Whom did you say you were looking for?" the Old Dowager asked, and gave a sigh of infinite boredom.

The reporter decided against the call of his dignity. He wanted to go; to run as fast as he could; to get lost somewhere in the idle spaces of the heath. But prudence made a greater claim on his decision. He looked at the photographer who recognised a signal had passed. They exchanged glances. The reporter started a leisurely retreat towards the pavement. The photographer followed close behind. They started to deliberate in whispers. The reporter was afraid the Old Dowager might close the door and put an end to their enquiries. He was going to consult his notes. He was smiling over his shoulder for the Old Dowager's attention. He was searching his pockets. A hand-kerchief surprised him. He buried it quickly in the inside pocket of his jacket. Then a tangle of twisted tissues emerged. The lining of his coat was a rubbish heap. He abandoned the tissues to the pavement, and dried his forehead with the end of his sleeve.

He was hating his job; and it made him hate the woman who stood in the door. She showed no desire to cooperate; yet she wasn't in a hurry to send them away. He wasn't sure who was the target of her spite. The painter seemed an obvious choice. She might have been antagonistic to the tenant. She didn't want his affairs associated with her house. He didn't blame her. People who were likely to attract public attention ought to have a place of their own. It was a crazy notion. Thirty years after his first job he was still without the remotest prospect of buying his own house. He was pacing frantically up and down; and the Old Dowager watched him as though he were a hound confined to the narrow circle of its kennel. She made him nervous. He couldn't remember the painter's name. His error gave a new edge to his frustration. He didn't know how he would report this failure. The name, the name, what's his name? His impatience was mounting. It was building up to a positive loathing of every obstacle in his way. He tried to ignore the photographer's zeal. Priority! The assignment was to be given priority treatment. He was working his tongue like a key through the gap in his teeth. Priority treatment. The order had come from above. It increased his rage. He didn't really want to do this story. But the order came from above. He was nursing an attack of envy; but he couldn't tell exactly who was to blame. Now it was his editor. Then a glance at the second floor made him select the painter as his villain.

"I didn't care to do this story," he started to grumble.

He was having a mild effect on the photographer's mood. But it would have been impossible to curb the young man's zeal. It was his first break with a big feature. He was making his debut in the fitful gamble of recognition. But the future held no hazards for him.

"Did you find out why they're trying to build this up?" he asked.

The reporter's mood had prompted the question. He wasn't sure why they had chosen him for the photographs. The name, for crying out loud, what's the name?

"I never heard of his work before."

"You will," the reporter gravely said.

"They're giving it one hell of a build-up," he said. "What's the reason?"

The reporter was no longer cautious when he spoke.

"They're expecting a big story to break," he said.

"About this painter?"

"Not to do with him," the reporter was answering in the quietest voice. "It's about where he comes from. They're expecting big trouble on that island."

Now he looked as though he had suffered some cruel deprivation of his rights. A theft of opportunity had always visited malice on his career. He was exhausted by his struggle to be better known.

"It doesn't pay to be born where life is stable," the young man said.

"Doesn't pay to be born a lot of things," the reporter advised.

Now he looked wise and reliable as he paused to instruct the youth. Shakespeare was wishing him well; revealing the origin of his own neglect.

"Were I in England now, as once I was, and had but this fish painted, not a holiday fool there but would give a piece of silver. There would this monster make a man. Any strange beast there makes a man."

The photographer was staring in confused alarm. But the reporter went grimly on.

"When they will not give a doit to relieve a lame beggar, they will lay out ten to see a dead Indian."

Some dead Indian had suddenly restored the photographer to his senses.

"What the ass is this bastard's name?" the young man said, chewing his lip. "Perhaps she might ease up if we knew." He was growing increasingly fearful of losing his chance.

The reporter shook his head and let his eyes rove mournfully over the empty sky. Humiliation had made him cease to care.

"Let's try again," the young man begged.

He photographed the address, the garden enclosure, and the window on the second floor. The dog ran out from the side gate, and he photographed the dog.

"Come back Vulcan," the Old Dowager said.

Suddenly the dog stopped, braking its speed; then reversed to the door.

"Who gave you permission?" the Old Dowager asked again.

"Be a sport," the photographer said, "I can see you're all right."

She was going to smile; but glanced to where the dog was scratching his ear with an angry paw.

"Hello Vulcan," the photographer said.

The dog lowered his glance and stiffened his tail. The photographer continued talking to the dog; but Vulcan was indifferent to his welcome. His tail grew more erect; the mouth trembled; there was a low growl.

"Now be quiet," the Old Dowager said.

"When last did you see the tenant?" the photographer asked.

"There are no tenants in this house," the Old Dowager said.

She frowned and turned to go.

"What do you mean no tenants?" he said. He seemed to accuse her of lying.

"I say there are no tenants in this house," the Old Dowager repeated.

It was a fruitless effort. The reporter finally called it off.

But the Old Dowager was sorry to see them go. They had taken some portion of her delight. She wished they had recognised what she was feeling. Her scorn had given way to a look of ecstasy. They might have seen it if they had been patient enough to wait. She had come very near to putting them at ease. It's true Teeton was not at home; and she had welcomed his instructions not to let anyone from the Press come up to his room. She supported Teeton in this attitude; but she would have liked the men to know that she had played a part in these decisions. She had been letting her mischief work itself up to this point. It was a harmless role which she had given herself: a momentary joy in the power she held over anyone who sought her permission to see Teeton. She had never taken so keen a delight in her stewardship of his interests. The Exhibition was like a reward for every service she had rendered him; and the invitation to tea was a testament of his devotion to her.

The weather was on her side, surprising the grass with its sudden burst of heat. The heath was on fire. She could see beyond the first hump of trees where a young woman lay, face down and almost naked in her bath of sunlight. Her shoulders rose in curves above the huge pillows of breasts. The Old Dowager would have thought such exposure indecent if she had seen the girl at any other time. But she saw with different eyes today. The men didn't know that they could have won her approval. And yet she wasn't sure. It was just possible that she might have allowed them the benefit of the doubt. But there was something like impudence in their failure to remember Teeton's name. And imagine that, she was saying as she looked around for the dog. Come to see the painter. The tenant on the second floor. Her jaws had tightened again; and the look of scorn took natural possession of her eyes.

The reporter had done his best; but the assignment would have been as fruitless if it had been anyone else. She had held her ground behind the door, waiting to make sure they had gone. Later she opened the door and gave the street her final inspection.

"Now we can look after our business," she said, stooping to nestle the dog's head under her arm. "It's not a man's work, prying and spying into people's affairs."

The dog trotted behind her, doing a tango with his tail.

The Old Dowager was resuming work on her hair, trying out new clips; measuring a curl that had escaped down the creamy track of her brow. Vulcan watched her, puzzled, approving; basking in her praise of his attentions.

"Do you think it was right to accept Teeton's offer?"

For the hundredth time she was inviting the dog's opinion; and when she turned from the mirror, showing her eagerness for an answer, Vulcan's tail seemed to spring erect, like a flag displaying its loyalty. And the weather had approved. The bedroom had achieved a perfect glow. The Old Dowager could feel the warmth spread across her shoulders. She was like a girl again, struggling against the first warning of excitement; fearing there might be some flaw in her self-restraint; some brigand of an emotion was about to ransack her secrets, expose her delights. There were such armies of them: these little monsters of joy, deep in hiding where reason couldn't reach them; giving their soundings at the most unguarded moment; as though they wanted to subvert the normal laws of the heart.

"I think it was really sweet of him." Again she was depriving Vulcan of his neutrality. "Isn't it nice of Teeton to arrange it in this way?"

The dog had reclined on his haunches, aiming his chin at the face that smiled out of the mirror. The Old Dowager was massaging her brow, ironing out the covers of flesh over the horns of her cheeks: a face once laden with a thousand desires.

"So nice of him," she reminded the dog.

She rose from the bed. She was retracing the stages of preparation. She wanted to avoid a rush. She hadn't heard Teeton come in; but then he was a man; he could always afford the discomfort of being rushed. She was going to be on time, not exactly on the dot; and not having to apologise for a moment's delay.

"How much time have we got?"

Vulcan lowered his chin and sniffed the corners of the bed. The Old Dowager shook the clock and put it to her ear. She was going to set the alarm for a call at four, just an hour before her tea with Teeton.

"That means we've got an hour. Just enough for a doze. Keeps the temperature even."

Vulcan seemed to find these admonitions to his taste. Already he had begun to rub his body against the bed. He was getting ready to slide his flanks down, and knot his tail under. But the Old Dowager had deceived him. The dog anticipated she would make for the bed; but she was lowering herself on to the rocking chair. She wanted to stay upright. She was taking precautions against any delay by remaining fully conscious of the clock.

"So nice of Teeton. To choose me. Of all people. To celebrate the exhibition all on our own."

She was awake. She was arguing with herself to stay awake; for she wasn't going to take the slightest risk with sleep. The briefest interval of sleep would have been wasted on her body. But the Old Dowager was a prisoner of her own imagination. Some force had started a cleansing of her fears; she was learning a freedom she had forgotten. She could hear Teeton's maps like a sudden clap of sails about her ears. It must have been true. Now she knew it was true. There was still time to discover the delights of travel. Some promise of luck had begun to intoxicate her senses. She was shaking the islands like a fist of marbles through the air. The crunch of shell and pebble wouldn't cease singing in her ears. Now she knew that it would never be too late.

Sleep had taken her captive. She was travelling back. Soon she was losing her hold on the chair. She couldn't resist the gradual fall of her body. It was bringing her down. Ever so gently. The wind opened her hair and latched her hands to the rim of the sky. She was a parachute sliding down; tossed up and over bank after bank of cloud. A forest of leaves fell from the sky. She was helping her lover to build his safety. It was necessary to shut out her husband's voice. They couldn't pretend he wasn't there. His head was climbing past the roof. They saw him go, a sack of diamonds on his back. But his voice was coming over the wind; and her lover was afraid. Higher, he was begging, he had to build his hope much higher. Afraid, he had to be trained out of his fear. The clouds were breaking up like stone. Here, I am here. Safe, you are safe. He was taking her hand. White and handsome in his youth. The sky was caving in. The wind was folding up her hair. Down, her body was a parachute coming down. Safe, you are safe. We are ready. She had found his heart at last. I am here. She knew how to guard his fear. He was burying his mouth inside her ear. Her lips were sucking up the sky. A tide of fire had caught the wind. Down, she was coming down. Her lover was a bed of cloud. You are there. He knows we are here. But you are safe. Their love was warning that he would be back. But I am here. Safe, I know your love is safe. Down, coming down, she was trying to resist the call of the wind. She had come gently down. Safe, I know your love is.

"I am here," the Old Dowager heard herself shout. There was a shadow of cloud over her eyes. The room had the feel of early night until she heard Vulcan bark. His tail was whipping against the bed, but he didn't move. His eyes were watchful, as though he couldn't be sure whether the Old Dowager was awake.

"There you are," she said, turning her head away from the dog. There was a look of apology in her glance when she faced the wall. Then the mirror returned her laugh.

"Was someone calling?" the Old Dowager asked, stretching her hands out to greet the dog. Vulcan seemed to understand there was something she was asking him to forgive. He raised his paws up to the chair, and licked his tongue over the Old Dowager's hands. She started to laugh again.

"You mustn't tell," she said, making a parcel with his ears. "We can't let Teeton know everything."

The dog buried his head in her lap.

"There, there," the Old Dowager smiled. "It's time I was ready. And not a word. What did I say? There, that's right. Not a word. I think I hear him now. Not a word, you hear?"

Vulcan began to patrol the room. He ran to the cupboard where the Old Dowager was sorting the hangers laden with her clothes. He watched her count the buttons on the blue dress she was going to wear. He was scratching his tail as he watched the Old Dowager spread the dress over the bed. She was climbing out of the skirt she wore; and Vulcan threw himself on to one side and tried to roll his flanks over the rug. The Old Dowager was tunnelling her hands through the sleeves of her dress. Vulcan thrust his paws up and balanced them like stilts. He was a clown. He had suddenly remembered the oldest of his tricks. He saw the Old Dowager weighing her hair, watching the mirror for some fault in the bun which looked like a wheel at the back of her head. Vulcan rose on his hind legs, closing ranks like a soldier on parade. He lost his balance and fell. The Old Dowager smiled at him from the mirror. He looked down sharply at his paws. He was threatening the rug to tear it apart. He started to bark, three short, sharp blows of sound struck out at her face in the mirror; then a whinnying cry, soft and slow like the noise of wind forcing the springs of a door.

The Old Dowager was ready. Vulcan had seen that she had nothing more to do. He would have to start barking again. He knew when the Old Dowager was going to take him along. He could always detect the sign. But it hadn't come. He walked past the bed. He looked down at the rug as though he was about to sprawl full length across the door. But it seemed too soon to disobey. Instead, he sat upright. He was uncertain how to bring about her delay. The Old Dowager must have forgotten him.

Vulcan followed her up the stairs; but the mirror on the landing had brought her to a halt outside Teeton's room. Now she drew herself up, poised for her last, important enquiry. She looked at her face like a stranger whose past she had vaguely heard about. Cautious and fragile, her hand climbed up to the mirror and touched the nose which was imprisoned in the frame of glass. It was no more than a second's contact when the Old Dowager suddenly withdrew her hand and turned to see whether anyone had seen her. She was standing outside Teeton's room. The mirror was opposite his door; and the Old Dowager got the feeling that he might have seen her arguing with the face which the mirror said was hers. But no one had appeared.

"I'm so sorry," she whispered, and the mouth in the mirror moved as though they were agreed that no apology was necessary.

She hadn't noticed Vulcan crouched beside her. She was still busy preparing a face for her meeting with Teeton.

"You think he would like this?" the whisper was enquiring, and she stretched the line of eye shadow further up the socket of her left eye. One lash seemed thinner than the other; and the lipstick suprised her with a double shade on her mouth.

"Perhaps I should make you a little gayer," the whisper was advising, and she thickened the pink shade on her lower lip.

"Now there, that's better, much better."

She stood back from the mirror and looked for any defects which might have showed up in the sudden burst of sunlight which came from the skylight.

"I think he would like that," the whisper agreed, and she turned towards the door. For a moment she paused, and glanced over her shoulder at the length of her body which seemed to grow from the landing to the marble top of the mirror. Vulcan started to bark.

"Now get away," she said, ordering him with both hands to descend the stairs. Like a child, hurt by rebuke, the dog hung its head and moved shamefully down the stairs.

"Are you there?" the Old Dowager asked, and knocked twice on the door.

There was no answer.

"Is anyone in?" she repeated.

The Old Dowager was now talking to herself, counting the days forward, pausing with grave deliberation as she followed her memory from Tuesday to Wednesday.

"Then Friday," she said, now certain of the date.

The Old Dowager let her hand seize the doorknob; but she didn't want to be responsible for turning it. It would have been too rash an intrusion to find Teeton there, compromised by circumstances which she should not have witnessed. This would have been an error she could never have got over. She threw the door wide open; but held herself back and out of view; so that Teeton could make use of her delay. A single word would have been enough. But there was no answer from the room; not the slightest stir of welcome when she called out for Teeton. It was then the Old Dowager decided to go in.

The table had captured her attention; it brought her immense relief to see the preparations Teeton had made. It had been laid for two; and the Old Dowager's lips seemed to hold on to the smile which had come over them. She began to make apologies for Teeton's delay. She was debating whether she should stay; and then she thought she would. But she would leave the door open as a warning that she was there.

The Old Dowager turned to retrieve her handbag; and suddenly the feeling came over her, like a bolt of ice freezing her movement. She had seen her doom in the body which was about to fall off the divan. And in the very instant she had reversed towards the door. She closed it; she could hear her hands in a tussle with the key. She locked the door. But her eyes hadn't deserted the body for a moment. She watched it with a fearful knowledge of its condition. She had seen it for what it was: a corpse which might have been playing the part of being alive. The Old Dowager's eyes were playing havoc with her judgement. They were providing the dead body with its grave, debating with the still, suspended leg the right moment for burial. She didn't recognise the face of Nicole, taut and white as frost. It was as though death had deprived it of any individual features.

"Where are you, Teeton?" the Old Dowager heard herself crying. "Teeton, Teeton, where are you?"

But her voice had no influence on her gaze which remained on Nicole's body; restoring a natural posture to the limbs, tidying the hair. The Old Dowager's gaze had started some glow of fire which seemed to strike life into Nicole's face, bringing a calm, steady illumination into the dead, open eyes.

"Teeton, Teeton," the Old Dowager's voice was crying again. "Do you know of this? How did it happen, Teeton? Tell me, Teeton, what have you done? Are you in trouble?"

She was piling question upon question, appealing to Teeton in his absence; yet hopeful, it seemed, that the dead body would speak. Some dormant and impossible faith was coming alive in the Old Dowager, encouraging her to hear the dead voice say what had happened.

The Old Dowager looked to the door; then she covered the maps with her gaze, investigating the slightest evidence of danger. She straightened herself, avoiding support from the table, and made her way quietly towards the window. She wanted to get some kind of assurance from the street that Teeton was safe; that her name would be free from blemish; that the house would not have to suffer a future of disrepute. She was hiding her face behind the map, juggling the glances of one eye round the edge of the window frame. Then she decided to withdraw. She might have attracted attention from the street.

The Old Dowager felt undermined by some possible witness from the street. She stepped back, nodding towards the maps, as though she was grateful that they had given her safe cover. She turned her eyes to the divan, memorising Nicole's face, appealing for some sign of Teeton's whereabouts. It was as though his absence had now made her duty clear. She couldn't share the discovery of this death until she had heard from Teeton. She would have to stay where she was; a guardian of Teeton's safety. Until Teeton arrived, she would have to keep watch over the dangers which this corpse implied; she would have to keep watch over Teeton's absence.

"Where are you? Teeton, where are you?"

The Old Dowager straightened the dead leg, so that it now lay in place on the divan. She helped the hands complete their meeting over Nicole's breast. She was guiding the head towards a more tranquil space of pillow. She thought these were the gestures of farewell which Teeton might have made. His absence was like an order to protect this discovery from any stranger's intrusion; a plea to be company to Nicole's corpse.

"Teeton, Teeton, Teeton! Where are you?"

Her tears came like rain through a vigil which seemed to have no end.

Two

Where was he? Where had he ever been? There would have been accounts which got no further than the witness of the eye. Roger and Derek had seen him; Jeremy had heard from him. He had gone, slipping from the extreme precipice of mind, to seek some remnant of solace from the Gathering. He had been present in these places; and these places, by common report, would confirm that he was there. But where was he? No one really knew; nor was Teeton able to say.

At five o'clock he was safe. He had kept his oath to be out of reach. The merchants would open and close the Exhibition without the connivance of his visit there. He was on his way to receive the crown of the Old Dowager's favours: her arrival for tea. He was late; but this private, little triumph had made him gay. Then the headline broke from the evening paper: San Cristobal Bomb Attack. A torrent of fire had been rained on the island. Cattle Wash had been blown to ashes, the village now buried by flood; man and fish carried equally to their skeleton doom.

Where was he? The Old Dowager had disappeared from his memory like a cloud. The tea cups shattered the air; the dog was chasing its flaming tail. He had descended from the upper deck of the bus. His mindless pilgrimage had begun. Where was he? Where had he gone? Where had he ever been?

Some lunatic clarity of mind must have brought him home. He could hear the chimes drift up from the heath; but the clocks had lost all power to measure time. It seemed the stairs had taken Teeton by his feet up to his room. He stood outside the door. It had never been locked. His memory must have taken him elsewhere; but the smell of this landing held him there.

"Where were you? Where were you, Teeton?"

It seemed the door had given way to the Old Dowager's question. And Teeton followed the voice inside. She was guiding him gradually back to the terrain of his room. He came abruptly up against the boundary of the table. This wasn't his normal course of entry; and he realised dimly that the Old Dowager was piloting him away from the divan. His hands had found the back of the chair. The Old Dowager hadn't spoken until she warned against the light. Teeton's first effort of speech was apology; he was learning, like an infant emerging from some fretful babble, to say that he was sorry.

"I am sorry," Teeton tried again. "So sorry about the tea."

"Teeton!"

"So sorry."

"Are you in trouble, Teeton?"

Teeton's hands were asking for some light.

"It's safer in the dark," the Old Dowager warned. But she had got a candle ready.

"What is it? Why are we without light?"

A flame sprang up from the head of the candle. Slowly, Teeton discovered the surface of the table, the outline of the cups. His memory was struggling to liberate him from this strange universe of darkness which held the room under its spell. There was a stupor of night over everything.

"What is it?"

"Listen, Teeton, listen to me. Carefully."

"Are you in some trouble?"

"No, Teeton. Are *you*?"

He reflected on all her meanings.

"Am I?"

"Look, look over here."

The Old Dowager was paving a track with the candlelight. Now the flame struck the body; and Teeton's eyes suddenly blazed open on a pool of white fire.

"Nicole, my God, Nicole." The flame seemed to lift, leaving a mould of shadow over the face. "Is she, is she really?" Teeton sought the Old Dowager's eyes.

"Dead. I found her."

"You found her?"

"Yes. I alone." The Old Dowager struggled to protect him from every risk of involvement. "Do you know? Do you, Teeton? Do you know anything? Anything at all?"

"She was pregnant." Teeton's voice failed him.

"Would it be?" the Old Dowager was asking; but some code of discretion urged her to expel the word, murder, from her thinking. "An accident? Would it be an accident, you think?"

"I don't know," Teeton's mutter had returned. "The abortion, maybe. I don't know."

Yet he felt some dreadful premonition that he knew. He heard Jeremy's voice announce how Randa died.

The Old Dowager's mind had come alive with strategy.

"Now, you must be calm now."

"But ..."

"Calm, Teeton. You must be calm."

The Old Dowager made a chimney with her hands around the candlelight. She was in a fever of foreboding. The scandal of an enquiry, the taking of names. She had begun to examine each sample of crime. She wouldn't submit to such an ordeal. She couldn't abandon the house to public rumour. She thought of Teeton; and quickly buried any instinct to question his association with Nicole. It might be ever so hard to prove his innocence. And his guilt, the Old Dowager reflected, his guilt would put him in greater need of her protection. His safety couldn't be distinguished from the honour of her name, the integrity of the house. What hidden force of malice could have released such disaster on her age, shattering her peace of mind?

The Old Dowager was whispering action, signalling Teeton to pull himself together. She could only direct the safety of this burial; but he would have to carry the body.

"You didn't see her arrive?"

"No. Never saw her. Never heard her. Just found her."

The Old Dowager was trying to advise against delay. She didn't trust the stuttering flame of the candlelight. She had taken her hands away, cooling them with swift feverish stabs of breath.

Teeton could hear the Old Dowager whispering like the sigh of wings floating through the night.

"No calls at all?"

"None."

"From no one?"

"Nothing."

The answers fell without any trace of sound from the Old Dowager's lips. Her mouth was a shadow torn in halves through the whispering flame of the candlelight.

"Now. We must go now."

"Go where?" he asked. "There'll be a search."

"Now. We must go now. To the garden."

"And then?"

"Be calm, Teeton. You must be calm."

"And later, what happens after?"

"Attend this matter first, Teeton."

The arrival of disaster had given the Old Dowager a boldness he hadn't seen in her before; as though this death had, in some way, increased her hold on the living; sharpened the edge of her confidence. It had reinforced her defiance against the forces which now threatened her house. They would sink her name in a pollution of rumour that might never end. Teeton seemed feeble before the authority of her will.

He wanted to cover Nicole's face; but the Old Dowager was muttering haste; warning that it might be fatal to delay, fatal for him; for the house, for everyone.

"How will we explain?"

"To whom?" the Old Dowager scolded him.

"Someone must know she came here."

"Who could say when she left?"

The Old Dowager had claimed the last word, the decisive whisper. Teeton was hiding the dead face; wrapping Nicole's head in his arms. The head felt like a fruit in his hands. He couldn't let his feeling be touched by memories of Nicole alive; affection would have shattered his nerve, render every limb of his body useless before the desperate emergency of the Old Dowager's plan. He could hear the sigh limping from her lips: 'who could say when she left?'

The corpse was swung over his shoulder. He saw the circle of candlelight melting like a coin at the foot of the stairs. The Old Dowager was treading over her whispers as she slid down the passageway. The wind swiftly killed the candle flame as they emerged into the garden:

"Beyond."

"How? Where?"

"The trunk."

"Ants."

"Underneath."

"The tree."

"There's an opening."

"The tree trunk."

"Underneath."

Under cover of the tree trunk they had finally made Nicole's grave.

Part Two
Under the Veil

8

One

The Old Dowager put her hand on Teeton's knee. She let it rest there for a while, hoping that this gesture would be assurance enough. He was in good care.

"But where are we?"

"We'll soon be there," she said. "It's not a very good sea this morning."

He looked over his shoulder at the bleak hump of rock from which the pilot had launched the boat. The streets had disappeared into the mainland; but he could see the small white cottages wobble their roofs before the mist began to press them inland. Already, the edge of winter was on the wind. The Old Dowager had taken her hand away, observing that Teeton had become a little more composed.

"But where are we?" he asked again.

"In the North Sea," the Old Dowager said. And her manner was calm as an attendant repeating directions which everyone should know. She might have said: we are on earth, or in our boots, or somewhere under our skin. The Orkneys were coming dreamily into view.

Teeton was hoisting the lapels of his overcoat. He stretched them beyond his ears and held them firm, as the wind fought against his grip.

"How much further is it?"

"The cold's beastly, I know," the Old Dowager said. "But it won't be long."

Teeton wanted to ask about their departure from the house; how long did she plan to be away? But the wind fell sharp as an axe on his teeth; and he shut them in, lifting the lapel of the overcoat across his mouth. He couldn't straighten his memory out; couldn't come on any reliable clue that would lead him back through the stages of the journey. The Old Dowager was his only certainty. Now she looked so much stronger than he had ever seen her; and somewhat younger.

The Old Dowager had taken precautions against the weather, belting her coat securely round her waist. She looked a trifle anxious.

Her glances passed too quickly from Teeton to the pilot. But her hands were bold in their grip, light and sure when she stretched them out against the waist of the boat.

An island was emerging out of the mist. It looked like a broken bottle left in a pool of ink. The pilot was talking over his shoulder but the wind had swallowed his voice. The engine had begun to change its rhythm; the boat was cutting its speed down, reducing its movement to a drift. The Old Dowager pointed to the shore with one hand while the other relieved her belt. Teeton didn't stir. He was watching the water churn its dark surface into small fountains of milk. Now his memory was at work, awakened by the call of hotel service. The pilot had already swung himself on to the land, lashing the rope out of the water, pulling the boat forward like a reluctant goat. It grazed the pier, bouncing like rubber off the pillars of stone that shouldered the bridge: a narrow neck of timber which swayed as they walked over to the land. The Old Dowager was in secret consultation with the man.

"There," she said, returning her attention to Teeton. The stone cottage barely showed its roof behind the slope of a hill. "As good a place to rest as any."

Teeton was trying to find some other signs of habitation. It seemed there was nothing but briar and rock beyond the cottage. Every glance came up against a hill. The road from the pier had suddenly disappeared over a slope of gravelled plain. A dirt track was the only approach to the cottage: a twisting patch of brushwood and stone.

The land opened into cracks, some wide and deep enough to swallow a man. Teeton paused to assess this ancient damage to the earth. The Old Dowager had advanced into the lead, lamenting the welcome which they had got from the weather. Teeton struggled close behind. He couldn't trust his step where the track, slanting sharply, threatened to turn him upside down. The pilot was almost lost from view. He staggered up the track, bent in two by the pile of luggage on his back. Teeton had forgotten that he was there. He was struggling to come into line with the Old Dowager's stride. Her feet must have had some special knowledge of the terrain. She ignored the obstacles which rose in her way. She scaled the last ridge of dirt, and shouted to him to keep a close eye on her course.

"It's knowing the bends," she said, and stood for a while to let

Teeton rest. The slope made a careless dive into the valley of stone and gravel before his eyes.

"You couldn't walk there," said Teeton, pondering the sharp descent of the land. He thought the cottage would tumble roof down into the pit of the valley.

"It's knowing the bends," the Old Dowager said, showing him through the door. "Easy as a drink after you've known the bends."

Teeton stood in the doorway, gazing across at the iron spires of hills. He felt the wind like a sickle cutting a space inside him. He was afraid he couldn't support his strength much longer. His mouth was dry. There was a sound of rockets pounding in his temples. The Old Dowager recognised his need and hurried forward with the chair. She set it midway between the fire and the table in the dining room.

Teeton let his body sink carefully down. He felt the cottage distribute its ancient comforts around him. The air was warm. The Old Dowager had already assumed her chores. She swept her hands over the furniture. She climbed the brief flight of stairs that led to the rooms above. Teeton could hear her patrolling overhead. She was irrepressible in her eagerness to organise his comfort. He saw her descend the stairs, calm and sure like a sovereign come at last into her kingdom.

"Your room is on the other side," she said, pointing beyond the large sitting room. "He'll arrange it for you."

"Who?" Teeton asked, as though he had been alarmed to hear there was someone else. He had forgotten about the pilot. The Old Dowager gave him time to recollect their crossing from the mainland.

"I haven't told him anything," the Old Dowager was saying, "not yet."

Teeton must have read her lips, for there wasn't any trace of a sound in her words. Her whisper was like a stutter of air escaping. She had set her eyes on guard towards the door.

"Not yet."

Teeton had become alerted to the Old Dowager's thinking. There might have been some flaw in their safety. Her secrecy had increased its influence on him, and he put the door under close scrutiny.

"What do you mean not yet?"

The Old Dowager regretted what she had said; but she treated it lightly, concentrating on the more important task in hand. And that was to put Teeton at ease. She wanted him to detach himself from any misgiving about his safety; to get himself used to the security of the cottage.

"He is a kind man," she said.

"Who is he?"

"He is in charge," said the Old Dowager. "He looks after the place."

She was giving her information a certain lack of importance; but her whisper had scarcely gained in sound. Teeton tried to reason himself into a more secure frame of mind. Any danger which threatened him would fall equally on the Old Dowager. And it was impossible that she would be careless about her own safety; that she would invite disaster on her own head by giving information where it didn't belong. But he didn't find it easy to be rid of the pilot.

"You know him well?" Teeton asked, relaxing his watch on the door.

"A long time," the Old Dowager smiled, "a very long time."

She looked more at home as she answered; but Teeton was reluctant to ask any further questions. There was, he felt, some hint of intimacy in the Old Dowager's acquaintance with the pilot. This recollection may have given her some cause for joy, but he felt no inclination to probe it further. Nor did the Old Dowager show any sign of telling him more about the pilot. Teeton found himself drifting through the stages of their journey from the house; and the danger signals came on again. He was sure the Old Dowager had noticed what was happening but she seemed set on ignoring anything that might disturb him. He was wondering about the pilot. Where did he fit into their company, into what, for Teeton, was the secret relation which he and the Old Dowager had to the journey?

It was her tendency to whisper about the journey which struck a dangerous vein in his memory. The fire sprouted a candle fire before his eyes. 'Nicole,' he heard his breathing warn and saw the fire devour the fallen trunk of the tree. The geraniums and roses fell dead as ash. Suddenly, he looked up at the Old Dowager.

"The date," he said, "what's the date?"

But the Old Dowager showed no surprise. She had heard him make this plea before.

"You need to rest," she said.

"But the date, the date," Teeton went on. "What date is it?" He was almost frantic with the need to know.

The Old Dowager walked leisurely towards the chair. She put her hand on his shoulder, and a moment later drew it gently away.

"That's what you kept asking all the time," she said. "Ever since we left the house. For a week you never said a word except to ask the date. Don't you remember?"

Teeton was emerging from a nightmare he had had in some foreign city. The milk. Glass as in Glasco but you go, you go to Glasgow. The hotel was like a dairy.

"It was only at Kirkwall," the Old Dowager said, "only then it didn't seem to matter any more."

"Of course, I remember," Teeton said in order to avoid any further talk about the journey.

He looked down at the fire; then followed the wide, high sweep of the wall. He was trying to think about the Old Dowager's choice of the cottage and the length of their stay. And what would happen if Nicole's body was discovered before he was on his way? On my way, he was thinking; and the force of error had suddenly struck a terrible blow at his lack of judgement. He hadn't told the Old Dowager that he was leaving. It stood before him like a trap, mocking at him, teasing him with the thought that he could hardly break the news of his departure to the Old Dowager at this time. This was certainly the wrong moment to tell her what he had always known. It could only appear as an incredible exercise in deception. And what a devastating blow he would have dealt her! To choose these circumstances. Now that she had exposed herself to the possible charge of murder on his behalf. For a moment Teeton wondered whether he would have to escape without her knowledge; and he was dumb with shame. Would it be possible to leave her alone?

Entangled in his doubt, he hadn't heard the Old Dowager speak. She was asking him about Nicole. But her voice was so calm; so lucid and cheerful in its tone, that Teeton found his attention had already taken these responsibilities out of his control. The Old Dowager had, it seemed, relieved him of his immediate fears; separated him for a while from all the nagging particulars that were about to erode his confidence.

"The girl," the Old Dowager was saying. "You're quite innocent, I'm sure."

"I knew nothing about it," Teeton said, weighing the implication of such a question. It hadn't occurred to him that the Old Dowager might have been in doubt.

"Why would she have been looking for you?" he heard the Old Dowager ask.

"At that time?" Teeton's hand moved like a fan across his face. "I don't know."

"You knew about the abortion?"

"I knew she was pregnant."

"But the abortion? You did mention that in the house."

"I don't believe it was that," Teeton said.

The Old Dowager couldn't judge how much he knew.

"I found a painting behind the divan," she said. "Portrait of a woman."

"What portrait?" Teeton got up from the chair.

"It wasn't her face," the Old Dowager said, "but she must have brought it with her."

Unsure of what he ought to say, Teeton decided that he should sit.

"Where is it now?" he asked her.

"I put it with your things," she said.

Teeton shook his head as though he wanted her to understand that she had done the right thing.

The Old Dowager was gazing steadily at him. Now she looked up and away, as though she had heard some voice order her to call a halt to her questions. Teeton hardly noticed the interval; made no conscious observation on the silence which came between them. It seemed the Old Dowager had emptied his memory of everything except the fallen tree trunk under which they had buried Nicole. He was leaning forward, his head now held like a stone between his hands.

"From five o'clock," the Old Dowager said, rousing him from his preoccupation.

"Five o'clock," Teeton echoed her, trying to get his bearings.

"From five o'clock until you came," the Old Dowager said again, "I stayed with her. Watched over her."

"Nicole." Teeton said, feeling it his duty to supply a name.

"Watched over her," the Old Dowager said, ignoring Teeton. "How many hours would that be? It was like eternity, sitting there, not having a hope you would come. I just watched over her."

Teeton saw the Old Dowager brush her cheeks with the back of her hand; a swift, casual movement like a stroke of the duster. There was a shine like tear stain between the eyelashes. Her eyes appeared to swell with mist.

"I must have looked like her," the Old Dowager said softly, almost in a tone of private reflection. "How old was she?"

"Nicole?"

"The girl," the Old Dowager repeated, as though she hadn't quite heard Teeton. "How old would she have been?"

"About twenty-four, I'd say."

"Twenty-four?"

"Or thereabouts."

"I would have been her age," the Old Dowager said.

"When you were that age?" Teeton ventured.

"I must have looked just like her," the Old Dowager said, as though her mind had gone a little astray. But she had ordered it back with its strange cargo of live graves and panting skeletons. She was defying the mist to flood her eyes.

Teeton leaned forward, and found her knee with one mild stroke of his hand. He was relieved by the silence that came. He was looking at the Old Dowager, glancing up and down at the smooth, pale slope of her profile. Teeton thought there was hardly a wrinkle anywhere.

"How old did you say the girl would be?"

Her voice had surprised him.

"Twenty-four." After a moment's reflection he added: "A year less, maybe."

"I was about that age," the Old Dowager said, risking her glance across the ceiling. "My husband used to watch over me like that. Just as I watched over the girl in your room."

"Nicole was dead," said Teeton, struggling to discover the Old Dowager's meaning.

"I know," the Old Dowager said. "But I was alive. Perfectly alive. At her age and with the same wildness in my limbs. Such wild feeling. But it was the only pleasure my husband would allow himself. I must have looked like her in his eyes. Fresh as a rose in spring. And laid out in my coffin. He had built it himself, my husband. Yes, he did. Always had a gift for shaping things. Couldn't have been a more stylish coffin in the country. Handle bars in silver, and the lining of silk from end to end. He'd prepare my body himself; white veil and the lace nightgown in black. Wouldn't have any other shade but black. Transparent, so that I showed all through. God, how frightened I would be sometimes. The way he watched over me; watched over his corpse. After he had made me ready for burial, he would wait by his coffin, and watch over me. The only pleasure he would have of me. For years. Until he went away."

The Old Dowager stopped abruptly. She looked up at Teeton as though she was afraid to go on.

"You're sure you didn't know about the girl?"

Teeton was repeating his denial; but he had hardly given thought to the Old Dowager's question. He was shaking his head in alarm. He was overwhelmed by the Old Dowager's account of her experience as a young wife; her curious identification with the dead body on the divan. Ten hours, he recalled. It must have been ten hours that she had kept vigil in his room; watching over Nicole's corpse as her husband had once kept watch over her.

"I believe you," said the Old Dowager.

The old proprieties of conduct had been restored; and the signals had gone up, showing where silence should take over. The thought had come to her—not with the force of a charge; but it had crossed her mind that Teeton was not unlike her husband. He might have been cast in the same mould as her husband. She looked at Teeton; and smiled, conscious that he was perplexed. She was glad she had revealed herself, grateful Nicole's death had freed her and Teeton from the code which had ruled their association in the house.

They heard the sound of footsteps outside, an irritable drilling of boots that crushed the stones. The Old Dowager became utterly composed.

"He is back," said Teeton, as though he needed to have the Old Dowager's assurance.

"Yes," she nodded. "He was getting your room ready."

Teeton watched the heavy, grey shawl of light heaving against the window. It was an hour before noon; but the room was sinking under an early twilight. The wind was playing drums with the door. He was beginning to feel the strain of these surroundings: the air of desolation which seemed to cut the island off forever from its mainland: the absence of neighbours. He hadn't yet found any signs of another house nearby. But the wind had floated a call of sheep roaming somewhere. Wind and sheep and this melancholy silence inside the cottage.

He tried to focus some proper judgement on the Old Dowager's account of her husband's habits. But his mind wouldn't force him from his affection for Nicole. Why did she choose the room? Teeton felt a sudden thrust of anger at Nicole; and was, in the same moment of awareness, ashamed. He couldn't restrain the thought that Nicole's arrival in his room was an inconvenience. That was the word Teeton had been trying to expel from his mind; for he felt it to be a blasphemy to speak about her in this way. But the thought had come on him; attacked him without warning.

Now it was the Old Dowager who dominated his attention. He needed her. He was at her mercy. It was going to be difficult to put himself beyond her care. He had to get word to the Gathering. They emerged from the necrophagous world of the Old Dowager's dreams as his only certain redemption. It had never been so lucid; so urgent; so concrete a truth: his need for the company of the Gathering. It was a humiliation to be here on this frozen grave of an island, listening to the howling threats of the wind outside.

"Listen, listen," Teeton said, as though he was speaking to a stranger.

"Is there anything the matter?" The Old Dowager was prompt and solicitous as she turned to him.

"I must be out of here soon," said Teeton; and as quickly his glance had found the floor, avoiding the Old Dowager's eyes. He had felt a certain grossness in his manner; a deliberate abuse of the Old Dowager's feelings.

She looked at him as though she acknowledged every feeling which his silence now betrayed.

"Rest a little," she said. "You won't be any use if you don't."

"I'm sorry. I don't mean to be ungrateful. But ..."

"I know," the Old Dowager came to his rescue, "I know, I know. You need to rest."

Teeton kept still; but he was trying to shut her voice out; to protect himself from her advice. He couldn't afford the luxury of convalescence. He was in trouble; real bad, deep-down trouble. For this was his last chance to return to his own roots. He knew that this need would never bless him with its passion again. And if he failed it now, there could be no remnant of hope in any future which remained to him. He must be off this island soon. Now.

"Lunch," he heard the Old Dowager call to him. "You can't live on milk alone."

Two

"He didn't eat with us," said Teeton, and glanced at the empty chair.

The Old Dowager reflected on the cutlery which had been laid for a third place. But she didn't appear to show any interest in Teeton's observation. The game was back in play; the unheard remark, the momentary lapse of sight; the sudden treacheries of memory. Now her silence was total. The Old Dowager might not have heard at all. But Teeton found it more difficult to adjust. It was as though the change of terrain had modified his aptitude for the game. He was now inclined to be insistent; to repeat himself until it was obvious that he had to be heard.

"Why didn't he eat with us?" Teeton asked.

The Old Dowager could find no strategy that would save her from reply.

"He has his ways," she said, "a little moody, you might say."

"Is that the reason?"

"He's shy of strangers," the Old Dowager ventured. "But not to bother."

She was diverting their attention to the fire. It was the pilot who had fetched the wood and got it blazing while they were having lunch. Teeton had yielded to her guidance, slanting his eyes, without any shift of body, to watch the wave and billowing dance of the flames. It was an enormous hearth with a base of red stone and a wide partition of brick at the back. The flames had room for prancing. The sparks floated; shot like rockets up to the massive black brow of the fireplace; then crashed, and a drizzle of soot fell into the fierce white centre of the fire. Teeton raised his head to improve his view of the fire. And the Old Dowager observed him closely, noting, with a mild sense of triumph, that the fire had captured his attention. But Teeton had been somewhat detached from what he appeared to be doing; and the Old Dowager was alarmed when she heard him speak again.

"Yes, but I have to bother," said Teeton. "I don't know him. So I don't know how to treat his moods." He had exchanged no words with the pilot.

"It will come out all right," said the Old Dowager. "He is not a bad man."

"But if we have to be here," Teeton began; and suddenly stopped. He realised that he had no intention of reconciling himself to being there.

"We'll have to make it work," the Old Dowager promised, completing what Teeton might have said if he hadn't checked himself.

Teeton thought it would be safer to withdraw all interest in such a proposition. He was unresponsive, almost indifferent in his tone of dismissal.

"Not that it matters," he said. "There won't be time for that."

"You're so impatient," the Old Dowager scolded him. The voice was gentle, familiar in its solicitude; and Teeton felt a momentary warmth come over him, awakening his old gratitudes for everything she had done.

The Old Dowager hadn't freed herself from the spell of the fire. She was glad when Teeton went quiet, taking it to be a sign that he was getting used to the cottage. And this was the only duty which now consumed all her thinking: to make him feel welcome and at home; to prove herself reliable; a guarantee of his security. The fire had come to her aid.

"The man," said Teeton, "the pilot who brought us over."

Teeton had denounced his interest in the fire. The Old Dowager sensed his agitation.

"I've told you not to bother, Teeton." She was trying for a tone of firmness which might, with luck, conceal her worry.

"The boat we came in," said Teeton, "is it his or yours?"

The Old Dowager looked relieved. She began to laugh. Teeton might have shown his irritation if he hadn't been surprised by her reaction. But the Old Dowager was genuinely relieved to learn that there was nothing more serious to his question than the ownership of the boat. She was still smiling as though she had been rewarded by some fleeting moment of joy. It was an aura of delight; a strange radiance from her eyes which influenced Teeton; for he found himself laughing too.

"Of course it's his boat," the Old Dowager said, ridding the last chuckle from her smile. "It's his and mine ..." She was serious, almost grave. "Which means it's also yours while you're here. It's ours. The boat belongs to all of us."

Teeton offered no reply. He couldn't dispute the Old Dowager's generosity; but he recognised her need. She was determined to make him feel an equal part of everything that went with the cottage. He didn't think it appropriate to bring the Old Dowager back to the real point of his interest in the boat. He let his attention drift back to the drama of the fire. But the Old Dowager had started up her chuckle again.

"You remind me so much of him," she began.

"Of him?" Teeton asked, indicating the room overhead where the pilot might have been.

"No, no, not him," the Old Dowager went on. "I mean my husband. So much like him."

She brought her shoulders further back as though she had now relieved herself of some pain. She turned her gaze on Teeton, and let her eyes travel slowly, playfully over his body.

"So much like him," she said again, giving her comparison new emphasis. "That's just how he would have asked about the boat. Is it his or yours? Just like that."

Teeton looked a little embarrassed; as though this association had caused him some offence. But the Old Dowager had been so jealous of his safety, so protective of his interests, that he felt no impulse to show his displeasure. And it struck Teeton that there was a sense, deep and subtle and even dangerous, in which she had achieved some powerful hold on the roots of his emotion. She had trained him to forgive her; to find some reason for diminishing any offence, however wounding it might have been. And he noticed, with a feeling of something like amazement, that he was smiling, claiming his share of the Old Dowager's mischief; conspiring with her, it seemed, at the sacrifice of his own natural response.

"He couldn't have looked like me," said Teeton, smiling at the obvious difference in skin. "Not in a million years."

"Not in complexion," the Old Dowager said, and she had dismissed her smile from service. "But in a deeper sense. He had that same private way you have. Keeping the other person out. In the nicest way. He was very much like that, my husband was."

Teeton had also taken leave of his smile.

"You couldn't mean that as a compliment, could you?"

The Old Dowager had sensed the serious note of appeal in Teeton's question.

"I loved him," she said, after careful reflection. "I never stopped loving him although he deserted me."

She had spoken with cold and grave conviction; as though she wanted, by this admission, to declare that there could be no greater compliment than her love. What greater compliment could there be? And her voice had worked its influence on Teeton. It seemed that he was feeling some regret for casting doubt on her loyalty.

"I didn't mean to be rude," he said.

The Old Dowager looked at him now with such force of will, like one whose power of forgiveness knew no limit; who recognised the extraordinary privilege that goes with being able to confer it. Her eyes shone, bright, calm; and they made him think of glass; a mirror that wouldn't yield the reflection it had caught.

"Just like him," she said, "must have your way."

"You weren't offended?" Teeton asked, talking to her like authority to a child about to be enraged.

"What about?" the Old Dowager said, relieved that Teeton now looked so much at home. "What's there to be offended about?"

The fire was offering its distraction again. The Old Dowager was still looking at him, dancing her eyes down the back of his neck; selecting the nipples of his ears for scrutiny. Teeton could feel her gaze working slowly over him.

"I'm sorry I asked about the boat," he said, hoping to bury all reference to her husband.

The Old Dowager hadn't foreseen her next question; but it had come, quick and careless, like a shield protecting Teeton against his apology.

"Why did you ask about the boat?" she said; and her shoulders came forward to resume their familiar stoop.

Teeton had the answer ready; but he had decided to turn it down. He was thinking that it might be necessary to make his own escape. Revolt had schooled him in the ways of boats. He had a working knowledge of motors on water. But he wasn't familiar with the currents which came between the cottage and the mainland. Born a cradle from the sea, he knew the penalties which could follow on careless action. He sat quiet as a snail while the Old Dowager waited.

"I think we might go to the other room," she said, prodding him gently out of his silence. "The view gets better there."

But Teeton didn't move, although the Old Dowager had got up in the same moment her suggestion had been made; and Teeton noticed with vague admiration this absolute marriage of word and action whenever the Old Dowager wanted something to be done her way. So subtle and strong in manipulating a wish. She saw that Teeton didn't stir; but she didn't take so ominous a view as to make her call his lack of movement a refusal. She was weighing the empty plate on her hands. She thought it was time she gave them something to do; and it allowed her a chance to judge Teeton's mood.

"That fire doesn't look very strong," she added, making a noise with the plates.

"I prefer it here," said Teeton. "I think I'll stay here."

The Old Dowager returned the plates to the table, and slapped her hands for warmth. She walked towards the fireplace. She had begun to hoist a fresh log over the smoking embers. Teeton made an offer with his hands.

"No, you won't," she said, restraining him from coming to her help. "But since you're going to be here, then we must see that you're warm. And comfortable."

"It's fine here." He had confirmed her disappointment. The front room was the pride of the cottage.

"There you are," she said, poking the blaze and hearing a whistle of sparks chase up the chimney. "That's better. So much better."

Teeton looked up and communicated his thanks without saying anything.

"Is that better?" she asked, and forced an opinion from him.

"Much better," he agreed.

The Old Dowager had failed to get him out of the dining room;

but there was some compensation in the thought that he had, at least, expressed a preference. She started to clear the plates away. Teeton was about to get up; but the Old Dowager had anticipated his help, and promptly waved his offer away. He felt no inclination to persist, and she noticed that he was very prompt to obey.

When the Old Dowager had left the room, Teeton stood, stretched his arms to make an arch above his head; flexed his thighs; and then walked over to the couch. The fire was getting ready to launch a new act in its drama. There was a heavier veil of smoke; and the rivalry of colours seemed more subdued. The flame was more homely, tamer in its ascent. Everything was easier to watch, more subtle in its connections than it seemed before. Then he heard the Old Dowager return.

"Teeton!"

There was a strange hush to her voice; but Teeton wasn't quite free from the absorbing drama he had built around the fire. The Old Dowager noticed that he didn't respond. She called out again, and Teeton caught the tremor in her tone.

"Something gone wrong?" Teeton asked.

"No, no, no," the Old Dowager said, blankly staring across the filleted range of hills. "I don't see him anywhere."

"The pilot?"

"He hasn't been in here since I left, has he?"

"No," said Teeton. "What is it?"

"But he should be here," she said. "And he's nowhere. Nowhere."

She was marching from the front room to the dining room in such a frenzy of question and speculation. She was beside herself with worry. He couldn't understand why the pilot's temporary absence should produce such an effect of dislocation on everything the Old Dowager tried to do. Teeton's obsession with escape returned him to his questions about the boat. But he seemed reluctant to put any greater strain on the Old Dowager.

"You think he went back to the mainland?" Teeton asked.

"He would have told me," the Old Dowager said. "And what would he have to go back for?"

"I don't know," said Teeton. "But then I don't know anything. Who is this man?"

"Please Teeton. The question's where. Where is he? He gets so afraid of strangers."

"But who is he?" And a note of violence, unknown to the Old Dowager, had charged into Teeton's demand. "Who the hell is this man?"

The Old Dowager went pale with fright. It was the first time she had ever experienced this roughness of language from Teeton. His voice now frightened her, as it repeated:

"This man, the pilot, who is this man?"

"His brother," the Old Dowager was trying to explain, "he is my husband's brother."

Now Teeton became nervous for her. He was overcome with shame at the violence in his manner. He walked over to the Old Dowager who was trying to compose herself, sweeping a hand over her face. Teeton took her arm and walked her slowly, nurse-and-patient-wise, back to the chair.

"It doesn't matter," he was saying. "Why does it matter so much? It can't matter that much. And he'll be back. Wherever he's gone he'll be back. You can't get lost that easy. Not on an island this size."

She was recovering under Teeton's cheerful optimism. He was coaxing her like an infant out of worry; now glad to see her regaining confidence. She looked almost pleased to see him in this role, to feel his hands nursing her out of her panic.

"He gets afraid of strangers," the Old Dowager said. "That's bad."

She offered Teeton her hand and made to get up from the table. They were both walking into the front room. There you could see the pier, the rugged goat track of a road where they had arrived. But it was difficult to see below the drop of the land.

"What makes him so afraid?" Teeton was asking her. "What's wrong if he went over to the mainland?"

But the Old Dowager was concentrating her attention on the distant shimmering folds of mist that came down to the sea.

"I come here once a year," she said, "never more than once a year. I believe he knows we're in trouble."

"But how?"

Teeton was horrified to learn there could be such a source of danger. "What does he know? Who would have told him?"

"I told him nothing," the Old Dowager said, "but he knows something. I feel he knows something."

"You don't trust him?"

It was Teeton's turn to be in peril. It would be true to say that he was now shaking in his boots. To have come this far to make himself a stranger's catch. Whatever the dangers, he would have been safe with the Gathering. At any rate he would have known what was happening. There could be no suspension of judgement, no necessary secrecy.

"Why don't you trust him?" Teeton insisted.

He wanted to know; and yet he wanted to spare the Old Dowager the burden of her knowledge. For a moment she looked as though she were in agony; crucified by some fearful discord between herself and the man whom Teeton had thought of only as the pilot.

"All right. Let's talk about it later," he said, leading her back to the dining room. He turned to break the fall of a log which was about to plunge past the rail.

"Should I get you a drink?" Teeton offered a small gin. "What about it?"

The Old Dowager was staring up at him. She had managed to smile.

"That would be a help," she said, and sat down.

"A small gin it will be then," said Teeton, recalling the noises of the Mona bar.

"Thank you. And what about yourself?"

"The same," said Teeton.

There was a promise of delight in the Old Dowager's eyes.

"I didn't know you took gin."

"Taking it now," said Teeton, wheeling her glass between his palms. "There you are. And not a worry. Husband's brother or no husband's brother. You are not to worry."

They made a clink of salute with the glasses. The fire was up, cocky and prattling and full of confident sniggering as it swaggered against the brick walls of the fireplace. It had thrown a mixture of rose and purple over the Old Dowager's cheeks. There was a curious beauty in her eyes: a beauty of dark seas, and the tackle of mist sailing up into an ocean of cloud. The Old Dowager was going to lean forward when the opulence of this mirage was torn away. Every skein came down; was rent, as though a hidden flare of lighting had burnt the clouds to ash.

"I'm here," the pilot's voice announced. "Where I belong."

He had literally walked out of the wall. The Old Dowager dropped her glass. And Teeton's hand had knocked his over the table as he jumped back. The man had not moved. He looked like a sentry where he stood, nodding his head to assure Teeton that his eyes were seeing right. Yes, it was the wall. Teeton was staring at a gap, the width of his body, through which the man had let himself out. The plaster was swinging on either side, displaying twin doors that looked like the shoulders of a harp. Teeton didn't notice that the Old Dowager was about to faint.

"I must retire," she called out, pointing to the man who was her husband's brother.

Teeton watched him cradle her like a child and carry her up to her room.

Three

He must have been a man of very striking presence in his youth. All the signs of an ardent and virile strength were there. The eyes, almost sky blue, betrayed no squint of age. His cheeks were firm and smooth. The wide sensual mouth. The high brow, with a gentle tilt where it met the first silvering roots of his hair. He wore it long, wild and careless. It was leaning everywhere. He had a farmer's confident hands.

The dining room now felt much too small for the three of them. Teeton had hardly touched the supper; but the warning was clear that he had finished. The man chewed in silence, fast and ravenous, never raising his head much higher than the altitude of his fork. The Old Dowager tried to look composed. She would study the pilot's face, the fighting jaws, the lips moist and bursting with the sweat of gravy; then she looked across at Teeton to assure him that everything was in control. Improbable as it might seem, she knew the circumstances which they endured.

Teeton thought only of the boat; and the earliest crossing to the mainland. He had a furtive vision of the Old Dowager's garden; the casual foraging of some animal which might have given a clue to Nicole's corpse. Quietly, secretly, he had begun to curse himself; to curse the folly of his act in coming here. But what else could he have done? He had scarcely known when he was on his way. The Old Dowager had taken his safety in her command. There was no alternative to her plan. She had moved according to her interest which, in the circumstances, was also his. He wanted to deny himself any shadow of an excuse. But she might have acted otherwise. Suppose she had called in the police; assumed his innocence and taken the risk that everything would be all right. Alternatives arose and disappeared, extinguished by the logic of his circumstances. Yet he didn't want to submit to the view that there was nothing else he could have done. If he absolved himself of error, it was because he felt it would be idle to bury his mind in what had gone before. His business was to concentrate on what would happen now. He would have to depend on every move the Old Dowager made. Did she have some plan for his return? He couldn't trust the pilot's sanity. His madness could be the greatest danger of all.

There was the sudden rattle of a knife falling on the plate. The man had finished his supper. The Old Dowager indicated the bottle; the man understood that he should pour. Teeton watched him fill her glass with wine. Before any offer had been made, Teeton raised his hand to say that he didn't want to drink. The man returned the bottle, and also went without a drink. It looked as though the meal had formally come to an end. All knives and forks had been laid to rest, and no one spoke.

The Old Dowager was making a monocle with the mouth of her glass, looking for her shadow in the wine. Teeton studied the white, stewed veins of the brussels sprout. The nibbled slab of steak was drying out on his plate. The prongs of his fork seemed to grow upward like a plough. The man had given himself a pause; he sat still, as though his digestion got under way with an interval of meditation. The Old Dowager must have found her shadow in the drink. She had brought the glass down, piping her breath on to the wine. Teeton's hands changed duty. The right stood up and moved into place under his chin. His stomach started to grumble; but the noise stayed in, like an undetected break of wind.

The man's hand had reached forward to a box on the table. The lid went up; then fell back, displaying the cigars in a row. The man selected one; paused and watched the cigar hang like a finger from his hand. It might have been an invitation to Teeton. But the man's hand rose; swallowed the cigar; then vomited it up between two fingers. He leaned forward to meet the candle stick halfway; scorched the end of his cigar; and dismissed the thin effigies of smoke which travelled over Teeton's head. The Old Dowager was preoccupied with the sediment of wine. She seemed to read the grains that floated over the bottom of the glass.

Slowly, as though every stage of the action was against his wish, the man was getting up. He stood. The Old Dowager was about to get rid of the glass. The man inspected the ceiling for a while; returned his glance to the candlelight. The Old Dowager was still getting rid of the glass. The man stretched his hand over the cigars, fingered the lid as though it were a leaf; then turned it slowly on to the box. Erect again, his shoulders had begun to steer him away from the table.

He said: "Goodnight."

The salutation seemed to strike forward at the wall; then bounce and ramble back on its return to the table. The Old Dowager had finally got rid of the glass.

She said: "Have you had everything?"

The question seemed to chase after the man; caught up with him at the point of exit from the room; and called him to a halt. His chin was in reverse over his shoulder. It had answered for him.

The Old Dowager said very firmly: "Goodnight."

Teeton didn't look up until the man was out of sight. And suddenly he became aware of the weather. The wind was making war outside. He couldn't imagine how he had ever found the courage to travel by air; couldn't, by any measure of sanity, comprehend the scale of such a risk: that he had often sat somewhere under the sky, borne through these murderous currents of air. There was such fury of wind lashing outside the door. The winds swept over the broken hills, pounding like thunder on the night. Some giant of incredible speed was dragging nature up by its roots; waging an Armageddon over the cottage. There was a sound like the bursting of pipes against the window; the widening push of an enormous crowd backed up against the walls; a stampede of air. It was marching through every crevice of his skull.

But Teeton hadn't been aware of the slightest noise when the man was there. Now he had gone it seemed the cottage was about to break up like a box. Any moment the walls might collapse; and the fire disperse like dying stars through the night.

The Old Dowager said: "It gets windy at this time of year."

And it seemed like an age since he had last heard a human voice. The Old Dowager hadn't suffered any change. There was no sign that anyone else had been there. She had begun to collect the plates; tidying up the banalities of an ordinary day. Teeton couldn't distinguish who was the more improbable of the two: the man who imposed this silence; or the Old Dowager whose calm, domestic poise seemed to annihilate all memory of the meal. Teeton was beginning to doubt that he had ever known her; for it seemed impossible that anyone could have managed these encounters with such facility. He watched her now as though she were a stranger; and felt all the years of their acquaintance suddenly contract into the shock of a moment's blind collision; a blind awakening from a blow struck by some force you couldn't identify.

There was some curious bond between the Old Dowager and the pilot. He evoked a perplexing conflict of responses from her. When he was present, the Old Dowager's eyes made her appear submissive. There was a tendency, almost a need, it seemed, to obey his wish. And yet there was a confidence in her manner when she spoke: the way she had said goodnight, as though it were an order for him to go. All through the meal she had treated this silence as though the man were a pet; some favourite discomfort which had long lost the power to become a nuisance. Yet Teeton was sure that if, at any time, she had felt some fleeting inconvenience, it would have been entirely on his own behalf. Like a person who had deliberately invited danger because it might reduce a deeper pain detected, suddenly, in someone else.

Teeton's discomfort had been acute; but she had decided to take it over; to claim, as her own, some portion of that pain and fear which he wanted to be rid of. He watched the Old Dowager. He had been stealing this enigmatic watch over her ever since the man left the table. Now it seemed that he wanted to ask her some question which was clearly beyond the reach of words; of any words that he could find to satisfy his meaning. It seemed to be outside the province of normal communication: how to express the nature of this take-over; the total assumption of another's wordless emotion. And for a purpose which appeared so honourable; which seemed, and, indisputably, must have been, entirely to the Old Dowager's credit. Her conduct had the purpose of putting him at ease; of training him to adjust to the necessity of being in control of circumstances he couldn't trust, and a man who was mad. But he felt the Old Dowager had been endowed with a gift that would see her through any crisis he could conceive. For the moment he could recognise only one difficulty which had to be managed at all costs. He had to return to San Cristobal; had to free himself from any obstacles of nature or the law in order to accomplish his return. The highest point of danger, in this moment—and, perhaps, for all time—would be his failure to do so.

Gradually his stealthy watch over the Old Dowager began to change; to transform itself back to his familiar glance, solicitous and normal as the need of his lungs for air. He felt this startling change of emphasis in his feeling towards her, as though he had suddenly discovered what he had always known: his confidence in the Old Dowager. She would manage it; she would, indifferent of risk, see him through. But—and something had turned slightly sour—but. There was a widening gap in his calculation; some nightmare chasm that was about to separate him from his real intentions. The omission now struck Teeton as incredible. It was hounding him, battering him with shame down on his knees to make some confession.

'You haven't told her you are going. You should have told her you were going. If you had told her you were going.'

Teeton shifted to shake himself free of these moral indictments. They had arrived on time; and it was the wrong time. He had to treat them as officials, in ignorance or haste, must often do. They had to be put away for further treatment, souvenirs for the future. And he thought he had found the strongest argument the heart could offer. He believed the Old Dowager loved him, as a son, as she might have loved her own offspring, had she been blessed with any. And the conviction grew in Teeton. If she had taken such risk to protect him from suspicion; to save him from any charge of complicity in Nicole's death; then it was small benefit to confer on him now an offer of forgiveness for such ingratitude. October 10. The date had lodged like a bone in his throat.

For the first time his error seemed to lose the force of doubt. In the house, the morning the Old Dowager had got the paintings ready his secret had struck as a malevolent breach of trust. Now—and for the first time since then—it seemed to lose its force. It had promised to be small; to remain negligible—not in itself—but beside the Old Dowager's certain largeness of heart.

Teeton had put himself on trial; and he was coming out, at last, to get her acquittal. The Old Dowager had caught him again, unawares, in that frenzied shaking of his head. It was the second time she had noticed it, but the game was on and she willed her eyes into a momentary blindness. But the code was threatened when it happened again. He had started some doubt in her mind. And she told herself that he could not, for the moment, be at ease. The plates had formed a ladder under her hands. She stretched forward and took Teeton's glass.

"There you are," she said.

Teeton jerked his head up at the sound of her voice. He saw the glass in her hand; but he didn't expect her to speak. The silence had prolonged its influence on him. She was pouring him a drink.

"Thanks." He passed the glass from one hand to the other and back, as though he hadn't decided whether he wanted the wine. Then he said thanks again, very quickly, and drank it in one draught.

"Gracious Heavens!" The Old Dowager was approving. She might have been saying, 'I didn't know you could do it'. Then she found a reason that made his action seem quite natural. "Of course, you didn't have a drop at supper."

"Thanks again," Teeton repeated, now wholly recovered from his private meanderings of hope and doubt and promise. "Could I have some more?"

"That's what it's there for," the Old Dowager said, recalling the publican's advice in the Mona bar. "Or would you give the gin another chance?"

"Later," said Teeton, taking the glass. He had quite forgotten his lack of taste for gin.

"You will give the gin another go?" The Old Dowager was teasing him.

"I don't see why not," said Teeton.

"Then I'll help myself to one as well," the Old Dowager said.

Teeton was watching her again. This enigmatic, probing glimpse had come back. There was a gradual resumption of normal intercourse. The warmth of the drink was about to enclose them; to provide them with some shield against the fear of intrusion. Yet the moment's relaxation had suddenly brought Teeton's mind back to the meal and the absence of the pilot. The Old Dowager was clearing a space for the gin.

"Listen."

"Did you say something?"

"You heard me."

"So I thought," the Old Dowager conceded. "You were going to say something."

Teeton had found his courage. He felt the mild sting of the gin dissolving round the edge of his tongue. There was a taste like sulphur at the back of his throat.

"I wanted to tell you before we came here," said Teeton, and paused as though the effort was about to obscure what he wanted to say. The Old Dowager took a sip of the gin. Her eyes were avoiding him now.

"It's your memory again," she said, "it needs a rest."

Teeton was quick to deny this, fearing that he might let the opportunity slip. He was looking at the Old Dowager, summoning her attention back to him.

"My memory is perfectly all right now," Teeton said. He didn't relax his stare. His eyes were candid and fearless as they called on the Old Dowager to listen. He wanted to defy any suspicions that he might have forgotten what he had begun to say. And he wondered, for a moment, whether the Old Dowager, fearful of what she might hear, might have been trying to exploit his previous lapse of memory; might have been trying to persuade him that his recovery was far from complete. But his memory was sound; ready and urgent to come to his aid. Yet some habit of reluctance had been getting in his way.

The Old Dowager had become his priority; he began to feel a quickening of guilt; soon it would break loose and submerge all other interests, reducing his own needs to a lack of importance, threatening them finally with extinction. His wish for the Old Dowager's happiness had put Teeton on the defensive. A deeper truth now tormented him. She might forgive his failure to let her know of his plans to leave England; but he was afraid she might also imagine some link between his decision and Nicole's death. Then his omission would no longer be seen as failure. It would become a refusal, a private and devious calculation to look after his own safety; to leave her stranded without explanations that would satisfy the law; without hope of escape. For she had no place to go; no other home; no refuge beyond this barren island.

The Old Dowager's safety; the protection of her name; the total vindication of her character before the judgement of all who knew her: these had suddenly become Teeton's sole responsibility. He was slowly losing the argument for his own safety. Some new and exacting morality was coming remorselessly to birth, forcing its code of duties out from the womb of his conscience. He would have to commit himself to any danger which threatened the Old Dowager, share in any punishments that were to be inflicted on her as a result of Nicole's death. It would be the only way he could prove beyond doubt, satisfy the sternest demands of her loyalty, that there had been no connection between Nicole's death and his decision to go home. The Old Dowager had become his conscience.

Teeton hadn't taken his eyes off her; and she seemed in no hurry to be informed. He was listening for the blast of the wind; but there was only a tremor of air rubbing against the windows. The volume had diminished. The sound came from afar, a slow, leisurely fall through the distance like the retreating march of an army.

The Old Dowager seemed to feel a little safer. Teeton's warning of a new danger was a false alarm. Peace had arrived; a peace that may have been fragile, precarious. But it was on their side. She could feel its presence confer some novel reward for her decision to bring Teeton here. It had certainly been a rash venture; but that was how it had to be. There are moments which allow of no other action than what ordinarily amazes by its rashness, its unreasoning boldness. She noticed Teeton had withdrawn his glance in time to avoid hers. He looked strangely melancholy, calm, almost remote, as though he had chosen to forget all the hazards which they had, so far, survived. His mouth grew docile; his eyes appeared to be on the verge of sleep. He was drifting away from the morbid priorities that had held his mind a prisoner; drifting free from his earlier conflicts of safety and escape. He was drifting deeper into the Old Dowager's care. This was the only duty which now ruled her heart; and kept her passion alive: to see that Teeton was at ease.

Teeton's hands had begun to stir. He raised the glass, holding it up to break the path of candlelight pointing into his eyes. The flame seemed to throw itself against the glass, dividing into small, squat daggers which sparkled over the gin. The Old Dowager was considering the hour; turning over the idea that it might have been time for them to retire. The day had been crowded with events; but it was almost over. It was as though their initiation had found them worthy of the island's refuge. The most hazardous stages of their adventure had been overcome. Teeton had finished his second gin. He returned the glass to the table and made a lid with his hand over it.

"What's the date?" he asked.

"The date," the Old Dowager started to answer, quickly diverting her attention with a note of banter. "Would you have a date to keep, Teeton? It's the only thing you kept asking when your memory came back. What's the date Gran? The date, the date. Do you remember that?"

Teeton nodded that he couldn't remember asking her the date before; but he had resisted her attempt to distract him.

"What is it, anyway?" he asked again.

"I'd have to look," she said, searching the bare walls for a calendar. "But it's not a thing you bother about up here. You're so far away. But I know it's Thursday because that's the day the vegetables come. Everything gets measured by the day, by the name of the day, that is. But the date. I'd have to look."

She had gone on speaking to the slow, searching turn of her eyes round the walls, pausing to check with her memory where a calendar might be found; and the search had taken her to the man. His absence had struck her as a warning to put an end to any further search. She felt she could postpone the matter since it wasn't urgent. She had started to push herself up from the chair.

"I'll have to look for it," she said, coming unwillingly halfway to her full height.

Teeton showed no signs that he would restrain her. The Old Dowager was surprised. She waited; delayed, it would appear, by the late arrival of her memory.

"Now where would it be?" she asked herself; and lingered as she stood straight, having no further height to go. She remained standing; repeating the question for the general attention of the room; appealing to carpets and the wall for guidance. She was perplexed by Teeton's failure to respond; as though the game had lost the power to enforce its normal rules. She considered—sensing some margin of hope—that it might have been Teeton's memory. The game had fallen clean out of his memory. She hadn't moved.

"Is it so very urgent?" she asked, risking a serious violation of her rules.

"I'd like to know," said Teeton. The tone was dry, without hurry.

The Old Dowager must have been desperate for the safety of the game; for she had, by some unpredicted thrust of curiosity, decided to press the matter further.

"Couldn't it wait until tomorrow?"

"I'd feel better if I knew tonight."

"At this hour? It must be going on midnight."

"Nevertheless."

"Why, you astonish me, Teeton." Her reluctance had made no difference. The Old Dowager felt shaken by this strange insistence. For a moment it made him appear truly foreign. He was still waiting.

"Perhaps he would know," said Teeton, with a toss of his head towards the ceiling.

"But Teeton!" The suggestion had brought the Old Dowager back to her seat. "He would be asleep by now."

Teeton looked up at the ceiling; then across at the wall where the man had appeared. The Old Dowager made no secret of her distress. The game had really been abandoned; every rule demolished.

"You wouldn't want me to wake him?" she said. Then with accusing emphasis: "Simply for that."

"It's not so simple," said Teeton.

"Are you all right?" And it was clear there was no prevarication in her question.

"Quite," said Teeton, "quite all right."

The Old Dowager didn't know what to do with her hands. She tried to scratch them; to clasp them. She was at a loss what small, familiar service she might give them to perform. But they lay on the table like a pair of crutches which had no one to carry. Then the gin became an ally; and she put an end to their idleness.

The Old Dowager poured herself a drink. Barely conscious of her offer, she had passed the bottle to Teeton. And it struck her as though it might have been the act of a stranger who wasn't sure she should take the liberty of pouring the other person's drink. She held the bottle up, astonished by her failure to go on and do what would have been so natural a moment ago. Teeton couldn't ignore this curious suspension of the bottle, waiting for him to rescue it from the Old Dowager's hand. But he didn't take it; nor did he feel any special inclination to do so. Instead, he raised his glass; brought it right up to the neck of the bottle. He held it there, inviting the gin to enter. He couldn't detect any movement from the Old Dowager's hand. But the trickle had started; then a spasm of drops that crashed on to the bottom of the glass. But his hand offered no help; stayed immobile like the Old Dowager's; so that it seemed the gin had poured itself. It was making a fitful, tremulous entry into the glass which was suddenly under flood.

They were both astonished by the overflow.

"Well, well, well," the Old Dowager was rebuking herself. "We must be out of our minds."

Teeton was asking for a saucer. The Old Dowager shoved it forward to catch the first spill of gin.

"Thanks," said Teeton, bringing the glass down. "No damage done."

"Whatever could I have been thinking?" the Old Dowager said. She was still under the spell of this strange insistence in Teeton.

"I couldn't understand why you didn't pour it," he said. His voice was low, nondescript, a noise that passed without intention.

"I don't know," the Old Dowager said. "Somehow I thought you were going to take it."

"But that's strange, isn't it? You were offering to pour."

"Yes," the Old Dowager said. "I can't imagine what came over me."

She was considering the prospect of sleep. This seemed an appropriate moment to suggest that they must have been under the strain of the day. They had become careless with fatigue.

But Teeton was wide awake. The Old Dowager couldn't have persuaded him otherwise. She realised that she might have to make her departure alone. She didn't favour such an arrangement on the first night. It would have been more in keeping with her duty to be the last to go. But there was no alternative; and the Old Dowager started to prepare herself for a departure that might pass with a minimum of formalities. She had to formulate an apology that could be received with the right lack of notice.

"Before you go," said Teeton.

"How did you guess?" she said. She was almost cheerful.

"I must know the date first thing tomorrow," said Teeton.

"Of course, of course." She must have repeated this agreement three or four times without pause. She had been relieved by his willingness to let it wait.

"The very first thing," she said, coming into her stride, glad she could at last encourage his indulgence.

She had started on the signals for departure.

"You won't be needing anything more?" she asked.

Teeton reflected. He knew where to find his room.

"You're turning in now, I suppose."

"Just about," she said. "But you needn't hurry. There's no reason you shouldn't go whenever you choose."

"I know."

He wanted to be alone. But he was also haunted by the need to have her stay. Just for a while. Tomorrow he would be more at ease; he would be able to give her all his attention. Without the restraints of guilt. He would be more at home.

"Gran," Teeton said suddenly. "Before you go."

"Is there anything," she intervened, ready for his slightest need.

"I am going home. I should have told you before. Before we got here. I had already made plans to go home."

The Old Dowager was slow to follow what urgency there could be in these announcements which were, in the circumstances, dangerously impractical.

"It's much too soon," she warned. "It couldn't possibly do you any good to go back. Not so soon. It's hardly a week since the girl, since we, well don't you see? What good could come from being back in the house so soon? Don't you see?"

There was electric in the pause that stretched Teeton's hands out across the table. He had found the Old Dowager's arms. He held them, close with comfort.

"You don't understand," Teeton explained. "You've got me wrong. I mean I'm going home. Back to San Cristobal." His touch weighed like burning velvet on the Old Dowager's arm. "I wanted to tell you before. I should have told you before."

His pause came up again for testing; but it achieved no reply.

"Before what happened at the house," Teeton said, "that's why I got rid of the paintings. I sold them so that I would be able to go back. I arranged to go almost immediately the Exhibition was over. I was going to tell you then. That afternoon. When we arranged the tea. I wanted to make it a little farewell. Just the two of us. Private. Because I'm grateful. You can't imagine how grateful I am. There had never been a house like that, nor a room like that. For me never. And I wanted to let you know what you did. How you made it so. I was going to tell you everything that afternoon. Over our tea. But then. Well. You know what happened. But you see. I mean. I still have to go. That doesn't change. That's why I was anxious to know the date. I have to be out of here. You see?"

Teeton couldn't bring the burden of his news to an end. It seemed his sense of justice had started him on an interminable course of appeasement. If the Old Dowager had, by chance, seen no criminal error in his failure to tell her the news before; then it was certain his agony would have made her discover one. But Teeton couldn't tell what she had found. And when he begged her to see the innocence of his omission, he couldn't be sure what she had seen. She said nothing at all. The Old Dowager would not speak.

Teeton had anticipated that he would be relieved after he had done his duty. But he couldn't have been more gravely in error about the result. He had liberated himself from the torment of an omission which, perhaps, should never have been allowed to acquire the attributes of secrecy. It was not his intention to be secretive. He had a sense of regret when he knew that he would have to say goodbye to the Old Dowager; and he understood that she would have experienced a similar emotion when she heard. There would have been a difficult moment or two during the days that remained; but they would have known what to expect; and expectation often makes the object of its achievement familiar long before it arrives. The day of his departure might have been a climax which had no power to disturb. It might have grown stale after the vivid surprise and hurt of a timely warning.

But Teeton was now alarmed by the appalling treacheries of Time; the incredible difference which the actual process of timing can make to the most harmless event. The minutest change in the order of incidents, some slight reshuffle in the phases of an intention that had no specific future, may start a terrible dislocation. Like the blankness of mind which he barely experienced as he tried to look at the Old Dowager. It wouldn't have been a reliable truth to say that she was quiet. There was some other quality in this total absence of sound. He realised that his previous sense of guilt was slight, a negligible burden beside the shame which menaced his sanity. He was ashamed, felt sunk in shame. And it seemed to him, in the extreme lucidity of the moment, that this shame was an atmosphere in which he had always lived. It was as though this moment, made sharp and frightful as knives by the Old Dowager's absence of sound, was pure in its brutality, pure in the menace which reflected this shame which had been with him always. From the earliest, invisible fungus of birth, it had been soil to his loins; pulse to his heart; vein and artery to the miraculous flow of his blood: this shame that now looked up at him from under the veil of his skin. This shame which now warned him that it could be the most terrible chemistry of human action: hidden and destructive.

He had no control over the flight of his mind. He was no longer able to pilot the course of his thinking. But it seemed he had been transported out of the room, borne by some collective demon past the tyranny of the winds into the presence of the Gathering. His sojourn with them was swift, without words, like people met for worship; obeying some ancient and unwritten sanction of the blood. He had closed his eyes as though sight was a curse whenever it offered him the Old Dowager's face.

The candle was about to surrender its last thimble of light; a small pool of wax boiling and scorching the stem of black wick to death. He was back in the company of the furniture. But the Old Dowager was being lifted gently from her chair. Teeton hadn't heard anyone arrive; but the man was there. He didn't know how long the pilot had been there. He couldn't say what impulse had brought the man out of his sleep to see whether the Old Dowager was still awake. But he was there, his back now turned on Teeton as he settled the Old Dowager in his arms, and carried her like a lamp up the stairs.

9

One

It was a week since Nicole had disappeared; a week to the night since Roger had threatened Derek's life. They had been careful to avoid each other. A silence like doom had descended on the house. Roger wouldn't risk a visit to the Mona until he had made sure that Derek wasn't there. The publican had registered their separation and was heard to say there was nothing like a disaster to put old habits in reverse.

But O'Donnell had spared no effort to intercede. He had paid no attention to the great variety of rumour which had accumulated since Nicole had disappeared. He had shown no interest in what might have happened to her, as though he had lost all taste for the gossip of the pub. He would contribute no opinion to the lavish accounts of what might have happened.

But his loyalty to the men had come fiercely alive. He held several meetings with the architect, and each with the purpose of arranging some strategy that might bring Roger and Derek together again. It was an intense, agonising exercise: this close collaboration with the architect to heal a friendship he hadn't thought could ever be broken. They had worked like couriers, inventing messages which neither Derek nor Roger had sent. But every effort had been in vain. Nothing could be made to work.

When Roger and Derek spoke again, it was the calamity of homelessness which brought them together. Four nights after Nicole disappeared, their rooming house was burnt down. They had been plunged back into the roots of their previous feeling. Moreover, it seemed that Roger had suddenly lost all capacity to survive.

The fire had started on the top floor; and according to the architect, his first awareness of disaster was the blast of air that struck from O'Donnell's room. O'Donnell was not at home. He had gone to the heath again that night, armed with his torch and in murderous rage. He was looking for the woman who had been giving him her treasure, and all of it free. He was wild with fear that the worst had happened. Her gifts were proving a poison he was afraid to make known. He hadn't told anyone what his doctor had reported;

but the architect had sensed that he was in danger. O'Donnell had begun to drink at a lunatic rate.

The demons were attacking him again. The lights in the Mona had begun to dip, but there was still a quarter of an hour to go. Friday was always a boisterous night; and this was no exception. The saloon was like a tourist ship. The regulars were not out in force, but the crowd knew the worth of their numbers and made the place their own. The publican met them like a foreign tribe, courteous and watchful.

But the small bar was tense. The architect was trying to get O'Donnell away. Derek sat in the corner, waiting for Roger to return from the lavatory. He didn't like the way O'Donnell was staring at the barmaid. She was reminding him of his poisonous treasure on the heath. The architect stayed on duty, diverting the small bar's attention away from O'Donnell.

"I know she did it," O'Donnell was accusing. "I told the bitch where I lived."

The barmaid had turned away as though she was afraid of hearing some kind of evidence she didn't want to have. O'Donnell had started his accusations again.

Where shall O'Donnell sleep? He was trying to say. He looked straight at the architect, but he was afraid to speak. He thought he saw the architect smile with teeth like a rat's. He was observing the trap that was the architect's mouth. Caught, he was caught. Hit it and run. The architect had stalled on him. He hadn't gone for the treasure on the heath. Catch what cunt you can. He heard a roar of applause come to him from the saloon bar.

He had discovered rotten treasure on the heath. Hit it and run. Catch what cunt you can, but keep on the run. Keep moving. Soon he wouldn't be able to run. His booty had dealt him a blow in the blood. You've got it. Jesus fucking Christ I've got it. Already he was preparing for the odour of syphilis to rise from his loins. Hit it and run. But nothing was free in God's bedchamber. He was going to pay the grimmest price.

There was a burn like sulphur round his groin. His penis would sprout a flame. He was about to leak with the muck of treasure he had found. The rot would soon bore a hole through his brain. He saw the bottles of whisky lean as though they were about to tumble from the shelf. The necks were slaughtered by light. They said it usually got at the brain. They would put him in a cage. His tongue would make the noise of a beast. Fear was churning him up inside.

So where does O'Donnell sleep? For the third night running he would have to make his bed on a lavatory seat. He saw a station porter in the door, his ignorant face spliced wide by a grin. The porter was the guardian of his shelter. His glance caught Derek in the corner. He was gazing towards the saloon in search of Roger. His eyes were like holes of fire in a block of coal. They frightened O'Donnell. He couldn't endure this slab of midnight that was Derek's face. But where does *he* sleep? They had found this coon somewhere to sleep. The Circle theatre was a mansion compared with the lavatory seat. Where does O'Donnell sleep? He couldn't tame his fury. Humpty Dumpty sat on a wall. The nigger didn't go through with the abortion. Whatever happened to the bitch he ploughed? He couldn't stand the look of niggers when they weren't laughing. It was hideous to see those cheeks of soot go soft with grieving. But the Circle theatre was a mansion compared with where the nation relieved its shit. He was shouting to Derek, friendship and malice inseparable in his voice.

"Take it easy," the architect begged him.

"Where's that coolie shit you call a friend?" O'Donnell enquired, looking round the small bar for Roger.

Derek felt a weight explode like a bullet in his eye. But he didn't look up. It would have been dangerous to look up.

"Has he found his little whore?" O'Donnell was asking. The voice had gone soft and grave like a cleric intoning. "Didn't he know all the time where that piece of white trash was burning? Didn't he know? Or do we have to tell him who's stoking her fire? Didn't he know that Teeton was mowing her grass?"

The architect raised his hand and tried to collide with O'Donnell's glass.

'Don't move,' Derek's tongue was wagging over his mouth. 'Don't move or you'll kill him.'

"Let's get out of here," the architect was pleading with O'Donnell.

"I'd known all along," O'Donnell persisted, pushing the architect's hand away. "There ain't a nigger whatever the shade who wouldn't ditch his closest friend for a piece of white tail. Married or single, it makes no difference."

'You'll kill him,' Derek's tongue slapped his gums. 'Don't move. You'll kill him if you move.'

"For Christ's sake shut your trap," the architect shouted and slapped O'Donnell on his mouth.

"Except you," O'Donnell went on as though he hadn't felt the architect's blow. "You wouldn't horn that shit of a coolie you call a friend because you're a coward. You don't think you're worth whatever he's got. Why didn't you punch up his arse when he called you a corpse? Little actor man. What a bitch of a ding-dong you had that night. And over what? A little midwest small-town whore doing the grand tour. Looking for some ethnic prick far from home; I know you don't like the bitch any more, but it took you long to learn. You're too slow to learn, little actor man. Hit it whenever Teeton brings it back. Just hit it and run."

The barmaid looked frozen where she stood. They saw Derek get up, and O'Donnell went suddenly still. But his lips moved like an idiot trying to learn the use of his tongue. The barmaid ran towards the saloon bar. O'Donnell was grinding his teeth. They say it goes to the brain. He'd known a man whose cock came off. The publican appeared, but Derek had gone. The architect felt a shudder run through his hands. Would they wait for O'Donnell outside? He was in no shape to defend himself. He heard the publican's voice offering its charitable welcome.

"What can I do for you?" He had chosen the architect for his service.

"Large Scotch and a gin," O'Donnell ordered.

"Don't mix your drink like that," the architect said. "Take it easy."

"Double gin," O'Donnell insisted. "Same glass."

The architect was trying to catch the publican's eye. It must have been obvious someone had to protect O'Donnell from himself. But the publican went on with his job.

"I'll mix my piss if I like," O'Donnell said.

The publican laughed and cautioned O'Donnell to hold his tongue. He had served the drink in different glasses. The architect tried to restrain him; but O'Donnell was beyond anyone's control.

"I've lost everything too," the architect said, "but we've got to keep cool. It's hardly the time to lose your head."

"I know whose head we'll lose," O'Donnell renewed his threats. "We'll get the bitch. We'll find her if we have to check every whore on the heath."

"But you don't know what she looks like."

"Look for the marks," O'Donnell said. "I kicked the bitch in her teeth."

A small group had formed around them, trying in turn to console O'Donnell.

"Did you tell the police?"

"I want to catch her first," said O'Donnell. "I want to handle that part myself."

The architect was paying for the drinks. The publican listened to the chime of the till and turned away with the comforting thought that it was closing time. 'There goes the end of a bum,' he thought as he dipped the lights and called out to the crowd to find their homes.

He saw Roger emerging from the urinal, and called out again: "Time for bed."

The barmaid came up to complain about O'Donnell. He had told her that she smelt like a herring. The publican sheltered a smile behind his shoulder and turned slowly towards the small bar. The barmaid watched Roger forcing his way through the crowd. There was a sound like the hum of kites in his ears. She leaned across the bar and whispered to him. She didn't like to see a man cry and she thought there were tears in his eyes.

"Your friend says he'd wait outside," she said.

Roger stared past her towards the clock.

"Any news?" the barmaid asked.

Roger nodded and continued through the door. The barmaid was offering him a drink; but he had gone.

"It's hard," she said, inviting a man to share her pity. "First his wife runs off and left him. Now the fire leaves him without a roof."

"A bad match it was," the man said, loud and lucid in all his views. "Never the twain shall meet."

The barmaid was aiming her rebuke when they heard O'Donnell's voice threaten to damage the publican's groin. There was a struggle to get O'Donnell out of the door. The barstools were tumbled about; there was a crash on the floor. O'Donnell was being dragged like a slain bull out to the street. The publican's face was scarlet.

"Bum," the publican was stammering. "Don't ever serve that bum again. Not in here."

The barmaid was revolted by the mess on the floor.

"Pity the bugger didn't go up in flames," the publican fretted. "The bloody fire should have taken him off."

"All right now," the barmaid was begging. "Let's get a move on."

The publican dipped the lights again; and then a darkness reigned over the broken stool. The light didn't go on again in the small bar.

It was a rough night for the publican: the lucrative curse which descended on the Mona every Friday night. He liked it no less than he hated those who made it such a feverish interlude in the week's takings. A seaman in his youth, he now watched with a calm and careful eye the slow departure of these strangers who had lingered behind. They seemed reluctant to go, as though they feared what was waiting beyond the door. They were tripping over their legs, heavy and slow and reluctant as cattle, drifting into the street.

"That's a load off your hands," the barmaid said.

He was about to answer with some anecdote. He knew the end, but he had forgotten how it began. The barmaid had retreated. She was shovelling the glasses into the sink. But her hands wouldn't keep their grip. She was nervous. She couldn't get over O'Donnell's charge that she smelt. She would have liked the publican to deny it. But it was difficult to raise the matter. She couldn't ask him to sniff her; and he wasn't a man with whom an employee could be familiar. O'Donnell had started a terrible doubt. She didn't trust her smell. She couldn't be sure she was clean. She couldn't be sure that she wasn't like the woman whom O'Donnell had kicked in the teeth. But she didn't give herself to strange men on the heath. She had to get the publican's advice. She saw him getting ready to check the till. But she was scared. She had to let her question move in circles around him.

"Do you want something?" the publican asked.

He had startled her by the way he knew. He never missed anything.

"Did you hear what O'Donnell said," she began, and hoped he

might answer right away, but he would never anticipate the end of a question.

"What did the bum have to say?"

"About this woman on the heath," she said, giving cover to her real question. "It's a terrible thing to say."

"What's the bum saying now?" the publican said, but he might have been talking to the till.

"Says it was she set fire to the house where he lived."

"Good luck to her," the publican said. He might have been conferring an honour on the till.

The barmaid couldn't go any further. He had killed any progress she might have made with her question. She had lost her chance. She returned to the sink. The till went on with its chiming. She heard the train scraping to a halt outside. The noise came up from the tracks below. The station was the width of a street away. The water looked sordid with the remains of beer. O'Donnell had made her afraid of the night.

The train must have lost some of its limbs. It looked squat and battered under the light. The platform was almost deserted. But the porter was yelling at an absent crowd to hurry along. It's all over now, all over for the night. He was giving his warning long after the train had gone. It's all over now.

He went to check the lavatory doors. He knocked on the door for Gents before removing the sign marked, out of order. The architect came out from the Gents; and the porter waved him to remove the sign from the Ladies which warned it was out of use. The architect knocked on the door, but there was no answer. O'Donnell was asleep. His snore was slowly gaining sound.

Two

October had given warning that it had arrived. The night was windy, and there was a steady chill in the air. Derek pocketed his hands, and bit his lips and screwed his eyes against the wind. He could hear O'Donnell's voice pursue him up the Hamden road over the hidden slope of grass that took them to the summit of the heath. He didn't want to loiter here but he was at the mercy of Roger's despair. He couldn't let him roam alone. While he was at rehearsals in the day, he knew that Roger would park for hours outside the cinemas in Leicester Square, hoping that Nicole might appear. Each night after the fire he had come with him on this fruitless journey to the Hamden road. They kept watch near the ruins of the rooming house, then patrolled the heath, hoping that she might be there. Then they would return to the Circle theatre where the agent had arranged for him to sleep. He would make sure the place was deserted so that he could slip Roger in without anyone's notice. It was a dubious arrangement; but Roger showed no interest in finding new accommodation. He wouldn't discuss what they might do or where they would go when permission to use the theatre had been withdrawn. Nicole had become the only kind of refuge that would satisfy his need.

Derek hadn't anticipated the effect her absence would have on Roger. It had encircled him. Like vapour, it seemed to expand and influence everything he did. He could formulate no thought, experience no feeling which didn't originate with Nicole. Her absence had become mirror to every glance his eyes made; the origin and echo of every sound that entered his ears. This absence of Nicole, like a universe which swallowed everything with its vastness, had enclosed Roger's mind. He would loiter at street corners like a tramp, enquiring of total strangers if they knew where Nicole had gone. He would stare into the eye of dogs as though he had seen there an offer that the animals would help him find her.

"What time would it be?" Roger asked.

"I don't know," said Derek, "but I suppose we'd better be getting on."

"I'd like to rest a little," said Roger, catching for breath.

Derek came up behind, labouring slowly over the rising neck of the track.

"We might just make the last train," said Derek, "but we'd have to go now."

"There's a late bus," said Roger, and begged him to stay.

"What's going to happen tomorrow night?" Derek warned. "The play. You know the play opens tomorrow night."

"You don't want me to be there?"

"There's nothing worth seeing," said Derek, "but I don't like you coming up here on your own."

"She can't stay away much longer," said Roger. He lowered himself on to the grass. "I thought O'Donnell might have some news."

Derek kicked the top of his shoe into the ground. He was carving his heel into the earth. The wind pillowed his ears and made a noise like sheets floating across his eyes.

He didn't answer; and Roger let the silence pass. Derek considered the danger which had tempted him in the Mona. O'Donnell's attack was forcing him to surrender his bitterest feeling. He had been caught without warning. Like the night he saw Roger tower above him with the knife. There were moments which defied resistance. But O'Donnell's performance had left a more poisonous wound. He hadn't moved. He couldn't move. He knew that he would have killed O'Donnell if he had moved. And yet it wasn't the racial insult of O'Donnell's charge which hurt him most. This gangsterish abuse was no different from similar attacks he had heard before. It was the lack of warning, his own lack of preparedness which disturbed him most. He had never seen O'Donnell in this way before; would have thought it impossible to find him in this role.

He wanted to let Roger know what had happened while he was away; but the event was too near. It seemed too recent. He had to give himself time to master the fear which O'Donnell had started in him. He was afraid for his judgement; afraid that O'Donnell's abuse contained some truth; afraid that his surprise had sprung from some source of self-deception. And he wondered whether his sense of personal integrity had been achieved at the price of some deliberate blindness. He had to postpone the moment when he would tell Roger what O'Donnell had said. And he heard O'Donnell's charge of cowardice strike again. Hadn't Roger surprised him too by the astounding insult of being a little actor man? And he wondered whether it could be true that some lack of awareness might have been the basis of his affection for Roger.

He felt like a stranger where he walked over the soft, familiar turf of grass. He was looking towards the hidden skeleton of the rooming house. His memory came vivid with every stage of the disaster which had struck them down. And he realised it was Roger's loss which had grieved him most. He had abandoned his own room to the flames; and all his energies were spent in a vain attempt to rescue what remained of Roger's possessions: the archives of unfinished scores, volumes of exercise books with notes of what had happened during their first year in England. The piano had made the room too small. But it was Roger's total incapacity which alarmed him. He didn't move until Derek came into his room and dragged him away. He made no effort to escape. He might have been grateful to be buried under the debris of the rooming house.

Derek had to take him completely into his care. For he couldn't overcome this nagging guilt for what he thought he might have done to Roger. It made him despise any virtue he had seen in bringing things into the light. He would have liked to burn from his memory every day which had contributed to his affection for Nicole. Derek had yielded to the conviction that he was the cause of the general misfortune which had overtaken them. He believed there was some truth in Roger's abuse of his virtues. He had come to see his own obsessions through Roger's eyes; and it made him feel there was some element of fraudulence in his passion for bringing things into the light. He wanted to exorcise the scourge of virtue from his feeling. But events had worked against him. He couldn't ignore the crisis which was making a cripple of Roger. His response was immediate; and all his instincts had driven him into a deeper comradeship with Roger who had to be rescued from his increasing despair. It was as though goodness was a quality which afflicted Derek: a germ he had to live with. He came to a halt, then turned, and walked slowly back.

Roger sat in silence, patient and still, feeling some promise of optimism tempt him to be cheerful. Some miracle might yet spring up from the grass. Any moment Nicole could arrive, walk out of the night, graceful and forgivable, an Ariel of mischief; apologising for carrying out these practical jokes; explaining that she was always there, on the heath, in the trees. But no one knew where to look; no one knew how to see. So she had come back at last. Now she had known how easy it was to frighten a man who was blind. But it would be the end of her mischief. Freed from these tastes for experiment, she was now ready to resume her calling; to make him happy, to teach him how to love her.

Derek called to him from a little distance away. He was persuading him to go. He was tired of this waiting. Yet he would have done anything to bring Roger some relief; and it dawned on Derek that he really meant it in the literal sense. He would have murdered Nicole if her death would have helped to free Roger from this state of stupefaction. For he had cultivated his own suspicions about Nicole. There was something strange and painful in her departure from the house that night. He had felt more deeply for her than ever before. But she had refused him every gesture of solace in her impatience to be elsewhere. She had gone in search of Teeton. He had tried in vain to curb his anger; but his suspicion had grown swift and deep with every rumour he had heard after she disappeared.

But he was careful not to place any greater strain on Roger. And he felt O'Donnell's charges closing in on him like the night. The risk was on the edge of his tongue, ready to be heard.

"Roger."

"Yeah."

"Did you check at the boarding house again?"

"Haven't missed a day."

"Did she go back to her place that night?"

Roger reflected that Nicole's room looked undisturbed.

"That's why I'm sure," Roger said. "I'm sure she can't stay away much longer. She hasn't taken a thing."

"You didn't miss anything?"

"But you saw for yourself," Roger replied.

"I saw that the portrait had gone," Derek said. "The painting Teeton gave her. Didn't she always say she would return it to him if anything went wrong between you two?"

Roger was pondering the note of complicity in what Derek was saying. Roger didn't want to challenge him. He had known of Derek's suspicion; it was part of the strange and sudden transformation which had come over Derek. There was something like hatred in his attitude to Nicole. But Roger didn't think it would last. When Nicole came back, her presence would be enough to restore Derek's affection. He thought for a moment how she had met Teeton. He had been living, at that time, in a bitterness of spirit he could barely contain. Until Nicole arrived. But it was Teeton who had really brought them together.

"I am sure the portrait is around somewhere," said Roger.

"And Nicole is around somewhere," said Derek, "just as Teeton is around somewhere."

"But Teeton is always going somewhere," said Roger. "There's nothing new about that."

"You don't think ..." said Derek.

But Roger had intervened.

"No," he said. "Teeton wouldn't have taken that on."

"I trust nobody," Derek said, "literally nobody."

His tone was aggressive; free of all doubt, as though he were giving some warning that no one should waste a confidence on him.

"Nicole didn't go with anyone," said Roger. "I feel sure you're wrong."

Derek's reaction was the same whenever he heard Roger speak in this way. It was a barren consolation; and it made him angry. It was, indeed, the earliest evidence he had for the feeling that Roger might have been going mad. He had become a slave to this curious certainty that Nicole hadn't gone off with anyone. Derek felt the urge to challenge him with some reminder of the past; to recall that he wouldn't always have said so; that it was, in fact, Roger's own charge of infidelity which had started them on this terrible trouble. Derek could feel his tongue burn with the wish to say it; to let fly every argument and particle of evidence which Roger had previously used to suggest that Nicole had got pregnant by another man.

"I know we don't agree about Nicole," said Roger.

"I certainly don't."

"You didn't always feel that way about her."

"That's why I think as I do now."

Derek was blunt, brief. He spoke with that strangely hypnotic passion of the recent convert; for his affection had been converted into a sudden hatred of Nicole. She had destroyed finally his passion for bringing things into the light. It was the only shock, apart from Nicole's absence, which could exercise some part of Roger's mind: this sudden and tragic transformation which had come over Derek. There was nothing else which could ever make the least claim on his attention: the disappearance of Nicole and this consuming hatred which now took root in Derek. He didn't know when Nicole would come back, nor what he would do to celebrate her return; but he was going to find her wherever she was, and by any means his imagination could execute. He heard Derek get up and walk away. But he had no desire to move. It was late; but it wasn't the moment

for him to go. He could hear Derek's voice in a broken angry murmuring of curses against himself.

Derek was quietly chewing his lips as he followed the vivid procession of lights which held the city up for view. Westminster was
rising from the river's mud. He used to love this view of the city, a
jewel in the night. But he had lost all interest in the promises of
this town. Derek watched the lights where the Circle theatre might
have been, and he felt the weight of the future crush his dreams.
Whatever his role—the servile waiter or the model that amazes with
its muscle—he saw his life assume the mantle of a corpse.

He knew what was happening in the city where commerce was
lavish with welcome, its heroes buried in floss, a history of ghosts
impaled on the monuments and spires that watched over the credulous
herd, frantic to be on time, chasing to beat the rise of curtains,
masochistic and servile in their thirst for pleasure; gaping with greed
for any novelty whose lack of meaning might pacify the rage of their
boredom.

Derek wanted to forget the season at Avon and his admirable identification with the Moor. It seemed ancient and remote as a legend
which no one could now verify. There was a taste of aloes in the air, a
nagging bitterness scraping at the back of his tongue. The wind was
chipping at his eyes.

Roger heard him return. A woman's voice drifted up from the
rim of the heath; but Derek was still in the muttering stages of his
monologue. His ambitions had taken a fall. They seemed no less
treacherous than Nicole's flight.

"I suppose we've come to the end of the road," he said.

Roger wasn't sure what he meant.

"Which road?" he asked. And Derek recognised a sudden, nervous
prying in Roger's voice, as though he had been anxious for some
fresh assurance.

"Tomorrow night will be the last time," he said. "I don't think
I'll play another corpse again. I've been dead too long. Somebody
else can have a turn."

"You really think you can give it up?" Roger asked.

"I've got to give up being a corpse," said Derek.

Roger was looking up at the sky. There was a shadow like roses
dissolving slowly through the night.

"It's not been a very long road," said Roger, watching the roses multiply.

"Seven years. That's long enough for me."

"It's taken lots of people much longer," Roger said.

"They knew where they were looking," Derek said, "and it makes a difference. Here I'm chasing a delusion."

"Chasing a delusion, you say," Roger answered him gravely, and looked at the sky again.

"Of course my career has been a delusion," Derek said, feeling the taste of aloes in the air. "It's time to call a halt. After seven years."

Roger was silent. He was gazing up at the chapel of sky, and then he saw it coming, the widening shadows of rose floating down, and branching out into streaks of light like scarlet ribbons blown about. The wind was making purple wreaths with the cloud. He had lost his tongue. He heard nothing for a while, as though his eyes had put all other senses out of reach. He could barely recognise Derek's voice shouting, "Fire, fire, it's a fire."

Derek had found his arm. He was shaking him.

"I see it," said Roger, and got up.

"God, it's near," said Derek, "I wonder who's got it this time."

"It's the Mona," Roger said.

"Are you sure?"

"It's the pub all right," said Roger, making ready to move.

Derek was now beyond himself with excitement. His rage was simmering. He thought of bales of liquor on the boil. Somehow he couldn't believe what he was seeing. But his eyes rejoiced as he watched the fire climb and spread like an arch over the railway tracks.

"O'Donnell," Roger shouted, as though he had dragged himself up from a dream. "Isn't O'Donnell in the station lavatory?"

"I hope he is asleep," said Derek, and held Roger by the arm, braking his movement down the slope.

"But why?"

"I'll tell you why," Derek answered. "I'll tell you later."

He was no longer in a hurry to go. He was grateful to Roger for this delay.

Three

It must have been the longest journey they had ever made. They had drifted down the gentle slope of the hill and over the heath spreading itself out into a dark, level stretch of plain. It looked like an aerodrome in the night with the feverish traffic of insects swooping their head-lights that opened and closed like eyes of fire; and the huge, brilliant flares exploding from the wreck of the Mona. There was a hum like engines turning off where the grass blossomed for a moment as the insects came burning to a halt. A wave of air was simmering over-head. Then the pavements met them, and the streets settled down, and they watched the night uncoil before them.

It was the slowest journey they had ever made.

The city had become a huge and foreign mausoleum where they walked. A procession of avenues marched them past the houses that rose like vaults, where everyone was asleep and shut tight in. And miles away the wave of fire rode after them with its cargo of ruins from the past. The photographs of Stratford rose in a rubble of smoking frames; and the charred skeleton of the piano floated its chords up to the sky, lamenting the day they had ever made this crossing.

It must have been the quietest journey they had ever made.

Until the West End lights besieged them with their curious geometry of shadows that marked the streets. A brief and fearful interval of waiting, and soon they had escaped the clamour and applause of the city's illumination. They had become invisible where they paddled their way through the murky air of the alleyways. And the Circle theatre rose like a tomb to let them through its forbidden gate.

It was the most fearful arrival they had ever made.

Each step echoed the silence of a grave with the after smell of theatre crowds. They hoisted their weariness up from the floor, and into the grim, vacant yawn of the stage. They might have come by chance into a cemetery of silent clowns.

But Roger called very softly to Derek who was ready to bed down at his side.

"If they come for me," he said, "you must not interfere."

"Who's coming for you?" Derek laughed.

"If the police come."

Derek sat up; then heard his confusion come in a babble of sound. "What are you saying? What do you mean?"

"If the police catch up," said Roger, "let Nicole know where to find me."

Derek couldn't move. All the bolts of lightning had struck him dumb.

"It's the Old Dowager's house tomorrow night," said Roger. "Tell Teeton I'm going to burn it down."

IO

One

Teeton was starved; but the pilot had taken charge of his hunger; had driven it back and further away until it was no longer part of his consciousness. He watched the man, afraid that he was going to burst. Another word, and his rage might have carried his body up in flames. But the man held no fears for himself. He looked solid and lasting as steel.

"But I warned her; from the beginning I tried to shield her with my warning." He was shaking his head, prodding the table with an irritable fist. "I should have taken her away; should have come and got her out of that house; out of your animal claws."

He had aimed his glance at Teeton; and his whole head seemed to tremble as though this sense of error, this failure to come to the rescue of the Old Dowager, was making him hate himself. Teeton didn't stir; couldn't summon any strategy to defend himself against this astonishing assault. He wished the Old Dowager would appear; but she was nowhere in sight. He hadn't seen her since the man had carried her from the table the night before. He had lingered in the room all morning; made those domestic noises that might call attention to himself; but the Old Dowager didn't come down for lunch. No meal was served. No one appeared. Until the man surprised him from the wall as he had done before. There was no welcome, no interval for adjustment to the night before; no reference to the Old Dowager beyond the charge which he had kept up with such ferocity. She must have heard his voice.

"Is it her money? Or is it the house you are after?"

He was drumming the table with his fist.

"She was lonely," he said, as though he had to forgive the Old Dowager her error. "I was glad when she said there was someone on the second floor. It made me happy for her. It was beneath her dignity to be in the pay of tenants. She didn't need to. But her loneliness was a terrible thing. And she had never forgotten what she had been through with that monster. Heaven curse his grave. The ocean isn't large enough to wash his kind."

There was a force of hurricanes in his eyes. He came close, as though he knew more than he could afford to say; but he couldn't restrain his shout.

"I killed him." He was quartering Teeton with his stare. "With these hands, I saw to it that he wouldn't breathe air again. And now, now, now. That she should descend from him to you."

His fist struck more rapidly on the table; four, five successive blows hammering his mistakes into the table. He should never have allowed the Old Dowager to live on her own. Reckless, he was scolding himself, she was always reckless with her passions.

"And you would have seen her weakness," he went on, as though Teeton might have read his mind; known through some magic what he had been thinking. "You would without a doubt have seen to that. Seen to it that every trap was laid for her undoing. And it's always been her undoing. She has never loved and not come unstuck, torn up into pieces when it's all over. Like how she is now. All crushed up inside, can hardly recognise herself. So crushed up. And for your kind, your monstrous kind."

His fist had finally struck down in a resounding crash. But he showed no sign of discomfort, not the slightest wince of pain, as though his rage had made his body proof against all feeling, naked and tough as the island's stone.

"Her husband was a monster too," he intoned, averting his glance from Teeton, "but of a different breed. Breeding alone came between him and your lot."

He was retreating from the table, his hands now fiercely bandaged across his brow. He stopped at the opening in the wall; glanced at the dark passage which ascended to the room above. But he didn't go further. Now he turned, pondered the walls of mist falling apart outside. Echoes, echoes, he heard such echoes in his head. He could barely see Teeton although his gaze was bearing down towards the table. There was such a tangle of clouds before his eyes, like burning smoke ascending from a pyre of leaves. He could dimly see Teeton; see, that is, a shape, a shape of something; some kind of creature which he had to recognise; some punishing eruption of nature. How could it be true? How could the Old Dowager have punished his heart with such a rival for her love? It was monstrous, monstrous beyond meaning, what this stranger had come to be for her.

He watched Teeton as he had often watched the island appear

slowly from under the dark veil of the hills. And he wondered what had made her bring him here: why should she have introduced this barbarous menace into his retirement? It couldn't have been a wish to hurt. Never, never. She wouldn't have been capable of that. But she didn't know the origin of his fears. He had kept her in the dark about his cell. He could sense a slight burning in his eyes; as though the mist had deposited a trail of acid on the air. It was clear again. He could see the table again. He could see.

He was walking back from the wall. Teeton followed his approach; measured every step which brought him nearer; the slightest movement was now magnified by Teeton's gaze. He was nervous; and he knew it. But he wasn't afraid; and he knew that too. He was alert; and he knew it was the man's rage which had given his alertness such intensity. It worked with such a force of duty on his nerves; this watchfulness which the man had imposed on him; so that it seemed to overwhelm him, offering no hint of limit; a superstition which had trained him not to relax his attention.

The man's admission that he had murdered the Old Dowager's husband, his own brother, had mobilised Teeton's guard against all danger. He was now on guard against the Old Dowager; on guard against this curious history of romance which she had built around him for six years, nurtured in secret and with such careful reticence. For a moment Teeton had come near to being deceived by his guard. He was softened by the Old Dowager's passion for him; curious about the partnership which she had kept going with her husband's brother who waited, patient, loving, grateful for the annual pilgrimage which she made back to the solitude of this cottage. Teeton had come near to a flaw in his alertness when he heard about the Old Dowager's reports of their meeting; his years of residence in the house; the improbable passion which he had aroused in the Old Dowager.

But the absurdity of the man's jealousy now frightened him; frightened him, that is, into a harsh and insane discipline of alertness. He was on guard against the menace of this man's knowledge. Teeton didn't know how much the Old Dowager might have told him; what change might have come over her since she heard of his plans for going home. He kept his guard against the likelihood that the man might have been informed about the burial of Nicole.

Teeton was looking at him, now magnified into a giant figure that crushed the chair with its weight. The fury hadn't gone out from his eyes; but it was underneath. His eyes seemed to contract and quiver from within. He had come forward; his splendid head almost hidden by the mane of hair that flogged the back of his neck. It fell like a cloud of hay about his face. Now it seemed as though he might, with a little luck, grow calm. His mood suggested there was some ground where they could bargain.

The guard had come like a tyrant into Teeton's eyes. There was a temptation to enquire about the Old Dowager; to wish that she would come down and relieve him of this rigorous vigil. What would she do if she were here? Where was she? But the questions had been struck down. Swiftly. Utterly. His wish for the Old Dowager had perished almost at birth. His guard kept the man's voice where it should be. The man watched him closely. He was lamenting what he had to look upon.

"I wanted to marry her," he said. "After my brother went away. I would have brought our daughter back. He knew she was our daughter. He knew it. Just as he knew the woman he called his wife by marriage was really mine, my own kingdom. Mine. She was mine. That's why he found it so easy to leave her behind. He had no claim of love on her. But he took our daughter. Out of spite. Her only child. My God! He could have allowed her some compensation. Her only child. My God, can you imagine it? Or perhaps you can, perhaps you can."

His eyelids spread like the wings of a bat as he waited for Teeton to confirm the wickedness of the Old Dowager's loss.

"Her only child," he cried, "hardly old enough to know her name. Myra was barely three when he took her to that forsaken hell of an island. To live on estates he had never seen. Knew nothing about although they were his own. He carried the infant off like a common slave. Took her with him. A single man with no interest whatsoever in domestic life. A man who'd never soil his hands with the cleanest chore. Never. Carried the infant off to bring her up among a tribe of monstrous butchers. Living with brutes. For fourteen years. And not a word, not a single greeting back to his country. Not one item of news whether that infant had ever survived. Out of spite. He was always one to experiment with spite. Revenge and spite."

Teeton watched him rise from the table. He felt an urge to speak, but he couldn't break through the austerity of his guard. He was alerted by the smell of danger; fiercely on guard against anything he might say, any question it had occurred to him to ask. He kept the tightest guard against his curiosity, against any tendency that might lead him to reveal what he knew. It wouldn't let him recognise the history which the man was struggling to revive.

His guard was following the man slowly down to the chair. He had come back, urgent and careless in his need to be heard. He had to free himself from the solitude of these miseries.

"And I made that journey," he was begging to be heard. "Fourteen years after his desertion. To see whether we couldn't be reconciled. It was a long time. Wounds might have healed a bit. And for her sake. Any mother might have asked a similar favour. To bring her daughter back even for a short while. A month if no more. My God! Can you believe it? Or perhaps you can. To my horror he had never told her a word of truth about where she came from; what she was doing there. He told her nothing, nothing that could make for interest or knowledge about a family; that he had a brother. God, I would forgive that maybe, but how can you forgive him the lies? Educated the child himself in lies, lies, lies. She never knew she had a mother who was alive. Never, never knew. That monster. Sprung from the same loins as myself, it's true. But a monster."

He had grown quiet. His voice was like the sound of a prayer. He was asking heaven to unlock the mystery of a wickedness that could be so contrary to ordinary experience. He had always hated that portion of their inheritance which his brother so perversely claimed. Remote and perilous in its ways, it seemed the perfect setting for his brother's genius. But he couldn't grasp the evil satisfaction which it had given his brother to plant such innocence in that soil; to impose his spite and his wicked pride on a child; to deprive her of every privilege that was the foundation of his own childhood. He couldn't comprehend the nature of such an intention, any more than he could cope with the horror he wanted to exorcise when he stared into Teeton's eyes.

"Lies, lies, lies," his prayer was echoing. "He has never uttered a syllable of truth about the smallest particle of his life. Lies, lies. Lies to his wife, to her daughter, to everyone who came before and after them. My God, to think of it. After all those years. Me, his own brother, that he could introduce me as a partner. That's what he told her. I was a partner in the estate. An absent partner in our estate. After fourteen years. To see her then. No longer a child. So beautiful, but with her head full of his riddles. Educated only by my brother with his taste for the dead. He always trafficked with the dead like the savages who worked on his estate. There she was. Trained to treat me as a stranger and a friend, her father's partner. Our daughter. There she was. The fruit of his revenge. Talking the language of the savage who was his servant. God, my God! I should have killed him long before. I should have killed him long, long before it happened."

He saw the mist break through the window pane, fanning clouds before his eyes. Echoes, echoes, he could hear such echoes in his head, like cries breaking from the mouth of drums; such echoes had arisen to swell his ears; such a clamour of sound as though the tongues of trumpets were licking with fire against the walls of his skull.

"The monsters," he cried out, hoping to revile Teeton with the habits of his kind, "I should have saved her before that black breed of scorpions seized the chance to crawl over her. God, God, the monsters. How they took her body, like cannibals feeding on some carcass they had never hoped, never dreamed they might ever taste. God, how they brutalised her beauty. For she was that: beautiful; an absolute beauty until they set the hounds upon her. Can you imagine it? Or perhaps you can, you can. Perhaps you can imagine how they made the hounds violate her sex. The animals. The very creatures which had been her fondest pets. Those monsters stirred up the animals' lust for her; and let them loose over her body. Just as they had seen their master do with some of them. His own field servants. Oh, yes, my brother, come from the same blessed loins, the same ancestry of privilege and blood; my brother himself had made this devil's crime a common sport upon his servants. Male and female alike. Trained his hounds to mount a human sex. That monster. I should have killed him before; could have taken her away before the monsters got at her.

"And heaven knows what became of her. Heaven knows what terrors the daylight strikes into her; but she couldn't come back. She wouldn't let me bring her back. I left her there. She'd just wander about, unknown, in a craziness set on her by your kind."

The clouds were lifting from his eyes. One hand was crawling across the table. Teeton watched it crouch and slither down his waist. It rose again, and settled quietly on the table.

"I may not be long for this world," he said, as though the mist had darkened his vision again, "but I know what I've learnt. That experiment in ruling over your kind. It was a curse. The wealth it fetched was a curse. The power it brought was a curse. That's why my brother found it to his liking. He knew it could deform whatever nature it touched. A curse I tell you. A curse! And it will come back to plague my race until one of us dies. That curse will always come back. Like how you've come here."

His hands made a violent hammering on the table as though he was helpless to redeem some error he had made. He looked towards the cell.

"And now she has brought you here," he fretted with himself, "not knowing my horror of your kind. I couldn't tell her everything. There are things you can't always tell. So she has brought you here. Not knowing. Brought you to my last corner of safety. Brought you right into the secret of my cell, that hole which would lock me in the wall if it was necessary. Ever since those monsters made me watch them craze our daughter. I had to have a corner where I might hide if ever they came after me. And here you are. Why did she bring you here?"

Teeton considered him; but the guard wouldn't allow his interest to trespass any further. He watched the man's hands; observed the admirable plane of muscle that moved under his shirt up to the sharp cliff of his shoulders. But Teeton took no risk with talking; he had felt the rigours of the guard intensify; yes, it was possible; possible beyond his wildest fancy that this watchfulness could have increased its tyranny over him; for it was clear to him now that the man knew nothing about the burial of Nicole's body in the garden. The Old Dowager hadn't told him—meaning, the guard promptly informed Teeton, that she hadn't told him *yet*.

Would she tell him? When would she choose to tell him? The Old Dowager had been with him all morning; she could have told him then, but she had not. Perhaps she was in the process of deciding; perhaps she was trying to frighten Teeton by keeping away. She had found the right strategy for making him stay. They had demolished the rules of their private game; and now she was confirming that she didn't care about their preservation anyway. She was prepared to come out from behind their codes; to come straight to the heart of their business. But it was necessary, first of all, to give him this fright.

The Old Dowager hadn't appeared; hadn't made any enquiry how he had been. It was the man who came, more turbulent than the wrath of thunder. Teeton saw him there; and the guard observed how narrow the margin was which came between Teeton and the man. He remained on the chair; very quiet, pinching the corners of his chin, meditating on his own question to Teeton. Why? Why did she bring you here?

The man was getting up; he had come erect. He was turning away. Now his back was turned. His hand was crouching under his shirt. He was walking towards the opening in the wall, his cell of safety. He had arrived. He stood before the gaping plaster. Teeton watched him stand; would not allow any movement to happen without the approval of the guard. The man stood there; and Teeton watched him stand gazing at the cell which he had built inside the wall.

But everything had come to a halt. Teeton could feel a weight of chains deaden his feet. He was trying to find some space for his toes, but a cramp, sharper than the fist of iron, was splitting open his flesh, nailing his bones into the floor. And his guard was about to panic; his guard had, indeed, fled. For he was scared to the roots of his hair when he discovered that he could not move. The cramp had finally nailed him to the chair. The man had turned, he was already there; a hand away with the knife descending slowly, and with care.

Suddenly the air was raped by gun shot; and the cottage shook. Teeton saw the body bend. The man went over backwards. His head came to a dead stop against the grate. Teeton couldn't tell what had happened to his legs. He was struggling to get up when the second shot broke through the bone into the man's head. But Teeton remained nailed to the chair. He hadn't moved at all; as though his feet were still in chains. He couldn't move. He didn't know whose air he was inhaling; whose lungs were in charge of his breathing. But he felt he was a stranger to his body. He was squatting in some foreign shelter of flesh and bone that could never be his own. He didn't know what sound his tongue should make; what language he could make his own. But he wanted to speak; to make some kind of noise that would let the Old Dowager know how he was feeling. She had saved his life; saved him by the grim necessity of killing the man.

The Old Dowager hadn't moved since the shots were fired. Teeton could barely recognise her as she put the rifle quietly down on the stairs. It might have been a toy. She had handled the rifle like a curtain rod. Teeton hadn't spoken. He knew what he had to say. But he had no language; no tongue that he could call his own. And he continued to stare at the Old Dowager as though he wanted her to find some cure for this impediment; this total speechlessness which had now made him prisoner in his own dark and distorting consciousness.

The Old Dowager came slowly down the stairs giving all her attention to the broken head where the ear was leaking blood. She didn't look at Teeton.

"He is dead," Teeton said.

"I did what I had to do," she said, resisting any impulse to look in his direction.

Teeton couldn't grasp her meaning, the incredible detachment which the Old Dowager showed as she stooped to hold the body on the floor.

"Fernando dear," the Old Dowager was appealing, "why did you say the storm took Myra too? Why did you tell me that she died?"

Her voice was like a miracle in Teeton's ears. Now she looked calm, almost impartial in her apparent lack of feeling. She didn't speak again, as though some subtle, and dreadful force of enmity was born in her silence. Teeton began to feel his guard go up again. The Old Dowager was capable of any action. The man's body was still alive and fresh with grief for the Old Dowager and her daughter. Teeton looked at the body; then tried to gain the Old Dowager's attention. But she had turned away, walking towards the front window with its view of the pier.

Teeton didn't know what noise of penance his tongue should make. He could only hear the chilling silence of the cottage, and an echo of the Old Dowager's daughter floated on the wind: 'It was Father's servant who organised his friends'.

He watched the body spread its dying on the early darkness of the afternoon.

Two

Teeton sat alone. The night was burying his hands in the crack of earth where he had shovelled the body underground. He had held the man as though he had known him before. He might have been a neighbour. It was uncanny the way he had lowered him into the ground: so calm, and scarcely aware that he was alone.

The Old Dowager had shot her husband's brother. She had killed her lover; put an end to her daughter's father. But she had left Teeton to manage the burial on his own. She didn't speak to him again. She had no advice to offer. It didn't seem to matter where the body was laid: in the cell which the man had built within the wall, or in an ordinary hole outside the cottage. The questions had come stammering from Teeton's lips, but she was no longer any part of what he was saying. She had withdrawn her interest from these emergencies. He couldn't grasp this lack of connection which she had displayed. She looked as though she had come to the end of all endeavour. Her silence was inscrutable. But he had followed her example. He did what he had to do. He had buried the body on his own.

He was calm and without fear, remote as the sky. He threw away the last fistful of dirt spiked with the gravel that was clinging to his hands. There was a tremor of light within the cottage. He decided it was time to go. He wouldn't stretch his delay much longer. He tested the safety of the ground with his hands. Then he got up. If he kept a straight course it would bring him in line with the door. He memorised the details of the path he had taken. He paused at intervals, stooping low to scrape the earth with his hands. He wasn't sure when the cracks would appear. It would have been safer to crawl; but the cottage was near. The light grew stronger against the window.

The Old Dowager was occupied with the flutter of the candle across the table. The light filled her hands which were turned up, the palms spread wide. She was about to close them when she heard the crunch of footsteps outside the door. She was arranging the angle of her glance to meet his entry; but she was careful not to look.

Teeton recognised the expression which was slowly building up around her mouth. For a moment he thought she was about to smile; but there was something too feverish in the tautness of her lips. Her eyes were lost in caves of shadow. He couldn't detect any change. She was sitting where he had left her.

His hands were cold. He walked over to the grate, but the fire was dead. He looked round the room, supervising the corners of the ceiling until his glance fell on the emptiness of the stairs. The rifle was no longer there. The Old Dowager must have taken it away. He had to regain her attention; but she wouldn't stir.

Teeton ran up the stairs and went into the dead man's room. He was inspecting the floor again. He lifted the carpet, and prised the laths which showed .the opening in the floor. He squatted down, and his hands found the top of the ladder which descended into the dark passage that opened through the wall. He was inspecting the cell for the second time. He thought the Old Dowager might have come up to ask what he was doing there. But there was no change in the sombre stillness which oppressed the cottage. He started back to the dining room. He would have to get the fire going on his own.

The Old Dowager couldn't tell what he was looking for; but there was something in his gaze which said he knew. She couldn't be sure what it was that he might have known. She had noticed the look of recognition which came to his eyes at the mention of her daughter. But she didn't care to speculate about what he knew. She had resigned all interest in the past. She heard him coming down the stairs. But their partnership was at an end.

Teeton sat at the far end of the table; hoping the Old Dowager might relax a little. It seemed there was nothing more to be said. He was drifting finally out of her care. But he was still within her power. She was free to defy his wish, free to refuse her favours. He felt a brief thrust of rage at the thought that his future was dependent on her mercy. He was determined to draw her out, to offer some bargain for their safety. He might yet redeem her loss. He would offer to find her daughter. He could help to restore this battered portion of her past. Then his departure would no longer have the power to leave this scar of treachery on their friendship. It would be slight beside the rewards of seeing her daughter. But he reflected on the time it might take, the hazards which grew with every moment of delay.

He was gentle, cautious, almost nervous in his approach.

"What shall we do now?" he asked.

But the Old Dowager didn't break her silence. She closed her hands, and deposited them sternly on her lap. She might have been expecting him to speak, to test her firmness.

"I believe your daughter is alive," said Teeton. He was looking for some hint of optimism in her response. But the Old Dowager didn't shift an eyelid. He was mildly surprised by her lack of interest. But he couldn't resist his need to strike a bargain. He could no longer trust his safety to the Old Dowager's care.

"I am sure we can find her," Teeton said.

He was alarmed by the look of hatred which burnt her eyes.

"You can arrange that too, I suppose."

She was shattered by the conviction that he knew; that he must always have known; and she discovered some animal treachery in his secretive ways. She saw the ancestral beast which possessed his kind, a miracle of cunning and deceit, forever in hiding, dark and dangerous as the night.

"The answer is no," the Old Dowager said.

Teeton's voice had suddenly failed him. He saw her rise from the table. She stood erect, her eyes now hard and dry like curves of rock. He was under the spell of her rejection, barely conscious of the distance which had come between them. She was making her departure up the stairs.

The wind had found its strength. It had started to pound the door; and a sound of hissing blew down the chimney. He stared into the gaping mouth of the fireplace. He was twisting the cold out of his hands. He seemed astonished to find himself alone. But a mood of calm was coming gradually over him. He concentrated on the hearth, and the lack of fire; and wondered where he would find some fuel.

Teeton knew he would have to organise his own escape.

Derek was waiting for his call. The light made a dwarf of his shadow, squatting on the floor. Half an hour to go. Or was it an hour? He couldn't be sure. But he was there, punctual as the boards which announced the show: *A Summer's Error in Albion*. A thimble of liquor might have cooled his nerves; but he couldn't find the phial of rum. The little cubicle closed in like a sentry box around him. He had a dressing room to himself. They had promoted him to the privacy of this little stable. Here he could hide from the press of reptiles who had been chasing after him. The evening papers had done him proud. He was suffocating from attention, from the malice and pity of the smiles that had hailed him. He was cracking under the strain of Roger's arrest.

The police had swept into the Circle theatre an hour after dawn. Roger had kept him awake with his warning. He didn't expect them to come so soon. But Roger had sat up, making himself ready for their arrival. Some instinct had given him a forecast of their coming. He looked so utterly at ease, almost grateful that they had found their man. The police had played the rules which made them take the suspect in for question. And they played it smooth. Roger had made sure that it wouldn't be rough. He let them know that he was their man. But they had a feeling both men were involved, and they took Derek along. They would have locked him inside with Roger, but the agent had intervened on behalf of his property. Derek came out alone on his agent's bail. The corpse was back and ready for its opening night.

Was it an hour to go? It might have been more. But he was there. Buried under the ruins of his clothes. A tramp's outfit. The coat sagged about him like a tent. He didn't think he could see the evening through. The little phial of rum might have helped; but it had got lost in the debris of the room. It was too late to escape. He had begged to withdraw; but the agent had made himself clear. He had his own arrangements to promote.

Derek knew he was on time. He hadn't left the little stable since the Press released him. He had forgotten the hour, but the afternoon editions were already exploring his career. There was no reason he should be afraid of what he had to do. But he was afraid. In the past he had entered this role without the slightest misgiving. Dead, he knew how to stay quite simply dead until the body was carted off. Now he kept going over minute instructions, as though his gift of self-mockery was no longer a joke. 'Every corpse has its own way of dying, its own angle of going stiff.' But his eyes and his mouth had forgotten their cue. They couldn't laugh any longer. They were guiding him through the columns of the evening paper.

His little museum of clippings had been lost in the fire; but the Press had dug up evidence of their own. He could recognise his face under the painted skin of the Moor. Two brief paragraphs had excavated the memories of an actor who had played in his *Othello*. There were pictures of Roger and Teeton as they appeared with Derek at the opening of the Stratford season six years ago. They were all on display in a miraculous resurrection of Derek's name.

He was already near collapse when he left Roger in the morning, but the flood of publicity was about to finish him off. The Press didn't lie, yet their story made him feel like a man who had been framed. But the agent wouldn't hear of his withdrawal. And Derek had the impression that the man had intervened with bail on this specific condition. The corpse had to go on. He could have been replaced on stage by a parcel on a bench; but the agent had suddenly discovered he was property. The arrest at the Circle theatre had given his career an extraordinary direction. What with *Othello* and Avon somewhere behind him, and the daily news of revolution raging in his native island; it seemed to the agent that the game of arson had come on time. It was what the property needed to discover its true price. Within an hour of hearing about the arrest, the agent had alerted every medium that carried news. They had rescued Derek from anonymity. They were kneading his name like dough, teasing the palate of every citizen with a taste for scandal.

The newspaper was slipping from his hands. He let it drop on to the floor. The room reflected the chaos of his confidence. He might have been stealing shelter from the weather. Was it half an hour to go? He couldn't be sure that he would get it right. He was looking for some sign of an exit; but it was too late to run away. Why didn't he withdraw from this solemn farce of a play in which his corpse would serve briefly as a point of reference, a landmark by which later events might be remembered? There was no change in the demands of this role, except the timing of the body's fall from the bench. There was no difference except in the plotting of his discovery.

In his previous experience he had always had to wait. But tonight the curtain would rise on the discovery of his corpse. Within the half hour he would be free. But his head was like a hive with advice. He was rehearsing the syllables he had to listen for; briefing his memory with excessive care. There would only be the girl's voice casually enquiring of the body: 'What have we got here?' Here, here. Only once, she says it once only. Here. And then the fall. Is it five or did he say ten seconds after Here. Only once, don't let her have to say it more than once. My back is to the audience before the fall. Eyes open if you like. Better keep them closed for the girl's sake. It's the girl's début. She's just fresh from drama school. Eyes closed. Have we got here? Have we got here? One, two, three.

He broke off the rehearsal to look for the miniature bottle of rum he had put away. He was rummaging through the garbage of his pockets; but it wasn't there. He swivelled himself round to see whether he had left it on the table. Lost, he gave it up as lost. But he made a tour of the pockets again; and the verdict was the same.

He was coaching his memory for the rise of the curtain. He felt a weight of fatigue bend him forward as he heard the girl's voice give him his cue. He let his head rest on the table. His glance surprised him as it fell on the little smile that came up from the tip of his boot where the sole was about to give way. And he was smiling back. It was a long time since he had felt such relief. It was the little bottle all right. It must have found an exit through the lining of his jacket. It had dropped into the fold of his trousers. He took it up and gave it a look of applause. It was souvenir size, almost the shape of his thumb. He glanced at the little ditch of space that opened round his trouser leg; then looked at the miniature bottle again. It might have been a toy ship that had got sunk. It was a generous double in any pub; but he didn't want to drink it now. It seemed a pity not to let it last. Souvenir size. Growing up from his hand like a swollen thumb. He was smiling.

He was prompting his memory again, inventing some bribe that might sustain his confidence. One two three. What have we got here? It's the other way round. He had forgotten his cue; he was lost in applause for the drink.

He saw the agent's face in the miniature bottle of rum; dredged up like a skeleton from a bed of sand. A fish or a man, it was hard to tell: the mouth was wide as a mammal's, the tiny eyes almost invisible. But the girl's laugh struck like a harpoon through the little helmet of metal which covered the bottle of rum. There was an ocean of laughter in his souvenir measure. He saw the summer walk up from the neck of the bottle: the entire backdrop of scenery that would soon deliver the girl emerging from a haven of swans. Like his first summer in London; his first discovery of these birds on the river, watching them assemble like a parliament, suspicious of strangers. The wind made dimples in their feathers, the long necks curling up and scribbling their perfect whiteness on the air; their wings unfolding in the wind, capsizing the children's boats, carving up the tide. And his Sunday mornings in the heart of the city, surprised by the magic of park and woodland drifting over acres of grass and lake away from the smell and cry of the city.

The girl was striding from the tiny shoulders of his miniature bottle; tumbling through the summer of leaves, young and careless as the wind. Like his journey through the islands of his childhood. He saw them swimming through the neck of the bottle. Before the chorus of birds at dawn, he would be up and gone, riding over stone and pebble through the lanes of the village on his way to the sea. He would watch the dawn arrive; and the sun come sudden and sharp; and the beach would shake and tremble from the violent embrace of the day. And his body would leap from the pulpit of rock, spread-eagle over the bay and drown his ears in a gospel of the waves.

Here, what have we got here? But the girl had fled with his cue. He was emerging from the islands, loitering for a moment in the safety of the theatre where he was born. Now the drama of his childhood rose before him as though some reservoir was about to overflow inside him. And the scenery of the Circle theatre gave way to the drama of his pentecostal days. Orphaned at an early age—he couldn't have been more than five—he had been rescued by the pastors of the Saragasso chapel. They were the first directors he had ever known. Simple and austere in their obedience to the word. They would allow no scenery of pulpit, no artifice of altar and incense to interfere. The power of the word was sufficient proof. It made them witness to the holy birth; carried them on a joyful pilgrimage from the cattleshed to a kingdom that was to come. The script didn't change, and yet no production was the same. The entire congregation was their cast, marrying word and movement. He had received the message through his body. The gospel was a dance which trained his legs and arms to pray.

The pastors had planted the seeds of all his future dreams. They had fed him on the miracle of Cana's wine. He had seen Lazarus come forth; knew why the camel could not go through the needle's eye. The pastors had made a parable of his own life. But they would never have believed; would have been horrified, indeed, to know that it was in this chapel that a boy in their care had discovered the secret of transforming legend into fact; discovered the magic of drama; and where the two and three were gathered together for the word, the boy's imagination had found its scenery and stage. He was born in the theatre; had grown up there; could not imagine an ambition that would take him elsewhere.

She talks to the body: 'What have we here?' He was getting back to his cue. Someone was knocking at the door; but Derek didn't stir from the table. He heard a voice enquiring whether the body had been found. They must have been calling for some time. The knock came again; but Derek was slow to let them know he was there. He was twisting the little cap off the miniature bottle. The call came again, and the knock was repeated. The cover had yielded off the top of the bottle; and soon he felt the sting of the rum split his tongue. It was fierce and sharp, like a spurt of acid burning holes in his throat. There was anxious muttering outside the door; then a sigh of relief. He heard the low, genial chuckle of the agent's voice assuring someone that they were all quite safe; he didn't think the body would set the theatre on fire.

Derek was swift on his feet, as though the reference to the fire had suddenly quickened his awareness of the dressing room. He finished the rum, threw the bottle on the table, and turned to unlock the door. The agent came in. He pinched Derek's arm, then embraced him round the shoulders and led him in silence towards the door. They parted without a word; and Derek suddenly felt the man's attention enter him like a dagger through the heart. It had sharpened his awareness of being alone.

He was carrying his body up the flight of steps, bearing it across the scenery which crowded the stage with summer. He would soon lower it on to the bench. But he was gazing at the scenery as though the apparatus of park and the trees would collapse in flames. His fear had come alive with the reference to the Circle theatre going up in flames.

He was already there; yet he felt unnerved by the sound of the voices which had been searching for him. He tried to share the agent's joke that the Circle theatre wouldn't go up in fire; but his mouth wouldn't let him smile. His lips were about to crackle with fear. He couldn't enter this comedy of danger which the agent had improvised and as quickly forgotten. Was there any chance the theatre might be set on fire? It might have been an opportunity for someone to try it; to do it in his name. He was about to take up the body's position on the bench. The cue had sunk beneath all memory.

He was brooding on Roger's arrest. He felt a thrust and prick of arrows ploughing up his mind for the seeds of some permanent disgrace. And the fruit of his guilt fell on him; it swelled and ripened within him. It was almost ready to smash his brain. And his conviction grew that he was the cause of Roger's downfall. At least it was he who had brought it on. It was his charge that Roger wouldn't know how to look on the whiteness of his child, couldn't bear his hereditary fear of impurity. It was his charge against Roger; his untimely disclosures to Nicole. It was his fraudulent stewardship of other people's lives which had brought such appalling disaster on everyone.

Derek was beyond the touch of the bench where his corpse was waiting; and he cursed the origin of his oppressive failure. He was piling obscenities on the pastors' virtues, on the ignorant chapel's exhortation to be and to come and to keep always clean. There was gall and brimstone in his blasphemy. And in this feverish moment of denigration he started to experience a strange relief. He was in control again. He could feel an awesome power of contempt reign over him and his surroundings.

He wished his previous fear would now come true. Why shouldn't the Circle theatre add its mite of sacrifice to the rooming house and the Mona bar? Why shouldn't it burn? He would have witnessed the agent roast alive if he had been given the chance. He would watch him burn like rubber. He was feeling the fervour of the pastors when they started to warn of the perils of hell. But he wanted to claim a pride of Lucifer. He was feeling like a man on the moment of some impossible task; an adventure unto death with no rewards but a crown of fire. It would have been a magnificent end to the body's career.

And there, he was now about to lay it down and let it wait to be found. Would there be time enough for someone to put an end to this brothel of actors and audience and the pimps who are paid to come and watch and recommend? There was an anxious shooing from some crevice far back stage. Derek didn't hear; didn't realise his body was not keeping still. He was groping through the thicket of his tramp's pockets for something; anything that might come to his aid; anything that would burn and explode this cauldron of a summer park with its artifice of nature on the run, and the girl, graceful as the swans that watch her wade leisurely through the summer air.

But the shooing was coming again, swearing with frenzy into his ears. Then he was startled by the hush which seemed to fall like vapour beyond the stage. The auditorium was being anaesthetised. Derek realised by this stillness that they were ready. He knew and loved that interval of the curtain's ascent; that tense, pregnant quiet, arriving and swelling, stage by gradual stage to its climax of absolute silence.

It was like the silence which would happen in his childhood when they waited on their knees; and stayed there, wordless and waiting until the pastor had, at last, found his voice. There was always that moment of dreadful silence: a beautiful silence as though the clouds had spread out, and come down like the hands of God to gather up every echo and build a barricade of silence over and around the chapel. It was such a rich and solemn hush which now hung over the auditorium. And it seemed to go on forever, as though there would be no end; as though there could be no end to this unholy wrath which had erected the corpse from its bench. There was a wildness of butterflies in the girl's eyes, and her voice went ripping through the footlights like a wail of angels in agony. The silence grew like the horror of the body which was now pricking its way violently through the girl's thighs. Some hurricane had torn her pants away, as the body struggled to split open her sex. And the audience saw it, almost watched it, as though the girl's scream had manacled every witness to his seat, made impotent by their lack of warning before so uniquely brutal an assault. They watched in speechless unbelief until the curtain raced down through that terrible hush and fell, trembling like a veil over their fury.

Derek was dragging his body up from the floor. The cast was terrified. They watched him where he stood as though some dragon of legend had been released on the stage. They were nervous to go near him. He was, for the moment, untouchable; protected by the privilege of the beast. For the moment this dragon could not be touched. He made no effort to escape; just stood there, his back turned on the girl as though he was waiting for her to get up and give him his cue; waiting for *A Summer's Error in Albion* to begin; just waiting to put his body through its death and be gone.

But the theatre had surfaced from the opiate stupor radiating from the stage. They had awakened to the nightmare of what had happened. The theatre had found its proper voice of fury. They were thirsting for the dragon's blood. They heard a cannibal rage call them to instant duty. They were gazing at the scarlet veil of the curtain which came between them and the stage. And they had a lucid vision of the cities submerged by endless tides of blood. No heart could possibly stay neutral here. All were agreed. Some monstrous shadow was spreading through the land.

12

One

In the basement room the Gathering have assembled for the last time.
There is no shade over the bulb, and the light fans out, chasing all
trace of shadow from the walls. It is sharp and fierce where it ascends,
blistering the cracks that race like streaks of cloud over the ceiling.
It sets a scorching blaze on the tattered edge of the carpet. Beyond,
a modest pile of luggage stoops in one corner: the barest requirement
of those who will depart at different times, by different routes, on the
long and fateful journey to San Cristobal. They have been puzzled by
Teeton's delay; but they have postponed any argument that touches
on his absence; and the voices ramble leisurely through an order of
events which they have been repeating like an alphabet.

"First flight out," Potaro says, drumming his thumb against his
brow.

CHACA-CHACARE: London stopping at New York.

SANTA-CLARA: Here we divide and make a fork in two ways.

CHACA-CHACARE: I branch to Bermuda north. The other fork fly south
to Florida.

POTARO: For final destination which is.

SANTA-CLARA: That's my business.

POTARO: Correct. Ports of entry.

FOREST RESERVE: Three.

POTARO: And Potaro's port will be.

FOREST RESERVE: I don't know.

CHACA-CHACARE: Each man to his own.

POTARO: Correct. Now for the protocol as they say.

CHACA-CHACARE: Army and police must be roaming everywhere. Asking all kind of personal question.

POTARO: Control yourself. You must answer like you back in school.
Show your clothes and your manners according to normal and
peaceful custom. Until you are ready to proceed in orderly fashion
to.

FOREST RESERVE: That's my business.

POTARO: Correct. And from the moment of arriving till we meet again, the code will continue. I Potaro must be nothing but a black shadow you never notice. Whatever emergency of accident. If hurricane or hooligan knock me down you do not know the victim.

CHACA-CHACARE: I proceed in ignorant fashion.

SANTA-CLARA: That part is in order.

FOREST RESERVE: Next stage.

POTARO: That is the flight for San Souci. At three o'clock. London stopping Madrid. And then? Then?

CHACA-CHACARE: He isn't here, Potaro. Not yet.

POTARO: I was forgetting.

CHACA-CHACARE: I have a bad feeling, a bad.

POTARO: Keep cool, Chacare, keep cool. He will be here.

CHACA-CHACARE: But it getting late.

POTARO: I say keep cool, Chacare. We finish this business first.

FOREST RESERVE: London stopping at Madrid for San Souci.

POTARO: Yes, yes. London for Madrid. It is a wider way round. Let us leave the reasons till he come. The Gathering will be on native soil two days after taking off. And now?

FOREST RESERVE: I wait out that week.

POTARO: October twelve to be correct. One week after San Souci arrive we assemble like how we sit here now. Destination?

FOREST RESERVE: Saragasso.

POTARO: In Saragasso cemetery we meet. Midnight by the chapel clock.

CHACA-CHACARE: An' if there is no hitch.

POTARO: Hitch or no hitch there must be no communication. By letter message or magic. Absolute none. Clear?

SANTA CLARA: Everything is crystal clear.

Potaro gets up from the table. He follows his glance round the room and pauses at the solitary entrance into the basement room. In the old days, the dark days he remembers like dirt, before his spirit converted him to war, this would have been a moment for prayer. In the days when he lived by the power of grace. He would have been eager to kneel in gratitude for any wish that had come true. He would have prayed because he was at the eve of his departure from a foreign land. But it is a long time since he buried the habits of his youth.

Pioneer of the San Souci revolt, there is no end to the list of charges he has survived. He will almost certainly be executed if he is caught. And he knows it. But he has come to the end of his sojourn abroad. It is a weariness of spirit which makes him desperate, and hurries him into a future which threatens to disown him and his past. He is Teeton's senior by ten years. He has known him since the days at San Souci, but in recent times Potaro has been shocked to recognise his own terrors in the younger man; shocked and softened in his sympathy for what he sees. He is anxious for Teeton, full of apprehension about his delay. But he doesn't let it show.

He listens with obvious attention to the murmuring of the Gathering; and struggles to resist the sentiment that creeps up to his eyes. It is the last time they will assemble here; the last time they will disperse from this parliament Potaro has cultivated underground. Already he prepares to leave the memory of this city behind him; to expel the punishing scars of its weather from his bones. But the verdict of his exile conceals a word of praise for the city which gave him refuge for a while. Dangerous and devious in its ways, he has always been startled by its power, the pride of assurance it displays, so brutal and confident in its capacity to survive.

The voices of the Gathering interrupt his meditation. Potaro turns sharply; then steadies his nerve before trying to curb their worry about Teeton's delay.

CHACA-CHACARE: But where is San Souci?

POTARO: He will come.

FOREST RESERVE: It is late.

POTARO: There's still time. From now till three in the afternoon. That's time enough. Is it past midnight?

SANTA CLARA: Past and gone.

POTARO: His passage done booked. What is there to do but name a last detail or two?

FOREST RESERVE: He was always punctual to the dot. But a week went by and not a word.

POTARO: The agenda didn't call for any word. We had no cause to meet until tonight. I say he'll come. Don't argue, Chack. It's not till three this afternoon.

CHACA-CHACARE: Not argue I argue. But I fear accident. What is to happen if there is accident of some kind?

FOREST RESERVE: I have a feeling it may be deeper than that.

POTARO: What you mean deeper than that?

FOREST RESERVE: Maybe some trouble attack his memory again. Maybe somebody near to him dead.

SANTA CLARA: Would he be in the same trouble as his friend. Judge Capildeo son. The music man. I didn't like how the papers play up his face with the other two.

POTARO: There is a bad mood come on the town. Whatever you do or don't do, nobody safe.

CHACA-CHACARE: I didn't like his face put up in public. Not in that way and for that reason. That is why I say what I say. Accident of some kind. It could be that.

POTARO: From now till three in the afternoon. We have time. Let the morning come first. He will be here. Until that flight move up in the air I stick by what I say. He will come.

SANTA CLARA: I follow Potaro. Let morning come first.

CHACA-CHACARE: I finish my say but I hope nobody near to him dead.

POTARO: Alive or dead. Near or far. It can make no difference. No grave or prison will hold us in this place. His heart will never reconcile to waiting here.

Two

It was over now.

He was crouching near the last ridge of heather, a crab among rocks. He was moving on claws. He could hear his hands scraping through the dark. His fists were smashing through the crust of the night. The fire was struggling to survive. He was crouching low; he had to soothe these sharp piercing arrows of flame which the fire had been screwing into his eyes. His chest was an apron of bone; he had ceased to feel the pebble and gravel of the earth. It had made a grate of his skin. He was coming up, sucking the air; coming slowly forward from the furnace of the Old Dowager's grave; on his stomach, a crab in flight, crawling through a roaring tunnel of wind. I'm coming; I'll be there. It was the call of the Gathering; his voice from the future. It came over the cottage. It told him the date. This was the date. He had made arson on the Old Dowager's body. She was burning away; burning his memory away. He had burnt the Old Dowager out of his future. He had burnt her free; burnt her losses; burnt her husband; burnt her lover; he was burning her into eternity. A crab among rocks, he was crawling forward, piloting his claws over these treacherous slopes of land: a valley of gravel and dirt, splinters of bone against his palms; root and fangs of the briar chewing at his knees, scraping a tattoo of the island over his stomach. The earth was swallowing the Old Dowager's body, melting her limbs, baking her bones. He didn't see her bleed; as though the fire had shot her body through with lightning. She had gone all white. A pure whiteness covered her skin; melted through her pores; converted her blood into a lake of cloud. A slow evaporation of her flesh. Her bones had dissolved like boiling wax. Thin pillows of cloud; like a gathering of islands exploded to dust. The Old Dowager's dust. Her skin was a map of dust; a fountain white with cloud. He was crawling forward, a crab among rocks; his eyes like needle points of flame whitening the dark; a trail of burning cloud groping ahead. He could see the cottage, a solitary tower, a desolate cloud ascending from the valley to supervise the dawn. The Old Dowager's body was behind him; her face had finished in a cloud, a white shadow that moved in circles. The wind had washed her smell away; the odours of scorching tissue; the acrid remains of her hair. The wind had made a total killing; her smell had been swept up; carried clean off. There was no memory of a smell left over her grave. The wind had snatched her smell; drowned her putrefaction; baled her odours up from the gravel and dirt of the valley; her smell was adrift, a tide of air drowned in the wash of the sea. He could hear it warning him to crawl forward, to go more quickly, turn reckless on his claws. He had to make it fast to that desolate boat. He would be safe for a while. The boat would restore his sense of the surroundings. He would be at ease for a while. Not safe. The engine couldn't offer him that. He couldn't expect to find safety there. But he would be at ease. For a while. Time enough to get used to what had happened; to learn the meaning of what he had done; to learn what the call of the sea was warning. He could hear it knocking against the shell of his ears. He had lost his taste for safety. It was an instinct that had now gone dead; a permanent loss of appetite. It wouldn't come his way again; the need to be safe; the normal taste for safety. Gone, it had gone down with the Old Dowager's corpse. But the boat was bringing him near. He could see it dragging him forward. He would soon be there. His claws now carried him out of these rocks; piloted him over this ridge of gravel towards the refuge of the boat. He would be at ease for a while. His claws would push him up; stand him erect. The altitude began to make him dizzy. It couldn't be otherwise. But it didn't influence his balance now; couldn't touch the savage lack of taste for safety. Dead, his need for safety had gone dead; was now burnt out. He could hear the wash of the sea. He was dragging himself up, struggling with his strength up from the pier. The boat was like a rock under his hand. The wind was pushing him about; had pushed him up. He was swinging his body into the boat. He heard the engine cough; and gazed ahead. He was gazing where a cave of fire began to open the sky. Calm, you are so calm. He was so calm. I am, he was struggling not to say, so calm. A trinity of voices came up from the floor of the ocean. Calm, Teeton was ready to move; and he was so calm.

It was an unlikely start to the day: this fierce and lucid thrust of dawn that burnt the chill of autumn away. He saw the sea leap in a sparkle of morning which had torn the mist off the iron spire of the hills. There was muscle in the wind; but his face was warm. The air was rubbing him gently. The island began to drift behind. He was moving away from the cottage. He knew it was there. The island was somewhere behind him, solitary and desolate in its vigil. It was watching his departure. He would soon be out of view, out of its reach, beyond the orbit of its shelter. He didn't want to look there again. The future had come between them. The engine made a noisy vomit of smoke on the water, but the wind had scrubbed it clean. He saw the profile of the mainland lift and shiver like the fangs of a jaw where the houses rose behind the ragged mouth of the bay. Near, he was moving forward and so near. He had come to the end of his safety. But he was calm; no pulse to his blood; no whisper of a beat from the cage of steel that covered his heart. Calm, Teeton was so calm.

There was a smell of fire on the morning.